AGENTS OF ORDER

AGENTS OF ORDER

FEDERAL AGENTS OF MAGIC™ BOOK SIX

TR CAMERON   MARTHA CARR   MICHAEL ANDERLE

DISRUPTIVE IMAGINATION

LMBPN Publishing
PMB 196, 2540 South Maryland Pkwy
Las Vegas, NV 89109

First US edition, August 2019
Print ISBN: 978-1-64202-460-9

Thanks to the JIT Readers

Dave Hicks
Micky Cocker
Diane L. Smith
Misty Roa
Shari Regan
Larry Omans

If we've missed anyone, please let us know!

Editor
The Skyhunter Editing Team

DEDICATIONS

For Dylan

— *TR Cameron*

To everyone who still believes in magic
and all the possibilities that holds.
To all the readers who make this
entire ride so much fun.
And to my son, Louie and so many wonderful friends who
remind me all the time of what
really matters and how wonderful
life can be in any given moment.

— *Martha*

To Family, Friends and
Those Who Love
To Read.
May We All Enjoy Grace
To Live The Life We Are
Called.

— *Michael*

CHAPTER ONE

Cara turned slowly to gaze out at the surreal landscape that stretched to the horizon in every direction. Above, too far to be seen clearly but nonetheless sensed as an urge to duck, an array of pointed stalactites hung, ominous and threatening. The ground beneath her feet was the cracked soil of a desert, its copper tint doubtless the result of the spilled lifeblood of those who had battled there before. The visible land faded quickly into darkness.

She finished her full circle to face two figures—twins and opposites. On the left was an ebony-haired woman clad entirely in white-leather medieval armor festooned with matching bands and buckles from the colorless boots below to the thick collar protecting her neck. Her ears were pointed, her cheekbones sharp, and her lips soft and lush. The elf's haughty expression suggested judgment. Cara shied away from it and turned her head to the being's mirror image. He wore the same armor but all black, and his features were identical with only the slightest firmness to his features to convey masculinity instead of femininity. White hair stood in dramatic contrast to the rest of his appearance, as the dark mane had for the other. He, too, gazed at her condescendingly from above his folded arms.

A hasty glance downward confirmed that she wore her most comfortable combat outfit—boots, tactical pants, and the tight black tunic ARES agents used as a base layer. The standard wrist-length sleeves were cut off at the shoulders to leave her muscular arms bare. The light wind that rippled through the area warmed her skin with its touch. She shook her head once and felt the weight of her long hair captured in a warrior's knot at the top of her neck, ensuring it wouldn't get in the way of the fight that was sure to come. The air seemed to vibrate with the imminent threat posed by the twins.

So, apparently, it's to be a battle.

The woman on the left laughed, and it was less cold than she'd expected. "Indeed, it is to be a battle."

Cara groaned. *Great, they can read minds.*

Now the man laughed, the sound identical to his twin's. "Yes, we can read *your* mind anyway, bearer."

She squinted in confusion until the moments before she'd landed in this place returned to her brain. Nylotte and Diana had stood over her and tightened the straps to secure her to a table in the basement of the Dark Elf's shop. She recalled thanking them and surrendering to the mental pressure of the paired daggers that comprised part of the Rhazdon's Vengeance artifacts, then remembered nothing more before her appearance in that desolate place.

She narrowed her eyes. "So, Angel and Demon, I presume." She nodded to the light and the dark in turn.

They returned the gesture with identical movements, obviously still amused. In response, she offered a sardonic grin. "I don't suppose we're here to chat about how our partnership will work?"

The duo laughed again and now, it sounded like real pleasure was present. Angel tossed her black hair dramatically. "No, talking is not—"

"— our preferred mode of conversation," Demon finished.

Cara sighed and rolled her shoulders. "I assume it's not one at a time, either, right?"

Together, they replied, "What would be the fun in that?" With that, they attacked.

Angel led the way and circled away from her twin as she stalked forward. Cara responded with her own evasive circle to increase the distance from her darker opponent and put his sibling in white between them. Angel was suddenly in range, her advance so fast it failed to register, and she swung a fist. The agent jerked her head to the side and the blow narrowly missed her left ear and she replied with a two-punch combination to the woman's sternum. Both strikes connected, but the layers of belts and armor prevented damage to anything other than her knuckles. *I wish I'd imagined myself some gloves.* She barely ducked aside to avoid the spinning back fist that slashed diagonally at her face. Immediately, she countered with a leg sweep, but Angel skipped over it with ease.

Midway through the motion, Cara caught a flash of black in her peripheral vision, and flung herself aside, and rolled as soon as she landed. Demon's first kick missed, but the next one struck her in the back and propelled her into a faster roll. She used the momentum to leap to her feet in time to catch his follow-up axe kick on crossed forearms. His eyes widened as she grinned and delivered a low front kick into his crotch that forced him to stumble back several feet. She frowned when he failed to drop in agony. He must've seen the question in her expression because he gave her a condescending grin. "Angels and demons are ill-equipped, to borrow a phrase, unless they choose otherwise. And, in battle, who would?" She fell back as Angel appeared beside him and they attacked together.

Okay, they're both fast, and body blows won't work. It's time to start breaking stuff. She backpedaled, blocked with the minimum required effort to conserve her energy, and waited for an opening. The duo fought as if they had battled together forever. They stayed out of one another's way and used opposing attack vectors that challenged her ability to defend against them. For all she knew, they did have eons of battle time as a unit. Diana had explained how ancient magic users had transferred the spirits of great warriors—willing or unwilling—into objects of power. This pair certainly seemed to have been chosen for their martial prowess.

Her distracted thoughts cost her as Demon delivered a punch into her shoulder hard enough to spin her around to the right. She planted her left foot and levered a sidekick at his chest, which he blocked with ease. Before he could retaliate, she drew her leg back and thrust it out again to smash his shin with her heel as he raised his limb to avoid her intended crippling blow to his knee. He cursed, hopped away, and limped in a circle to walk off the pain from the kick. *If I'm lucky, I fractured something. But somehow, luck doesn't seem likely.*

Angel abandoned finesse and rushed into a furious tackle that took them both to the ground. The woman was heavier than she appeared, and the elbow she drove into Cara's sternum robbed her of breath. She raised her left hand for a punch, and the agent used the instant of freedom to drive a knuckle into the base of her foe's throat in a single sharp strike. Her adversary gagged and curled to the side as involuntary panic at the fear of suffocation did its job. *I guess I'm lucky they need to breathe.* She rolled out of the way before Demon's foot stamped where her skull had been a moment before. He assisted his twin—sister?—to her feet, and they faced her again. This time, the haughty looks were replaced with at least minimal grudging respect.

Cara nodded. "Are we done here?"

The woman shook her head. "We are not. This is merely a pause for you to regain your strength." She straightened and clasped her hands before her. "In life, my brother and I were considered great fighters among the Light Elves. Most of our battles, of course, were like this. Training, playing. We mastered all the available weapons with ease, and our success and abilities afforded us the opportunity for a more advanced instructional regimen."

Without a notable interruption, Demon continued. "We chose daggers, for we judged ourselves the nimblest, the most agile, and the fastest. As such, we would study the weapons that would best make use of those skills." He gestured, and a pair of long blades appeared in their hands. Angel's shone with pure light, untainted by the red haze that suffused the landscape. Demon's radiated darkness. Cara startled when she realized she suddenly gripped ones of gleaming steel. The mirrored surfaces reflected everything around. The hilts were longer than the knives she was used to, and the blades were as well. They felt perfectly balanced, however, and she imagined she could throw them accurately. *Or, if not accurately, at least better than against the dude on the catwalk.*

Her opponents laughed. Angel softened her comment with a smile. "That was definitely a pathetic effort."

Demon tossed his own right-hand blade in the air and caught it cleanly without apparent effort. "You are correct, they will fly true. Although disarming yourself is rarely a good idea."

Cara grinned. "I'm never disarmed, though."

The twins exchanged glances and nodded in unison to her. Angel did the same knife flip as her brother had done. It seemed to offer them reassurance. "We are aware of your magical powers. They will not avail you here, but they are one of the reasons we permitted you to select us."

She was about to ask what the other reasons were when Demon growled impatiently. "Enough," he said curtly and launched himself at her. He approached at a sprint and lashed out with his right blade when he reached melee range. Swiftly, she stepped to her left and pivoted to bring her own left dagger down in a sharp diagonal to deflect his attack downward. She maintained contact until he could no longer strike her with it, then swiped her own dagger out horizontally and aimed at the place where his skull met his neck. He halted, ducked in a smooth motion, and kicked back with his heel. She blocked with a raised foot of her own.

Demon rolled forward and onto his feet, facing her as he twirled both knives. He waded in without hesitation and rained blows at her in a familiar pattern—down diagonal, sideways, up diagonal, then sweeping strokes from the top and the bottom. She recognized it from her own training, as the strikes followed the standard progression for basic practice. She scoffed. "You're toying with me. Knock it off, asshole."

Cara caught his next attacks with outward circle blocks to open his guard, then delivered a straight front kick to his sternum. He fell back with a gasp, then stood, coughed once, and nodded at his partner. "Very well, then."

She barely had time to reposition before Angel's blades whirled into an almost liquid attack. Where Demon had used straightforward attacks backed by raw power and with the potential to end the battle in a single blow, the woman was fluidity personified. Every move was arced and flowed and one motion led seamlessly to the next so that her approach resembled a dance as she closed. It was a style she'd never faced before, and Cara was hard-pressed to defend against the incoming daggers with no time at all to think of counterattacking.

Despite her efforts, she missed a block and allowed one through to slice a shallow cut across her stomach. The ice as the blade parted her flesh was followed by the warmth of blood welling free, but there was no time to examine the damage as Angel continued to press her. Their blades rang against each other and Cara lost count of the exchanges in the haze of defending against them until finally, her attacker stepped back and nodded. Demon stalked to his normal position and regarded the agent, who focused on catching her breath before the next challenge.

Angel looked satisfied. "Adequate. The raw skills are there, although a great deal of training will be required."

Cara frowned. "Yeah, well, maybe if I had lived through one of your long elvish lives, I might have gotten there."

Demon shook his head. "Seventeen. We were the human equivalent of seventeen when we were called to battle against Rhazdon. We will not speak of it further, but know that we were forced to slay many before we were overwhelmed, captured, and imprisoned."

She was amazed at how much they'd accomplished in a seemingly short time and horrified at the notion of teenagers as prisoners. Angel wore a grave expression as she continued the tale. "Neither will we speak of the tortures and torments endured during our captivity. We will only say that when the opportunity for release came, we took it, even though it was to this." She gestured at the scorched world around them.

Cara's mouth dropped open. "You mean this is a representation of where you live or whatever it is that you do?"

He chuckled. "Exist is probably the most appropriate word. Yes, the last bearer made it so."

A grin crept onto her face. "So, if I offered to give you the swanky sixties pad that was inside the bottle in *I Dream of Jeannie*, you'd be good with ending this now?"

There was a pause before the pair laughed in unison, the musical sounds a perfect complement to one another. Angel nodded. "Your memories show amusement at the idea, but it would certainly be an upgrade."

Demon tapped his daggers together. "However, there is a final matter to resolve before such things can happen. You have not yet proven yourself worthy of wielding us."

Cara groaned. "I was afraid you'd say that." She tensed for an attack, but the twins turned toward each other.

He sounded despondent. "I would take this burden from you, sister, if you would permit it."

Angel stepped forward and wrapped the dark being in her arms. Tears glistened on both their faces at some shared pain. "It is my turn, brother. You cannot protect me from the choices we both made." They parted with an exchange of nods. When the woman turned back to Cara, her face was hard. "Bearer. Thus far, we have judged your skills. We have deemed you potentially worthy of wielding us. However, you must prove your strength a final time."

She nodded. "I assume it's not like before, though, right?"

The elf woman shook her head gravely. "It is not. Rather than test you, I will try to kill you."

Cara gulped. "And this is the only way?" She was confident that being killed there, wherever it was, would mean death for her physical body in Stonesreach, as well. Hopefully, if the cut had also manifested, Diana and Nylotte were tending to it.

Angel nodded. "However, you have this one chance to walk away unscathed. Should you cease your attempt to master the daggers, we will vanish, and you need not die in the pursuit."

She frowned. "How many have reached this point?"

Demon laughed. "Some."

"And how many have survived?" she asked and turned her head to stare at him.

He sobered and looked down. "Far, far fewer."

Cara shrugged, the decision made before she'd asked the questions. "Well, what will be, will be, I guess. I'm many things, but I'm certainly not a quitter." She turned her gaze back to Angel and stepped into a fighting stance, her front dagger low and angled up and the back blade high and angled down. She bared her teeth in a grin. "Bring it, Casper."

The figure in white paused for a moment, then smiled, clearly having pulled the reference from her mind. She advanced, weaving her blades in circles and ellipses, and Cara focused on using quick strikes to deflect and block them while she learned the pattern. When she thought she had it and was ready to counter, though, Angel changed her tactics and forced her to skitter away and reset against a whole new set of attacks. The process repeated twice before her tiring brain realized what was up.

Shit. She can read my mind.

The conclusion was rewarded by a nod from Angel and an increase in the tempo of her assaults. There was no way she would be able to maintain her defense endlessly, and if the other woman could read her thoughts, there was only one option. She reached for the state of no-mind that Nylotte had been coaching her toward as a means of exploring her magic without burning herself out. It was a useful approach because she had experienced no-mind many times before in her martial arts training—those moments where the body merely worked on its own in the absence of conscious direction. Those occasions had always seemed like short trips to paradise to her and summoning them deliberately was invariably a challenge. It seemed to be one of those "The harder you try the farther away you get" kind of things. But on the barren battlefield, it came instantly at her call.

A small smile twisted Angel's lips as Cara began to intercept the sweeping blows with greater ease. After a minute, she had managed to work in ripostes and counter-attacks and blended elements of the circular style of her opponent with her own more direct style. When the opportunity came, she only realized it was there as her daggers tapped Angel's high enough to pass over her shoulders, which gave her an opening to stab her arms forward and plunge her own knives into the woman's chest. The keen steel slid through the leather barrier without hindrance. She shoved the blades in all the way with a shout, then tilted her head to apologize.

Cara stumbled forward as the resistance vanished. Angel reappeared ahead at Demon's side, unharmed. Both now wore sheaths on their thighs with the hilts of their daggers protruding. Together, they bowed to her and intoned, "You have succeeded and won the right to wield us."

She dropped to sit cross-legged as adrenaline fled and exhaustion swept over her. "Does this mean you two will listen to me, obey my wishes, that sort of thing?"

Their laughter rang in her ears as she fell out of the space. She woke with a start and a deep gasp to thrash against the bands that held her in place. When she looked down, her shirt was damp where the cut had occurred in the other world. Diana leaned into her line of sight, a worried expression on her face. "Cara? Are you okay?"

She laughed hoarsely. "You might want to rethink finding the sword, boss. Weapons with personalities are jerks." Her vision constricted into a tiny dot of light that quickly succumbed to the blackness of unconsciousness.

CHAPTER TWO

Diana hurried into Kayleigh's lab at a run. She'd listened in over the comms but wanted to be with her team for this particular experience. The blonde tech was in her usual place and Deacon, Tony, and Anik were gathered around the worktable. In the middle stood a speaker that fed the intelligence signal from the bugs they'd distributed throughout the Remembrance warehouse.

Sloan had pinged them earlier with a coded warning that Marcus was on the way, and they'd monitored the feed ever since. A glance at the nearby areas revealed that the two techs were partway through a variety of different projects, judging by the exposed wiring and tools carefully set aside away from the table's surface.

Tony grinned at her. "I love good investigative work."

Anik countered with a mock frown. "As if you did anything. It was all Kayleigh and Rath."

"Yeah, well, I was there in the idea phase. I'm an ideas man."

Diana snorted. "Uh-huh, sure, whatever." She slipped between the field agents' chairs to lean on the table and looked across at her housemate with mirth in her eyes. "So, did she tell you how she was thrashed by a twelve-year-old in—"

Kayleigh raised a hand, her palm out. "Stop right there if you value your life. I can have Alfred deploy the defenses against you, you know." After Nylotte's warning, they had increased the house's active and passive protections, some of which were now downright violent. The tech had assured her the AI would use them wisely, but Diana still felt a little nervous approaching the house in the moments before the system recognized her.

The others laughed, Deacon the most boisterously. He had been present for that battle, apparently, but was sworn to silence. She had considered the best way to blackmail him for the full story, but so far, his close relationship with the tech seemed to preclude it. *Until they take the step across the line into romance, of course, and I'll have leverage on both of them. Mwa ha ha.* She chuckled inwardly and pictured herself twirling a handlebar mustache but was jolted back to the moment by the sound of a slamming door.

Sarah's voice was more acerbic than usual. "What do you want? I have things I need to do."

In previous recordings, Marcus had been calm, maybe even bordering on cowed once or twice. This time, however, his confidence was obvious, as was his antipathy toward the Remembrance's head witch. "I have some information that might be important for you to be aware of."

She barked a laugh. "What could you possibly know that I do not, human?" The brittleness in her voice was a counterpoint to her bold words. Diana imagined that Marcus heard it as well because there was laughter behind his next statement.

"You sit here in your depressing office, plotting and planning and pulling at the strands of your web. You have secret discussions with Dreven using your little statue and feel confident that you are the master of all you survey." He paused, and she pictured the woman seething, inches away from drawing her wand and trying to strike him. *Which might be more difficult than anyone thinks, based on what Sloan's told us about his mechanical arm.*

Sarah's voice was a growl. "Do you have a point, other than insulting me?"

"Only to tell you that while you've been in here being so clever, our enemies have listened to every word you've said." Kayleigh frowned and looked at the table, hiding her eyes behind the mane of her hair.

The witch sounded murderous. "Explain."

Marcus laughed, seemed to catch himself and be about to speak, then laughed again. Finally, he regained his composure. "There are electronic bugs all through the warehouse. They must be in here, too. They wouldn't do the one without the other. And you had no idea."

"How did you discover this?"

"My people are good, and they're more interested in making sure our base is secure than in comparing the lengths of their wands."

Tony chortled, and Anik stretched behind Diana to slap him. Kayleigh hissed. "Shhhh."

The feed was deathly silent for several moments, and they exchanged glances. Then there was a sizzle and a pop, and the connection went dead. The techs both sighed, and Deacon said, "Well, I suppose we got almost everything we could out of that one."

Kayleigh shook her head. "Probably. But it's not enough. Not by half. We need a way to get Sloan out of there." Her despondent tone revealed that she'd hoped the bugs would be a path toward accomplishing that.

Tony tapped his fingers on the table. "We might go old-school while we have nothing else going on."

They all turned to face him. "Well, any idea you come up with is old by definition," Anik responded. "Do you care to elaborate?"

The former detective rewarded the quip with a raised middle finger and a thin smile. After the ensuing chuckles had subsided, he shrugged. "We put surveillance on her. Drones where we can—high up so she can't detect them—and people where drones won't work. Telescopes. Long-range microphones. The tried-and-true."

Diana frowned. "We don't really have the person-power for that, do we?"

He thought for a moment. "Well, if we do two shifts a day and use cameras and recording equipment while she's asleep, Anik and Hank and I could handle it. For a while, at least, until we come up with something better."

"We can probably rig some useful stuff to help out," Deacon added. Kayleigh nodded her agreement.

Diana pushed back from the table and stood, stretched her spine, and raised her hands high. "All right. Put together a plan and let me take a look at it. Anything that makes her life more difficult is a win for us."

After the initial outburst where she swept the walls and ceiling of her office with power to destroy any listening devices that might be there—and send a message to the human in the chair opposite her—Sarah had maintained her calm reasonably well. She'd discussed security improvements with Marcus and reasserted her position as his superior by virtue of her promise to discuss it with Dreven at a convenient moment.

And with Iressa, but he certainly doesn't need to know about that until it's time for him to die.

She'd spent another hour in the room to demonstrate her lack of concern, but it had been entirely unproductive. The sense of violation was everywhere, and the fact that he had been the one to reveal it made the feeling exponentially worse. With a growl of annoyance, she stood and opened the safe to withdraw the statue with a sly grin. *I'll use this occurrence as an excuse to justify my need to speak to Dreven alone and in the safety of my home. That will put Marcus even further below me, where he belongs.* She shoved it in her bag and headed to the door.

The witch kept her steps slow and stately as she descended the stairs. Marcus's people scurried about and checked the rest of the warehouse for surveillance devices, and her own were seeking any telltale signs of magical watchers. So far, they had found none. Since Wysse's death, Sarah had resisted naming another of the group as superior to the others, so she checked in with each individually before she departed. They'd also discovered nothing, as expected.

She stepped out the front door, cloaked herself in illusion, and turned to walk to the far side of the building. With a flick of her wrist, she opened a portal to a secluded corner of the parking garage that served her apartment and stepped through. It was a short elevator ride to the top floor and a shorter walk to her door, which swung open at a flick of her wand. She entered with a grateful sigh.

Since returning from the World in Between, her condo was her only true sanctuary. Even before the discovery of the listening devices, she had not believed herself secure in the warehouse. Here, though, far above the ground and protected by wards on all sides, she was able to relax. *At least as much as the memories will allow.* Lately, her sleep had been interrupted several times each night with visions of the creatures she'd met there, and the awakenings found her covered in sweat, her heart beating as if the endless flight from danger in her dream had been real. That was her most vivid memory of the place—running until her chest felt like it would explode but knowing that to stop was death.

Sarah sighed and dropped her bag, closed her eyes, and rolled her neck to loosen it. The thump as the statuette struck the marble floor was alarming, but she discarded her concern after a moment passed and no danger materialized. Sometimes, breaking magical objects resulted in volatile catastrophes far out of proportion to their size.

She wandered to her bedroom and gazed through the large windows at the distant horizon and the sun sinking slowly toward it. A quick change of clothes increased her comfort considerably, and she sat before her mirror to brush her long black hair. She peered closer, noting the increased length of the worry lines at the corners of her eyes. The frown that followed revealed the same changes at the edges of her mouth. *Things were easier when Vincente was here and I could be the power behind the figurehead rather than everyone's target.* She threw her brush across the room, but the gesture lacked any ferocity and it bounced lamely off the bed to clatter on the floor.

The necklace that permitted communication with Iressa never left her, and she stood with a surge of energy as it warmed to indicate that the council witch was willing to speak to her. Sarah had sent the magical request hours before and had been prepared to wait hours more if necessary. She strode down the short hallway that connected the bedroom to the living room and sat on the white leather couch. As she leaned back, she whispered the activation phrase and her mind went hazy as it was drawn elsewhere.

Each time she had communed with her patron, the locale had been different. On this occasion, she stood on a cliff that overlooked the raging surf far below. Birds flew overhead, shrieking at the indignity of having to deal with a human presence. As before, she wondered if they were in a real place and perhaps existed as shadows perceived only by the wildlife around them. As before, she found no answers in the setting, nor in the eyes of the witch who materialized before her.

Iressa possessed the supreme confidence that Sarah pretended to. Her face was perfect and her body the same. On Earth, she could be a starlet, the most in-demand femme fatale to ever grace the screen. On Oriceran, her desires had clearly taken a different path, one that her acolyte hoped to follow. Power and influence would bring all the other things she craved.

"Iressa. Thank you for responding so quickly."

The other woman nodded, then turned to stare out at the sea. "I had a moment. Events are in a lull, it seems. Hopefully, it will be brief. I expect a summons from Dreven any day now." The woman's sneer as she said the Remembrance leader's name fit Sarah's opinion of the wizard perfectly.

"I have not heard from him recently, either."

Iressa gave no sign of having listened. "What is concerning enough that you wished to speak?"

Sarah straightened as the memory of the invasion struck her afresh. "Our base was compromised. There's no telling how much our enemies might have overheard."

Her superior's gaze cut back to her. "Not of our conversations, surely."

She was quick to stammer a reply. "No, no, certainly not. I only speak to you from my own home and behind layers of wards. But of my discussions with Dreven, undoubtedly. And those with Marcus."

The witch's lips twitched, and Sarah knew she'd betrayed her hatred of the man yet again. "Yes, your most-loved co-leader. It's a shame he is still alive. We will have to do something about that at some point."

"He was virtually gleeful in telling me about the warehouse surveillance. Almost as if he had taken part in it." Suspicion grew at the notion, the same suspicion that poked her every time she thought of the enemy's murderous attack on Wysse and her sisters.

Iressa shook her head. "You do not need to seek new

enemies when we already have so many. Certainly, he bears watching. Killing too, perhaps, if the moment presents itself. But do not narrow your focus overmuch. We must be ready to strike whenever and wherever fate gives us the opportunity." She turned to face her again. "To that end, you will pressure Dreven to come to Earth personally to lead your group."

Sarah frowned. "Whatever for?"

The other witch laughed. "You need not know the reasons and only need to do as I ask. Rest assured, it is an investment that will bring great dividends of power and authority for us both ."

As if her superior had cast a spell with her words, warmth and desire spread through Sarah. Her grin matched the other woman's when she replied, "Well, then, of course I will."

Iressa strode forward, grabbed her by the arm and threw her off the cliff. She screamed involuntarily, then jerked to wakefulness on her couch. When she stopped hyperventilating, she stood shakily. *I hate it when she does that.* She shook her head and looked around, speaking her thoughts aloud. "Now, where the hell did I put that statue? I have an idiot wizard to manipulate."

CHAPTER THREE

"Son of a festering hobgoblin." Kayleigh's curse was muttered under her breath but still earned her a snort from Deacon's position across the lab. She frowned at the back of his skull. "Aren't those huge ugly-ass headphones you wear supposed to be noise-canceling?"

He waved, clearly unmoved by her comment, and returned to nodding his head in time with whatever music he was listening to. She sighed and picked up the tiny piece that had flicked out of her pliers a moment before and placed it inside the sensor boundary. A holographic image of the circuit board and of the miniature soldering iron she used to fix it appeared in her glasses and hovered above the work surface. On the second attempt, she got the job done without any drama and set the component in its proper place in the fist-sized electronic device beside her.

She raised the sides and attached the temporary restraints that would hold it together until the design was complete. Most of it had been constructed from off-the-shelf components, probably the only part of her job at

ARES Pittsburgh that Kayleigh disliked. *With a proper fabrication facility, we could do so much more. Well, that and more time.* She set the squat black box onto the table. "Alfred, check power and signal flow."

There was a pause before the AI's aloof British accent replied, "Functioning within expected parameters."

"Verify audio and video capture, recording, and playback."

"Verified. The device appears to be fully functional. Well done."

She shook her head. "Suck-up. Now download a local version of yourself into the box."

The AI sounded reluctant. "Are you quite sure that's a good idea? Having sophisticated and proprietary software sitting on rooftops?"

Kayleigh laughed. "Don't worry. Once we've finished testing, we'll put in a failsafe that melts the insides if anyone messes with it."

She hadn't realized that the computer system could sigh with such clear disappointment. "Installing." She drummed her fingers, quickly bored with waiting for the software to do its task. The clock in her peripheral vision showed that it was already ten-twenty p.m, which meant she'd lost track of time while engaged in her work, a frequent occurrence. She folded her arms on the table and rested her head on them, closing her eyes. *Only for a minute.*

Deacon's call interrupted her before she'd managed more than thirty seconds of rest. "Hey, Kitana, come over here." She was instantly in motion, his use of her gamer tag a signal he had something to share that excited him. His workstation was a wide semicircle of monitors, keyboards, and mice. He also used voice commands to interact with his systems but rejected her offer of a personal AI, claiming he didn't appreciate virtual assistants that were smarter than he was.

She stopped behind him and put her hands on his shoulders, kneaded a few times, and elicited a pleased groan. "Whatcha got, hotshot?" He clicked an icon and one of his screens was duplicated to the large wall-mounted monitor above his station. It showed a scrolling feed of information that was about as comprehensible to her as the Matrix code. She shook her head. "Okay, I'll ask again. Whatcha got, hotshot?"

He laughed. "What you're looking at is a list of transactions for an offshore gambling site run by our friends in Chinese Intelligence."

She scowled and clenched her fists, drawing a startled yelp from him. "Oops, sorry." *Not sorry.* "Interesting play. Both revenue and leverage?"

He brushed her hands off his shoulders and began tapping his keyboards. On the monitor, the feed was replaced with a weird combination of a mind map and flowchart that seemed to show the inputs and outputs of the website in question. "Seems to be. NSA spotted it first, we acquired the information through our usual channel, and I gave it a look in turn. It seemed fairly ordinary until I realized it was magically guarded."

Kayleigh didn't understand the interface of magic and tech in the virtual world of the Internet. She understood it a little better when it came to working with physical objects that combined the two, but it remained slippery. He paused, clearly waiting for her to give him some accolades for his accomplishment, and she remained silent. *I can't have him getting a big head. Plus, he's fun to mess with.*

After a few moments, he continued, "Anyway, once I peeled the magic back and hacked through the defenses—both of which were monumentally impressive efforts that no one here is sophisticated enough to appreciate—I managed to access a client list. In code, of course, but even the best proxy servers leave traces. One of those led to a person we're interested in. Care to guess who?"

If he's letting me guess, it almost has to be someone on the oversight committee. If it was an enemy, he'd simply come out and announce it. She considered all the potential answers but couldn't settle on a favorite. "I'd say Senators Greene or Cyphret. Please don't let it be Finely or Somers."

Deacon laughed. "Nope. It's Tomassi."

Her jaw dropped open in shock. "Seriously? Our boy Winston isn't as goody-goody as he looks?"

"So it seems. Apparently, he likes to gamble. He only does it from home, so that's something. He uses secure accounts—which I hacked, of course—that he fills with his personal funds. So he's not stealing from the government or anything. But it makes his overall financial picture much shakier than we'd thought."

Kayleigh shook her head. "Wow. This is unexpected. But that leaves him open to two different approaches—compensation and blackmail. Damn." She drummed her fingers on his shoulders as she thought it through. "Okay, we need to plan. And to do that, we also need a change of venue. Let's move."

As they reached the door out of the labs, Alfred spoke in her comm. "Installation complete. Now I finally have someone intelligent to talk to." She rolled her eyes. *Maybe I've given the AIs too much room to grow.*

The Tiki Lounge was one of Kayleigh's favorite night venues. It was island-themed with a fake-straw canopy over the bar and torches winking throughout. The weather was nice enough that the front window was retracted to let the nighttime breeze in, and Deacon headed to the long bar that traveled the whole way down the left side of the room to order drinks while she diverted to the classic jukebox on the right wall. It was filled with everything from Elvis to EDM, and she threw in a five and picked songs from Kiss, Rush, Pink, PJ Harvey, and then, after much consideration, added another from Rush. *We are indeed modern-day warriors, with mean, mean strides.*

She met her partner at one of the tall tables that made up the center of the space and lurched a little as the high stool wobbled. Deacon laughed, and she scooped the cherry from her Pina Colada and threw it at him. "First, shut up you. Next time, pick a table that doesn't suck. Second, I'm picking the drinks from here on out."

He grinned at her. "Got it. So, this is your party. What are we doing?"

She took a sip, pleased to taste that at least he'd ponied up for a premium rum. A short instance of brain freeze later, she regained the power of speech. "Okay. First, a quick summary. We know Clarke is connected to the Remembrance and to Chinese Intelligence. We also now know that Tomassi has a connection to them too, which complicates things. We can't simply plant a piece of information and grab Clarke since it might come from other sources. Who knows how many of the oversight committee members they've compromised?"

Deacon nodded. "So, either different lies to each of them, which would be really difficult, or we need to be able to trace any leaks."

"How would you do it?" She had some ideas but disliked all of them.

He shrugged. "I'd put a bug in their phones."

"What if they used a computer instead?"

"Yeah, I thought of that, too." He sighed and leaned closer. "It would have to be to be capable of jumping to any machine on a network, assuming they're stupid enough to use the phone on Wi-Fi."

She snorted and took another drink. *Okay, actually, this wasn't a half-bad choice. It's tasty and goes with the setting.* The flickering torches cast moving shadows and gave their conversation a conspiratorial feel. She copied his action and leaned forward. "I think we can assume such stupidity. But we'll think of a backup too. Maybe we can send Rath in to bug them."

He nodded, but the expression on his face told her he didn't like that inelegant solution any more than she did. "So, we need to have all the suspects in a room together." He paused, then added, "Actually, if we do it, we should do it with all the committee members."

Her straw made a harsh noise that revealed her drink was empty, and she visited the bar to buy another round. When she returned to the table, Deacon gave her a suspicious glare. "Why is there no fruit on mine?"

She put her head down, chewed, and swallowed before she donned her most innocent expression and met his eyes. "I couldn't tell you. Weird, right?" He laughed as she took her seat again. "Okay, I agree. All the committee members, as much as that sucks. What's the lure?"

"The location of the base?"

"They already have access to that information. Besides, we have to assume our enemies are smart enough not to try to attack us on our home turf." The defenses they'd put into the building were even more impressive than the ones she had installed at the house she shared with Diana and Rath. "Maybe the security agency, though."

Deacon shrugged. "It's not really valuable. Why would they care?" He snapped his fingers. "I know. Your home address."

She gave him two middle fingers in return for the comment, then the solution hit her. "A fake base. We tell them that a given building is a special facility where we train to take on the Remembrance. We can find a space and use an AI and a few simple bots to make it appear occupied."

He laughed. "You're going to repurpose Roombas, aren't you?"

"Do *not* mock the automatic sweeper." She scowled at him. "Those things are the perfect tools for the task as long as the figures on top aren't too heavy and are balanced properly."

His mirth increased. "Yeah, right up until the moment they all start calling for help together."

Kayleigh rolled her eyes. "Why did I recommend you

for this job? I'm sure there must have been a reason, but for the life of me, I can't recall what it might have been."

"My good looks? Big brain? Videogame skills?"

Her reply was louder than intended and drew a few stares from the other people nearby. "Ha. As if. You couldn't shoot your way out of a wet paper bag, noob."

He shook his head. "It's sad that you have to resort to demeaning insults. It's beneath you, really. Anyway, your idea is a good one. Maybe the agents can visit it from time to time in case they're being watched."

Her happiness vanished as she considered the next step. "Okay, but that leaves us nailing only the committee members. There's no clear way to implicate anyone else further up the chain. How do we do that?"

Deacon shrugged, uncomfortable again. "A virus. It's the only answer. It'll have to go to every single connection they make since we won't know how they communicate."

Kayleigh frowned. Their shared values on the matter of viruses and random surveillance were long-standing. "That's frighteningly close to the edge, privacy-wise."

He nodded. "I'll create the virus. You design the AI that will review the information before any humans see it and delete anything that isn't a lead. That way, we can preserve some innocent connections, anyway."

She stood, her second drink only half-finished. "Damn. I don't love it but it seems like the only option. We'd better get back to work. Sleep will be in short supply for a while."

CHAPTER FOUR

Diana felt decidedly rumpled as she exited the airport. With perfect timing, Lisa's cherry red Audi TT drew up at the curb with an eager growl from the engine. She threw her travel bag into the trunk and slid into the seat next to her best friend, who accelerated into the road before any words could be spoken.

She laughed. "Damn, woman, you drive more aggressively than I do. Have you always been insane or is this new?"

Lisa turned and flashed her a grin before she returned her gaze to the road and weaved skillfully between the slower cars. "It's not my fault no one here knows how to drive. They act like they're in a funeral procession or something."

She laughed as she checked to ensure her seatbelt was secure. "Well, you don't need to show off so much that you get us both killed."

"Pah. You can use your magic to save us if I screw up."

"Me, anyway. Saving you might be too great a challenge." Her friend jerked the wheel quickly enough to make the car lurch, and she straightened in alarm, then cursed as she laughed. "Wench."

"Witch."

Lisa got them to the restaurant safely, and they were escorted to their seats by an elegantly dressed woman with olive skin, dark eyes, and bright white teeth. Diana looked around to admire the restaurant's marble and wooden interior and noted all the staff at the posh Italian venue shared similar features. "Authentic."

Her friend nodded and her newly shortened blonde hairstyle bobbed with the motion. "Yeah, it's a DC thing nowadays in the fanciest places—trying to make it look like you've been transported to the home of the cuisine. So far, no one's complained and the restaurants are doing well, to say the least." L'Italia was full with all the high tables taken by people dressed for business.

She opened the menu and whistled. "At these prices, they don't get many tourists, eh?"

Lisa laughed. "Exactly. Don't worry, my company is picking up the tab for this one. Let me make it official. Are you interested in legal representation, Agent Sheen?"

"Not at this time."

She put on a resigned pout. "Fine. See if I take you to lunch again."

Diana grinned, but her reply was interrupted by the arrival of their waiter, who was true to form with dark hair and eyes and a physique that suggested he might spend his free hours rowing gondolas in Venice. He was dressed in black, except for the scarlet tie that tucked into his fashionable vest. They ordered lunches and glasses of red wine to go with it, and he departed. They caught each other watching him leave and laughed.

Lisa sighed. "I wonder if he's single."

"I could ask him for you."

"Really, no thanks. Speaking of which, how's Bry-bry?"

She rolled her eyes. "Bryant is fine. I'll see him later tonight, in fact."

"Sure, you have time to spend with him but only lunch for me."

"There's no need to be a jerk. You're welcome to visit whenever you like. You keep promising and failing to deliver. Which, you know, might be why your relationships don't work out." Her friend's mouth formed a perfect circle and she tossed a piece of bread at Diana's head. She caught it with a laugh. "Okay, okay, that one was over the line. I'm sorry."

Lisa folded her arms and glared over the small rectangular table at her. "You'd better be."

Diana drew an X across her heart with her index finger. "How's work?"

The other woman sighed and took a sip of the Chianti that had arrived a few moments before the bread incident. "Things seem to have quieted. It doesn't seem like they're keeping secrets or anything anymore. In fact, it doesn't seem like they're doing anything. I haven't heard of any new clients for the firm, and heaven knows I certainly haven't gotten any. Maybe I'm being frozen out."

"You don't sound like that idea particularly bothers you."

She shook her head. "It did at one point, but not so

much anymore. It's a job. I thought it would be a career, but that looks less and less likely."

"Are you planning to look for something new?"

Lisa shrugged. "Eventually, I guess. I'm not sure if I want to stay in law. I could be a hell of a lobbyist—and take people to lunch all the time."

Diana laughed. "You're aware that, generally speaking, it doesn't involve projectiles, right?" She leaned back as a different server, also quite handsome, delivered their meals. Lisa had chosen a sensible Sicilian chicken dish that had a luxurious-looking cream sauce. She had seen gnocchi on the menu and had been unable to resist, and the perfect little dumplings rested enticingly in a pesto sauce. The aromas drifting up from the entrees were irresistible, and for a while, they focused on eating. Near the end, as usual, they traded dishes for the last couple of mouthfuls.

When the plates were cleared and tiramisu and coffees on the way, Diana had run out of ways to avoid the biggest question at hand. She squared her shoulders and met Lisa's gaze. "Are you okay? Like, *really* okay? After…you know?"

The other woman nodded once decisively. "I'm fine. And I'm not simply saying that. At first, it was scary, sure. But once I got my wits about me, I realized there were only two ways the story would end. One, you would rescue me before the pivotal moment came. Or two, I would fight him with everything I had and either win or go out knowing I'd done all I could. Of course, I liked the first better, so I was more than happy when you and the Drow showed up."

She searched her friend's eyes but found no deception

in them. "So, no lingering effects? Nightmares? Flashbacks?"

Lisa shook her head. "Nope. It has made me train more seriously, though, so I guess ultimately, it was positive." She laughed. "It's damn far to go for a good result—to another planet and all—but whatever. It could be that I needed that kick in the ass."

"You've become harder since I left."

"Damn straight. When my guardian angel deserted me, I had to improve at taking care of myself in the first place. It's all good. It's a tough world out there, and every day, I am better prepared to deal with it." She pulled on the chain around her neck and the half-heart necklace pendant popped out. "Of course, I'm not dumb enough to be without this, either."

She laughed and pressed her own where it lay against her chest. "Good call, blondie. Maybe next time, you'll be the one saving me."

———

The trip from the restaurant to her hotel had been far more sedate, thanks to the downtown traffic, and Diana had used the rest of the day to nap, clear some paperwork, and get ready for Bryant's arrival. When he finally arrived, looking bedraggled from work, she pounced on him and made sure he knew how much she missed him. It was quickly evident that the feeling was mutual.

The next morning, she stepped out of the shower in shorts and a t-shirt with a towel wrapped around her hair to discover that breakfast had appeared. He was already dressed in his standard suit for another day dealing with the political side of ARES. That they'd managed to shoe-horn in one evening together was a victory given the chaos facing the agency, but the need to have this conversation in person had been the true reason for the trip. The rest was merely a bonus. *Super-bonus, actually.*

She dropped into the chair across from him and lifted the silver dome covering her plate. It was filled with eggs, bacon, toast, and waffles. A small caddy of assorted condiments and toppings sat on a cart nearby, with a mug and two carafes of coffee. She sighed. "You do know me well, Bry-Bry."

He choked on his drink, and she laughed while he dabbed at his lips with a napkin. "Bry-Bry?"

She nodded. "Lisa says hello."

"Ah, gotcha."

Diana retrieved her purse and withdrew four items that, to a casual observer, appeared to be D batteries. She pulled off one side of each to expose the adhesive and stuck them on the walls. Two probably would have been enough to defeat most electronic surveillance, but she wanted to be sure. They would emit signals across frequencies that should deal with everything from vibration microphones to spies with stethoscopes pressed against the wall. Spillover would take care of the ceiling and floor, which had more natural insulation anyway, Kayleigh had assured her.

She checked the app on her phone to ensure that all four were working properly, and the indicators came up green. Satisfied, she dug into her food and alternated chewing with talking. "So, we have a thing for you to do."

Bryant sipped his coffee and leaned back casually as if they were simply discussing the weather. Only the narrowing of his eyes revealed his concern.

She nodded. "Yep. Kayleigh and Deacon have discovered a few things. We need you to get the oversight committee together."

"That shouldn't be difficult."

"*All* the members of the committee." She pointed the butter knife she was using to put raspberry jam on her toast at him.

His eyes widened, and he leaned forward. "Now you have my attention. Not only Clarke?"

She shook her head. "We've had other pings. Tomassi is implicated too. At this point, we have no way to be sure how deep it goes, so we need them all there."

"Damn. The idea of getting rid of Clarke has a lot of appeal. Even Cyphret. But there's no telling how the makeup could change if more are involved."

Diana shrugged. "As long as the negative votes are the ones who lose their positions, it's a win, right?"

Bryant seemed unconvinced. "I suppose, but at least with Cyphret, Clarke, and Tomassi, you know which way they'll break. If we replace them with others, who knows how crazy or how persuasive they might be?"

She stopped eating and regarded him levelly. "If it gets worse, there are always options, right?" He'd discussed only the most superficial details of Project Adonis with her, but she was reasonably sure the oversight committee was no longer in the plans if that protocol was invoked.

He nodded. "Yes, but it would be nice, for a while at least, to have a group of people who actually support us."

Diana laughed. "You're so much more cynical than Taggart. You should quit being so enthralled with the trappings of power and give him his job back."

The inappropriate comment broke through his reserve, and he chuckled. "I would love to return Carson's office, desk, and responsibilities to him. In fact, when he wakes up —that very minute—I'll get him a secure phone and tablet and go back to leading ARES DC."

"You're in the big leagues now, buddy. Even if he does take the job again, you know you'll never lead a single team again. Jealous?"

Bryant rose, checked his watch, and leaned over to kiss her on the top of her head. "Entirely so. And now I need to go be powerful."

She stood and put her hands on her hips. "If you try to walk out of that door without giving me a proper kiss goodbye, I will shoot you." Wisely, he complied. As he broke the lingering lip-lock, she murmured, "I would have, you know."

He grinned. "Shut up and kiss me again, or I will shoot you."

Diana obeyed, happy that their priorities were in accord where it counted.

CHAPTER FIVE

Dreven remained silent as the others filed into their places. The ruined courtyard around them seemed extraordinarily still, even ominous as he cast the shield to protect them from prying eyes and ears. The entire place was somehow more decrepit than the last time they had gathered. *Or maybe that's the empty place where Ushev's presence used to weigh on me.*

The death of the underground gnome had been a shock to them all when Iressa had shared the news. She, of course, had been as unperturbed as always. Whether it was because she'd known for longer, having been present when it happened, or because she lacked any actual feelings, he couldn't hazard a guess. She was a threatening presence to his right, and he avoided looking at her.

Quiet reigned until Jakko initiated the discussions. "My operations were a success. The level of chaos in the capital city has increased considerably."

Pesharn, the towering Kilomea across the circle, nodded. "It is so in the city above Stonesreach, as well.

And within the kemana, things advance as expected." Dreven frowned as engaging with those in the underground community was technically not her prerogative to address, but he did not speak. To protest would seem weak and to congratulate her would seem like an endorsement.

Iressa's sultry voice spoke next. "Although the daggers are lost to us due to Ushev's incompetence, I continue to seek the sword."

He winced. The blame game had begun the instant she'd returned alone, and he doubted she was being entirely forthright about the matter. Lacking any evidence to the contrary, there was little he could do to contradict her. *Besides, there is little favor to be won here any longer. If ever we were truly a collective, we are now simply an arrangement of individuals whose purposes overlap at the moment.* He smiled inwardly. *However, perhaps it's time to sow some animosity.*

With that in mind, he turned to confront the woman. As always, she was dressed in a tight black dress that covered her completely and still managed to be revealing. Her dark hair fell in luxurious curls to frame her pale face. A hint of makeup on her cheeks and a red tint on her perfect lips finished the look. Her wry grin revealed that she'd noticed him staring. Again. *Damn her to the World in Between.* He gestured with his chin. "Why should we believe that Ushev is responsible for the failure of the task you both shared? It's rather easy to blame him now that he is no longer present to defend himself."

She laughed. "You have answered your own question. Had he not failed, he would be here with us. Since he is

not, clearly, he is responsible for the humans' acquisition of the weapons."

Dreven shook his head. "Perhaps you abandoned him. Perhaps you are working with the humans to undermine the rest of us." Her look of shock was quickly banished but suggested she had something to hide. *Maybe she did abandon him.*

Her face was beautiful when she smiled but shone with a far more cutting beauty when she scowled. "Do not throw accusations about, Dreven. How are we to know that you, oh noble leader, are not manipulating our efforts to your own ends? It seems very strange that your underlings have failed so many times, now, to eliminate the woman who leads our enemies."

He sighed. *I knew it was stupid to challenge her, and I did it anyway.* With a turn to face the Dwarf on his left, he changed the subject. "Let's deal with reality instead of spurious accusations, shall we? Perhaps it is time we changed the roles. Jakko, Pesharn, are you willing to seek the sword?"

They both nodded and looked surprised at the request but certainly prepared to accept the responsibility. The Kilomea asked, "As before, we will determine afterward who is to wield it?" Dreven confirmed that was the case.

Iressa spoke before he could continue. "And what, pray tell, do you have in mind for me, wise one?"

He grinned at her. "You and I have the same task since I would not want to risk our comrades' wellbeing by putting them in the same situation as Ushev was in. We will both target the enemy leader and remove her from the field once and for all."

Iressa nodded, having no legitimate escape from the cage he'd dropped around her. He caught smirks on the faces of the others and hid his own. *I may have signed my own death notice.* He watched her walk away, the ever-present sway in her step no longer enticing. *If that is the case, so be it. I've had enough of this illusory teamwork. It is time to finish with this ruse and claim the power that is rightfully mine. That will not be accomplished by playing fair with these fools.*

His master had chosen to speak virtually rather than in person, so Dreven portaled to his hidden chamber and awaited the mental prod that would indicate Lechnas's readiness. He had abandoned the long robes he'd worn in the courtyard in favor of tunic and trousers of a soft material and walked barefoot on the warm wood that made up the floor and walls of the space.

He had retrieved his meditation rug and knelt upon it in the center of the room. Before their first psychic meeting, Dreven's intuition had told him that facing his master in a subordinate physical position would be a good idea, both to help him condition his responses and in case the scarred man was somehow able to see his surroundings.

Unlike in previous encounters, where the summons had been a gentle pull that he had followed to find the man, this was a whirlwind that ripped him from his own mind and deposited him on a broad plateau of ebony rock with molten lava trickling in streams to either side. The acrid air made his eyes sting and water as he peered around for Lechnas.

He stood with his back to Dreven, gazing out at an empty horizon. His formal black attire was missing this time, replaced by elegant black chain mail and plate. A sword was sheathed at his right hand. Dreven rose to his feet, hunched in self-defense against the brutal wind that ripped through the space. It seemed to not touch the other man and only swirled around him before it moved on to the other available target.

The other man's voice was deep and angry. "Dreven."

He bowed his head and yelled over the noise of the wind. "Master." Lechnas gave an irritated wave, and the gale vanished. He stumbled forward as the resistance evaporated, then rose to his full height and clasped his hands behind his back. "Thank you, master."

"Your failures are becoming too many to bear."

He stiffened his muscles to control their trembling. "With respect, master, we agreed to let the others seek the blades."

Lechnas shook his head but did not contradict the statement. An unknown amount of time passed while he waited for the other man to speak again. He calmed his mind by planning the many ways he could act against the enemy leader. Finally, his master turned to face him. His expression was as neutral as always, and yet there was deep anger beneath, only visible in the depths of his eyes. Dreven saw it and felt twinges of fear in his core. He harbored no doubt that his superior could kill him with a word, regardless of the fact that they were not physically near one another.

"Other matters hasten toward their conclusion, and this ongoing resistance to our efforts on Earth has become more than a simple nuisance. If your people are inadequate to the task of quashing it, then you must handle it yourself." Dreven opened his mouth to speak, to defend himself but was halted by an upraised hand. "Whatever you are about to say, I do not wish to hear it."

The other man strode forward, and his spirit quailed. With each step, his superior seemed more threatening, more powerful, and more capable of instant and brutal violence. He stopped when his breastplate touched Dreven and gazed down at him. "Let me put the matter as simply as possible for you. If your underlings fail again, they and you shall all die. It is therefore to your benefit to ensure they do not fail."

He paused, searched his eyes, then stepped back with a nod. "It seems to me that the best way to accomplish this is to handle it yourself. I will not speak to you again until you have success to report. If it is failure that you would bring to me, I recommend that you run, far and fast, as it may prolong your life for a day or two."

His master waved a hand and Dreven sprawled on his back in his own chamber. His head smacked off the wall that had been a half-room behind him when he'd knelt to commune with Lechnas. He paused to let the fear that had built up in him trickle away, only to discover a large portion refused to leave. With an effort of will, he pushed himself up and ran his hands through his disarranged hair.

"Fine. If you wish to abandon subtlety, that's what we'll do." He muttered to himself as he cast the spells to warn his subordinate on Earth that he wished to speak to her. A separate corner of his mind compiled a list of the items he would need to bring when he went to the other planet to take matters into his own hands.

Success you shall have, my master, or my underlings' blood shall flow to appease you. And, one day, when the tables have well and truly turned, you will have cause to regret threatening me.

CHAPTER SIX

The warehouse was as crowded as he'd seen it since the earliest days of "Tommy Ketchum's" involvement with the Remembrance gang. The populations of both the magicals and the human contingents had been bolstered by aggressive campaigning after the attack on Wysse and the other witches.

Sloan had been a part of the latter group's strategy sessions with Marcus, thanks to his connection with Mur. Each time they noticed a different magical face added to the mix, they responded with three or four humans, ensuring the balance of power remained tilted in their favor. The human leader had beamed with pleasure when they'd realized Sarah would not name a new top witch or wizard for the arcane side of the house and perceived it as an acknowledgment of her diminished status with Dreven in charge.

Sloan wasn't so sure about that. *Of course, I might simply be paranoid. Each minute I spend in that woman's presence makes me more worried.* The madness in her eyes that had been ever-present since her return from the World in Between seemed more volatile lately as if she could snap at any moment and kill everyone around her for the simple joy of it. He'd shared that worry with Marcus, and the other man had laughed. "Let her try," he'd said, "and she'll be dead before she has time to cast a second spell." *Mental note—stay out of the way of the first spell.*

Tonight's gathering was a scheduled one, the twice-weekly meeting where assignments for petty thefts and territory-grabs were handed out. Marcus was vocally supportive and excited about the concept of sowing chaos, and the human side of the house secretly engaged in its own additional illegal and chaotic activities on the side. Sloan wasn't sure what became of the loot they stole as Murray and Marcus took control after the jobs and drove off on their own. His best guess was that they fenced the merchandise quickly and built up cash to fund some secretive plans of their own. Well, of Marcus' own. Murray wasn't really the type for secretive plans.

He made a slow circuit of the human side of the room, exchanging fist bumps and greetings with the people who'd been around long enough to know him. The newbies were a different breed, young and hard with things to prove. Marcus called them soldiers and a condescending laugh usually accompanied the term. *It seems like he's willing to sell people's lives cheaply to get what he wants. I suppose that's not particularly out of character.*

When his travels brought him into the tight circle formed by Marcus, Mur, and a couple of others, he was greeted warmly by all and warmest by Murray. Even though he'd kept up as much of a wall as he could, he had to admit that he liked the awkward lieutenant who'd carried Sloan with him as his own fortunes improved. The bald man now wore immaculate black suits—a far cry from their first meeting, which seemed like years ago. His gruff voice was filled with goodwill. "Tommy, great to see you. How you been?"

They'd seen each other only days before, but that was for one of Marcus's side jobs. While in the warehouse, appearances needed to be maintained. "Good, Mur, really good. Chilling. Living the life, you know?"

"Nothing better." He nodded at Marcus, who was engaged in an animated conversation with one of the new bloods. "The big man says that this will be an important meeting for the gang." Sloan's eyes narrowed. It was an odd thing to say, and he took it as a warning that he'd need to stay on his toes. He gazed around the warehouse with a more discerning eye and his scrutiny revealed patterns in the arrangements of people. The groupings that had appeared random now seemed intentional. Humans and magicals each separated themselves into small units that paralleled one another across the invisible centerline of the space like opposing teams guarding against an attack from the other.

Shit. If a battle is about to go down, I am completely under-equipped. He carried only his pistol, an unreliable automatic Murray had provided some time before. Sloan put a blank expression on his face and sent out his magic in the vague hope to get a flash of knowledge or intuition from someone more in the know. All it returned was a number of people feeling the same anxiety over the unknown as him. He turned to return to Mur's side when a blast of rage struck, so powerful that it almost overwhelmed him.

His talent was unpredictable at best and fickle and undependable at worst. He often thought of it as a sentient being that thrived on mocking his needs, which is why he'd trained himself not to depend on it. But when it worked, it really worked. He knew instantly that he had landed inside Sarah's mind. The ominous presence of her memories of the World in Between threatened her sanity, locked away behind a door that was far thinner than he would be comfortable with. The fear and anger that boiled there was now the fundamental layer of her personality, and it pushed eagerly to slip free of its confines.

Above it lay strata of anger, each directed at different people. Dreven, who he'd heard of but never seen. Marcus. Mur. Vincente, even, for creating the portal that had landed her in the nightmare she would seemingly never escape. Mixed fury and remorse for Wysse's failure to stay alive. The only positive thought seemed to be a hint of future happiness wrapped around a generic image of a woman. *Herself? Someone else? A girlfriend?* He had no way to tell.

Sloan felt her determination and realized she was about to emerge from the office above. He pushed the sensations deep inside and faded into the background to the left in a casual saunter, away from Marcus, away from Sarah, and away from any of the magicals who might somehow sense his own powers being used. It had never happened, but that didn't mean it couldn't.

The door above banged open with a metallic clang that echoed through the warehouse and stilled conversations almost instantly. The one chucklehead soldier who continued to speak was quickly shushed by his comrades as every eye raised to the entrance at the top of the staircase. Sarah stepped into the anticipatory silence as if onto a stage and paused to sweep her eyes over the collected audience before she descended halfway, a single ringing step at a time.

When she reached the middle, she stopped, turned, and rested her hands on the railing in front of her. Sloan shuddered at the memory of the rage within her, visible in the way her fists clenched around the metal. She nodded at the magical side of the room, then repeated the process with the other half, her lips twisted with a hint of distaste. *Imperfect self-control, which fits with what I saw in her mind.* He took another couple of steps away from the witch and circled behind a group of tough-looking men wearing matching biker jackets. Marcus had cast a wide net to find warriors for his cause, whatever it was.

Sarah's voice seemed to echo, filled with a confidence he knew she didn't truly feel. "My people. You are deserving of thanks. For weeks, we have shown those in this city what true power looks like, taking what we want when we want it without fear of interruption or prosecution." *That's one way to look at it. You could also contend that by doing small jobs, you stayed off the radar enough that no one cares.* "But now, we are called upon to do more."

There was laughter behind him from where Marcus stood, now surrounded by the leaders of the various groups that made up his power base. A brief tilt of her head indicated that Sarah had taken note of it before she continued without a change in demeanor. "It is time to think bigger. We must plan something so impactful, so audacious, that no one will see it coming. And I have exactly the thing."

She gazed at her audience, and Sloan flashed on her again. This time, he heard her thoughts. *We will get him to come here, and in the confusion, eliminate him.* It wasn't clear who she was thinking of, but a trill of fear vibrated within that it might be him before he discarded the idea. He was a small fish, and the level of antipathy she felt was enormous.

"When we were tasked to attack the stadium in Philadelphia, it was a ruse to draw out the enemy and eliminate them. A good strategic move, but one that met with only partial success due to failures by many who are no longer with us." Her smile was thin-lipped and cold. "We will do better here. A multi-pronged assault will separate rather than concentrate their forces, allowing us to defeat and destroy them. It will take the commitment and skills of everyone in this room, and others who have yet to join us."

He looked around and discovered that the people on both sides of the floor had been captivated by her words. Heads nodded, and the assorted criminals talked softly but with clear excitement at the plan. She finished the message perfectly. "And once we have destroyed them, the city will be ours for the taking." She gave a single decisive nod and turned to return to her office. Marcus strode forward and trailed her up the stairs.

Mur stepped beside Sloan and shook his head. "I might be a pessimist, but this seems like a bad idea."

He sighed. "I'm right there with you. I guess we'd better get to planning our end before our leader comes back and wants to know what we've come up with." The other man clapped him on the shoulder, and they headed to a distant corner to talk privately.

Sarah had barely settled behind the desk with an exasperated sigh when Marcus entered in a haze of anger. She gave him a thin grin and nodded to the seat on the opposite side. He shut the door gently rather than the dramatic slam she had expected and lowered himself into the chair.

His voice was slow and sleepy, which she'd learned was an indication that he was at his most dangerous. She slipped her backup wand carefully from its hidden sheath and held it under the desk as he spoke. "So, Sarah, what the hell do you think you're doing? Last I checked, we were working together."

She nodded. "Indeed. But I have had conversations with Dreven that you have not been privy to, and he has charged us with this task." She kept her voice level so he wouldn't detect the lie. She had spoken with their leader, that much was true, but the rest was on her own initiative. The wizard had appeared distracted and disengaged, which seemed to confirm what Iressa had told her about his current situation. *Once the plan is in place and we are committed, he will have no option but to come and join us to ensure its success.*

Her human counterpart shook his head. "And it never occurred to you to discuss this matter with me before you shared it with our people?"

Sarah grinned. "Of course it did. I chose not to. It's not

as if we have much choice, anyway, given our orders. What was there to talk about, really?"

The faintest whir carried across the desk as he raised his mechanical arm and she tensed, relaxing only when he had finished adjusting his hair and returned the limb to its neutral position. His expression revealed that he'd done it deliberately and was pleased with the result. He seemed thoughtful for a moment as he sat in silence, then shrugged and rose from the chair. "You're right. It seems as if there's only a single path forward. For now."

He departed, but the menace in his words lingered after him. *I need to convince Iressa that he needs to die sooner rather than later. Much sooner.* She waved her wand to close and ward the door, leaned back and closed her eyes, and set her mind free to invent clever ways to have Marcus killed.

CHAPTER SEVEN

Diana had been shocked when Nylotte summoned the tray holding the teapot and cups before their training session. Normally, the Dark Elf—the other Dark Elf—reserved beverages and conversation for after she'd reduced her student to an exhausted, sweaty mess. The tea set was different as well, a lacquered orange-red with some kind of ideographs sketched on it.

The drink itself was deeply flavored and bitter, befitting its claim of "smoked." It popped on the tongue and was harsh on the swallow. Either the taste or the caffeine, or both, was potent enough to increase her alertness level with each sip. Her teacher hadn't spoken and only nodded at her arrival and served the brew. *And I sure as hell won't say anything until she does. That's asking for trouble.*

Nylotte's outfit was also unusual. She had foregone her normal clinging clothes in favor of a loose kimono-like top in a deeper red than the tea set. It was folded closed but didn't appear to have a belt or any other fastener to hold it that way. She laughed inwardly at the thought of the uppity woman using Velcro on her wardrobe, then sobered as the Drow placed her cup carefully on the tray and rotated it into the desired position. *Damn. She's concerned about something.*

Diana set her own mug down and focused her attention on her teacher. Nylotte tucked a strand of her white hair behind an elegantly pointed ear and sighed. "As much as I do not wish to be wrapped up in the nonsense going on in this city other than through your training, it appears I have no option. Lady Alayne has spoken quietly to several members of the community about the growing discord in the kemana."

She nodded. "Does she continue to blame us for it?"

The elf laughed. "She does. I think it is more about keeping the general peace down here than actually believing you are responsible, though. She has not come out and said so, but it is readily apparent that she does not wish you, or anyone above, ill." The agent ran a hand over her forehead to wipe away imaginary sweat, and the other woman smiled. "That does not change the fact that the Remembrance has gained traction here, where we all assumed such things were impossible."

She frowned. "I've wondered about that for a while. Why have you considered yourself protected here?"

"Those who make their homes in Stonesreach mostly seek to disengage from Earth. I presume the same is true for a majority of those who opt for kemana life, but I don't know that for certain. As a result, we inhabit a kind of middle ground between the worlds. Why, then, would we involve ourselves with the very thing we avoid by choosing to live here?"

"I can see that, I guess. But if you wish to remain apart from the doings of this planet, why not return to Oriceran?"

The Drow smiled thinly. "There are many reasons." She waved a hand. "All are irrelevant, in any case. But it appears that the issues from above have spread here, and more widely than anyone anticipated."

Diana tilted her head to the side and fixed her teacher with a hard look. "You sound like you're referring to something specific rather than generalizing."

"Indeed." She nodded. "There have been several incidents of what you would call graffiti celebrating the words of Rhazdon from long ago. Incitements, threats, that kind of thing."

"And is there no way to trace the ones who created them?"

"It was attempted, of course, but with no success. The culprits masked their magic well."

She sighed. "And now you are involved. Why? Because of me?"

Nylotte shook her head. "I would have been a part of the discussion regardless because of the place I hold as one of the community's longest-standing members. Every Kemana needs a person who can buy and sell things that are, shall we say, slightly outside the norm."

It was the closest her teacher had ever come to admitting to anything patently against the rules. She felt a momentary surge of concern but remembered she'd already been over that ground and found the woman trustworthy. *Besides, who am I to judge? My hands aren't exactly spotless.* Her mental voice manifested out of nowhere. *"Are*

we going to discuss your failures? I have so many to talk about!"
Diana visualized pitching an imaginary fireball at her, and
her internal avatar fled, laughing.

She cleared her throat. "So, is there any way I can help?"

Her teacher snorted as she rose and levitated the tray
with her. "Take care of your nonsense above as quickly as
possible so the nonsense below fails as well."

Diana matched her motion. "That easy? Consider it
done." *Exactly what I needed, another thing to worry about.* The
warning from Sloan that something big involving a
stadium was imminent never strayed far from her mind
but fortunately, the baseball team was out of town for a
few more days. The day they returned was an ugly one,
from a strategic standpoint, as there were evening events at
both stadiums. They'd already alerted the authorities and
been denied AET support from nearby cities, which were
having their own issues. She banished the myriad of
worries into the future and focused on dealing with the
here and now.

Their cushions flew out of the space as her teacher
returned to the circle, having discarded the flowing robe to
reveal her normal garb of tight leather pants, boots, and
the same embroidered black top she'd worn the first time
they'd met. Diana was in hers as well—tactical pants, boots,
and a concert t-shirt, today's selection a retro Billy Idol
look. They took their customary positions opposite one
another and exchanged nods before Nylotte threw a fireball at her head.

The agent summoned her own fire and shaped it into a
curved buckler to bat the flaming sphere away. The Drow
waved her hand and the ball stopped moving, then curved

to the right in another searing attack. She mixed her magics, using telekinesis to slow it and the fire shield to smack it back. Her teacher responded by adding a second one, then a third, until they were engaged in some kind of odd multi-object tennis match.

The training style that had evolved between them as her skills grew was taxing, and she was aware of her strength flowing away. Nylotte called, "Siphon," and Diana gritted her teeth. As a means of extending her battle ability, the other woman had tried to teach her to draw power from incoming attacks as she defended against them. It required her to divide her attention, which inevitably resulted in one of the strikes breaking through. Still, she obeyed and pulled from the spheres when they impacted her shield to refill her reservoir of strength.

Her opponent added another sphere, and she did a decent job of dealing with it, but the fifth was too much. She yelped in pain as it caught her bare forearm and burned her and immediately raised several blisters. Expecting an attack to follow, she walled the agony off, but her teacher handed her a healing potion instead. "Only a sip, enough to reduce it to a light burn. We don't want you to pass out after the session."

Diana nodded and followed her instructions, then returned the vial. The Drow used her magic to trace a human figure in the air made of light, sketching a body with an oval of flame that flickered in one hand, connected to a long line that reached into the middle where a glowing ball pulsed. "This is what you are doing." She pointed at the shield. "You gather the power here and send it along this path." A flickering dot traveled into the center. "Then, you draw it forth again to use in your defense." It sped in the opposite direction. "Instead, why not employ it immediately?"

She frowned and tried to understand how she might do such a thing. "I get the idea. I'm not sure how to accomplish it, though."

Her teacher shrugged. "Now that you have the concept, your magical self will work on it in the background. Today, our goal is different."

The agent shook her stinging arm and clapped briskly. "All right, what'll it be?"

"Ice." She only had time to think *bloody hell* before the attacks were on their way. She reacted instinctively and summoned a wave of force to turn the spikes in midair and hurl them at the other woman. Her opponent made a lifting gesture with both hands, and the shards rose, turned, and rained down on her. By then, she had a force buckler ready to deflect them. She tried to draw energy from them but couldn't manage it and felt the strength flowing out of her again.

The attack ceased, and her instructor paced before her. "You have good reflexes but you cannot draw from a dissimilar power. So, to extract the energy from ice, you will need to create ice."

Diana groaned. She'd had almost no luck with ice so far. "Do you have any suggestions?"

Her teacher nodded. "One. Escape, or die." She raised her hands and before the agent could react, two cones of frost emerged, washed up and down over her, and encased her in a block of ice. She couldn't move and couldn't breathe, and immediately began to panic. Nylotte's voice sounded in her head. "Stay calm. You can do this. Now, expand your senses and investigate where the magic is touching you."

She did as she was told and drew upon her earlier lessons in power absorption to worm her way into the ice with her mind. She saw the individual crystals and how they were bound together. When the stars from lack of oxygen began, she mistook them for part of the ice at first. Fear set in, but she pushed it down ruthlessly and stretched her mind further. *Nylotte won't let me die. Probably. But I don't want to fail.* At the edge of consciousness, she found the magic that held the elements in place despite their desire to surrender to the room's temperature.

The block collapsed as she drew that connective power into her, and she sucked a deep breath in greedily as she dropped to one knee. She took a moment to collect herself, then rose to face her teacher, her hands clenched at her sides. Frost gathered around them, and she thrust them both out abruptly. Spheres of ice careened across the distance to the Drow in an instant, struck her in the chest, and passed straight through. The illusion vanished, and Diana spun to find Nylotte sitting on a storage crate, watching her.

She clapped slowly, half-sincere and half-mocking. "Well done, my student. You've found the key to ice. It will be a simple matter for you to learn how to pull it with your shield once you accomplish the same with fire."

"Was it entirely necessary to freeze me?"

The Dark Elf shrugged. "Necessary? Perhaps not. Effective? Obviously. Fun?" She grinned. "Definitely."

Diana shook her head, then realized she felt much less

exhausted than normal after a training session. She remarked on it, and her teacher nodded. "The energy you absorbed has essentially refueled you."

She stretched and felt the pops in her spine as her bones cracked. "I could get used to this."

The other woman turned serious. "All the more reason to locate the sword, my protégé. Once you've fully bonded with it, the weapon can act as a repository for power and give you additional resources should you find yourself in need."

The thought of that much magic at hand made her heart leap, but a sudden realization made it drop an equal amount. "Is it the same with Rhazdon's Defense?"

"Good intuition. Yes, it is. That, also, is able to store energy for its user."

"So someone wearing it will possess more ability to use magic here on Earth before becoming exhausted." She nodded. "Damn."

"That does about sum it up." The Drow cast a portal that led to the corner of Diana's bedroom, always kept clear for such things. "Now, go and find a way to bring these Remembrance idiots to heel before I have to deal with them down here, please."

Diana touched the brim of an imaginary hat. "As you wish, oh wise one." She skipped through the rift before her teacher could counter. *Ha. I had the last word for once. That'll teach her to lock me in an ice cube.*

CHAPTER EIGHT

Chan grinned when Rath and Max trotted up to the entrance of the community center. The troll smiled at his teacher and did a backflip off the dog's back, growing to his three-foot size by the time they'd reached him. He offered a fist, and the older man bumped it.

"Thank you for coming, Rath."

"Thank you for inviting. Must train."

The teacher swung the door open with a laugh and ushered them inside. Each of the previous training sessions with the man had been different. The first was very basic, and Rath had left it in possession of the pair of throwing knives that rested in the dog's harness. When he'd received them, they were dull and nicked. Since then, the ARES agents had taught him how to care for them and provided him with his own whetstone to use every day to keep them sharp and true. It was a calming ritual he performed before bed or before a patrol, depending on the night.

The second time had been all about accuracy. He'd thrown blades until his arms were sore but his aim improved with each toss. *Well, almost each toss.* The one that clattered off the wall near Chan was not a representative example.

Today's summons arrived via the walkie-talkie Rath had provided to Manny that interfaced with the comm the troll always kept close. The older man had passed on the message from his teacher instructing him to come to this location an hour after it closed. The last rays of sunlight were fading on the horizon, and the lights were all on in the surrounding businesses. The inside was deserted except for a cleaning crew, and Chan exchanged pleasant remarks with them as he led the troll and the Borzoi into the depths of the building.

In the gymnasium, which was large enough for two basketball games side-by-side, his teacher had set up a pair of obstacle courses. One was appropriate to his current size, but the other was much smaller. Max barked in excitement, no doubt registering that the second course was meant for them both. Rath couldn't contain his own grin at the thought. It had been some time since they'd worked on their skills together, having long ago become proficient enough that only occasional sessions were needed to stay at the top of their game.

On the bleachers at the starting end of the challenges, Professor Charlotte Stanley sat reading a book. A takeout cup with the logo of a nearby coffee shop stood beside her, and on the other side, her oversized black bag. Rath had once heard of a thing called a "bag of holding" which had infinite space inside it, and thought hers might be one of those based on the wide variety of items he'd seen her pull out of it.

Chan led them to the smaller of the two courses. "I've done some work on blades for your smallest form." He gestured to a small case nearby. Rath lifted the lid and discovered six tiny throwing knives, each about the size of a needle. They were held by a thin piece of leather with holes in it for the blades and a loop around the end. He looked up, and the weapons expert nodded. "To attach to Max's collar. This will at least give you something you can use from a distance while you're riding him if you find yourself in a situation where you can't change your size."

Rath hadn't worn his miniature gear much of late because he preferred his larger forms whenever he wasn't with Max. But ideas began to spring to mind about how they might work together in scenarios other than random patrols like they had when trying to capture the pirate for the first time. The memory inspired a frown as he recalled the man's end at the hands of the mysterious assassin, Amadeo. He shook his head and banished the worry. *Can't do anything now. Later, though. He's a criminal. I am the law.*

Chan helped him to secure the weapon strap onto the dog's collar, and Rath shrank to the appropriate size and climbed Max's fur to reach his back. He pushed on the leather to move it to the side so he would have a better draw angle and nodded. The man who now towered above him gestured ahead. "It's a simple enough course. Weave in and out of the exercise balls, go over the barbells, and through the suspended hoops. When you see a target, hit it. There are six, and they might not be where you expect them to be."

Rath tightened his grip while Max walked to the starting place indicated by an X in painter's blue tape on the floor. The dog's claws clicked against the wood, and he whispered, "Careful. Slippy. Watch footing." His partner gave a soft chuff of acknowledgment, and his muscles trembled as he prepared to run.

Chan clapped loudly. "Go!" His shout echoed off the walls as Max flowed smoothly into motion. The Borzoi was economical in his movements as he dodged between the exercise balls, which were set up in a slalom. They were the large kind, and Rath couldn't see over them. When the target appeared on the one to the left, he had only an instant to draw and hurl the slender piece of metal in an awkward cross-body throw. Still, working with Chan had improved his skills enough that the blade pierced the outer ring of the target.

There was no time to celebrate as the dog broke out of the pattern of large spheres and headed at an angle toward the barbells placed about a foot apart from each other. In the center of the arrangement were two targets, one to the left and one to the right, and another suspended at a high diagonal to the right a few feet behind them.

He drew and tossed at the one on the right in a fluid movement, and the knife struck in the middle of the X in the center. Quickly, he shifted position, drew the next, and threw it in the air to catch it in a better throwing angle. The dog leapt at that moment, but Rath focused and whipped his arm forward seconds before his mount's paws returned to the floor. The blade tumbled as it moved and embedded itself above the target. *Drat*. He had been watching old movies lately and had taken to using slang words from that era at random moments. *Dagnabit*.

The next one posed a challenge. The distance was

diminishing rapidly as he drew another blade, but the angles were all wrong. He scurried up the dog's spine, his balance sure on the ever-moving muscles as the Borzoi leapt as gently as he could over the obstructions. When he reached his partner's head, he still needed a little more. "Higher, Max." The dog obeyed and raised his chin, and Rath threw the weapon before he back-flipped to return to his position. He landed as the wickedly sharp metal sliced through the hanging paper and continued to clatter on the floor beyond it.

He had no attention to spare. *Four down, two to go.* He saw them ahead, one high and one low on the final hula hoop. The rings were suspended about a foot off the ground and weren't all that large, which required Max to pull his limbs in as he traveled through them. In turn, that made the ride rockier, and the troll wracked his brain to resolve the puzzle before him. The top one was easy, but he couldn't see how to aim at the other at all. When the solution came to him, and he grinned at Chan's cleverness. *Got me thinking about partners. Sometimes, partners have to separate.* It was a lesson he'd learned quickly at Diana's side.

Rath drew the final two knives and gripped one in each hand. He sighted on the top target as Max neared them and threw the blade in his left as the dog landed after leaping through a ring. The troll jumped back as the Borzoi hurtled forward, and as soon as the throwing lane was clear, he cast his final blade at the lower target, then touched down on the floor in the standard superhero landing pose with one arm out to his side. He looked up to see the slender shards embedded exactly where they were supposed to be. They had missed the center point, but both would have seriously damaged their intended targets.

He grew to three feet and dashed over to hug Max. "Excellent run. Best partner ever." The dog wagged his tail and licked his face, causing him to fall on the floor, giggling. When their celebration slowed, Professor Charlotte greeted them with a grin and Chan with a raised eyebrow. The man nodded at the other course, and Rath bounced up to take on his next challenge.

Later, after they'd cleared the courses and locked the community center—where it turned out Chan worked several days per week—Professor Charlotte treated them to drinks at the coffeeshop advertised on her cup. She chose herbal tea, and he opted for lemonade plus a bowl of ice water for Max. Chan's choice was a surprise, a frothy sweet coffee quite at odds with his general demeanor. His pleasure in the drink made Rath happy, as did his own selection, which had unexpected cherries swimming in the bottom to give it a nice touch of sweetness to balance the sour.

He hadn't been to this coffeehouse before and thought it looked fairly old-fashioned. When he remarked on it, Professor Charlotte laughed. "It's Bohemian, really, although it is from the past. But it's less about a time and more about an attitude."

Rath nodded. "Messy."

The others laughed, which was fine, but he hadn't tried to make a joke. It was about as cluttered with stuff—

pillows, especially—as he could imagine a place being. Fabric hung on the walls, and doorways had curtains. A pleasant incense filled the air with an unfamiliar scent. He took a deep sniff and sneezed, which made Max bark, which caused the others to laugh again.

Then, the woman sobered and shook her head. "I'm glad we're together, Rath, because there's something I wanted to discuss with you in person, rather than over the walkie-talkie." He shifted to face her where she sat on the bench beside him. "Honestly, it might be nothing, and I only mention it because things have been so unsettled here lately."

He nodded, and Chan touched her arm. "Whatever you're feeling is valid because you feel it, Charlotte. Just share it."

She gave him a small smile and looked down again. "Manny and I...well, we're fairly sure we're being watched."

Rath frowned and Max growled under the table. The troll's longstanding suspicion that the dog sensed his emotions like he did Diana's—and was affected by them in the same way—raised its head for a moment before being overcome by his immediate worry. "By who?"

She shrugged. "I have absolutely no clue. We've cast some simple charms to discover the source, but nothing has come of it."

"Would they find non-magicals?" He'd thought first of Amadeo, and the idea that the assassin might be hunting the Griffons caused his anger to spike. *No one threatens my friends.*

There was a pause as she considered the question. He assumed her habit of thinking every single thing through before speaking was part of her job as a teacher. "The ones we've used should be able to identify anyone, magical or not, but they're limited by distance. If we're being watched from farther away than our spells carry, they wouldn't manage it."

Another point that makes Amadeo a possibility. Max growled softly again, and Rath took it as a sign that he needed to quit centering his thoughts on the assassin. He grinned at a new notion. "Have idea. Willing to be cheese?"

She looked confused but Chan laughed. "In the mouse-trap, you mean?" The troll nodded, and the woman joined in the mirth.

"Rath, I would happily be the cheese if you have a plan to find out if anyone's watching us and who they are."

He grinned. "Oh, definite plan." He glanced at the dog beneath the table. "Sorry, Max. Gonna need Gwen for this one." The Borzoi gave a haughty sniff and put his head back between his paws, but the way his tail thumped on the ground told the real tale. *Sometimes together, sometimes apart, but always partners.*

CHAPTER NINE

When Hank had rolled the large delivery truck into the parking lot near the headquarters building, Diana had known immediately why he'd told her to look out the fifth-floor windows overlooking it at that exact moment. She'd groaned and headed out to see it.

As promised, it was a climate-controlled vehicle that offered the requisite space to carry the entire team and their gear. He'd already rigged a medical area in the portion nearest the cab, with a table and mechanic's chests filled with appropriate supplies secured to the walls. Benches ran along both sides, and there was enough head-room that they would be able to sit beneath the lockers he said he planned to install above them. Empty places awaiting weapons racks were closest to the back doors, and a large exit on one side near the front could be used for quick access to casualties or normal egress.

Diana had shaken her head and admitted defeat. "Well done. Don't break the bank, but if you're going to do it, do it right." She'd pretended not to notice the entirely obvious high-fives that Hank exchanged with Cara and Kayleigh. *It figures that the blonde brat was involved somehow. She's a menace.*

There hadn't been much time to devote to it since then as he shared surveillance duties on Sarah, who had been unusually mobile over the last couple of days. Worryingly, she and her people had been sighted near both of the city's sports fields as well as the college fields, the hockey arena, and even a minor league baseball park forty-five minutes to the south.

They'd worked on the assumption that the evening of the simultaneous pop concert and baseball game filling the two stadiums downtown would be the likely date. When Sloan's phone shifted to transmit mode and they heard the sounds of the gang preparing for an attack that night, it didn't come as a surprise.

They'd gathered at the base to gear up and her team expressed varying levels of frustration when she'd informed them that stun rifles would be the initial weapon of choice. Anik had been most vocal about the stupidity of trying to knock out people who were attempting to end your life but ultimately, everyone understood the need for a little extra care around the many civilians who would attend the events. It wasn't every day that one of the biggest names in music sold out a football stadium in Pittsburgh.

Cara had quipped, "And it's pop music. If we were talking heavy metal, that might be an appropriate sound-track for the fight."

Now, they bided their time sitting inside the damned mobile-armory-to-be on a side street a short distance away from the concert venue. They'd arranged to have the police clear the service road that led from one facility to the other so they could drive to the baseball field in less than a minute if they were needed there. Arguments had been made for both and ultimately, the question was decided by a game of rock-paper-scissors between Cara and Tony. The detective had emerged victorious, so they waited nearer the larger building.

Diana hoped his instincts were right, on the one hand, so they'd be in position. But all things considered, the best case would be an attack on whichever place had the fewest civilians to endanger. *Or no attack at all, but that won't happen since we are their real target.* Sloan's recording of Sarah's diatribe had resulted in a consensus that the woman sounded like she was coming unhinged. *It's better if she aims that crazy at us rather than anyone else.*

Kayleigh provided an update. She was in the core, as usual, and Deacon was exactly where he always was— surrounded by computers and monitors. "Okay, we have all the traffic cameras and police feeds up. Alfred is monitoring them for trouble. I'm focused on the two stadiums, and Warlock is watching the Arena and the big college fields."

"Who's covering the stadium to the south?" Diana asked.

"State police," Deacon replied. "There is a barracks nearby, so they're hanging out on site. SWAT is six minutes away if they call."

"Okay. How about that other thing, Glam?"

Kayleigh sounded smug. "Got 'em. Every police drone is hacked and ready to receive our orders."

The many uncertainties around her had revealed a side of Diana that she'd not known was there. Former concerns about respecting the other bureau's turf fell away, replaced by the need to use any and all available assets to save lives as effectively as possible. *If they don't like it, they can take it up with my boss—who's also my boyfriend. I think I'm safe, all things considered.*

Deacon's quick-speaking cadence betrayed his excitement. "I have action at the Arena. Two targets are headed toward the back parking lot and they're looking around like they're worried about being noticed. Stand by." There was a pause before two mugshots appeared on her glasses' display. "Low-lifes but magicals, so concerning. They have been arrested on small stuff before, but nothing stuck. Witnesses have a habit of disappearing before they can testify, apparently." Feeds from a traffic camera and what had to be a security camera on the facility itself replaced the pictures and showed the pair walking with a purpose.

Hank asked, "What's that at the back, there?"

Deacon paused, then answered, "TV production truck. They're doing some kind of special on the hockey team." Their targets were on a path directly toward it.

"I bet it would blow up really well if someone hit it with a fireball," Anik commented

That was enough for Diana. "Pick 'em up." Kayleigh would already have shared information with the police stationed inside the arena, and they would doubtless sweep the pair up in short order. They'd been cautioned to use stun rifles from a distance and had control of a stun drone to make a first strike with minimal risk. She dismissed the duo from her mind. "So, that's one distraction down. Where's the next?"

In the minutes that followed, there were more reports of suspicious activity at all the venues they were watching. Again, the police swept in to mop up what they could while the ARES agents waited. *The criminals had a good plan. If not for the insider knowledge, we'd be running around trying to respond to each incident rather than waiting patiently for the main strike to happen.* She sent a silent thank you to Sloan, wherever he might be at that moment. *Fortunately, we're smarter.*

When the first explosion occurred at the baseball stadium, the entire team flinched. Smoke rose into the sky a mile away, and she felt the truck lurch as Hank shoved it into gear and revved the engine in case they needed to move. "Glam, status."

Kayleigh's frustration came out in her sharp words. "Stand by. Whatever else they did, they also blew out the electrical system that feeds the internal cameras." They had logically tapped into the stadium's video lines but hadn't anticipated the possibility of them being compromised. *Okay, maybe we're not that much smarter.* A moment later, the tech was back. "Drones inbound."

The ARES drone supply had increased on an almost daily basis since Deacon's arrival. The techs built two basic models. The first simply slapped a sensor package on top of an out-of-the-box vehicle. They weren't fast but made up for it by being comparatively cheap and easily assembled. Rath had assisted in distributing charging and docking stations on the rooftops around the city. The drones' home bases looked like medium-sized black plastic road cases and remained closed except when accepting or discharging one of the aerial vehicles.

The second kind were based on the models the military, police, and AET used and were faster and more agile than the others. Despite her reservations, Kayleigh had armed them with stun weapons. Each carried an internal AI to prevent hacking or unauthorized use and possessed impressive built-in self-destruct technology. The tech was serious about her dislike of weaponized drones and trusted only herself and maybe Duncan with them.

The images from the leading drones slid into her vision as they sailed in from the outfield. One swept in each direction, curving through the walkways that capped the first level of seats and weaving to avoid the lights and signs hanging from the beams they skimmed under. More detonations occurred as they watched and small fires started but in general, it seemed less like magic and more like traditional explosives. That assessment was confirmed moments later when the drones identified several groups who ran and threw canisters to each side at intervals. A stun blast from the craft dropped a handful of them.

"It has to be another diversion. Glam, Croft, opinions?"

The two women replied in unison. "Agreed." Cara added, "Assholes. They are probably street soldiers recruited specifically for this. It could be a double-blind and they're only the first wave, but I sure as hell wouldn't trust them in a real op."

Tony, who had the most knowledge of the city's criminal element, nodded. "Total agreement. These aren't even the top of the bottom. They're like the middle of the bottom at best."

Diana gritted her teeth as adrenaline and certainty surged through her. A loud crash sounded nearby as a pyrotechnic display heralded the start of the concert. "Then it has to be the football stadium. Show me the cameras."

Her glasses filled with the feeds and the truck grew quiet as all the agents watched. Cara noticed the first certain sign of their enemies. "The one-armed scumbag is there. Camera four, lower right." Sure enough, the man they'd put into the Cube after the battle at the office building strode through the image, a bloodthirsty look on his face. *Damn. That seems like ages ago instead of only months.*

"We have one. Find me the other, and I'll be sold." It was only a minute before the AI identified Sarah and put her picture up for all of them to see. "All right. It's there. Warn the police on site. No changes to the plan. You all head in on the ground. Rath and I will go in from the top."

A quarter-mile away, the troll perched on the pinnacle of the highest point of the casino hotel, an antenna array of some kind. He'd been careful when he'd climbed up an hour before so as not to damage any of the delicate-looking equipment. A half-hour later, the crate at the base of the metal structure opened and one of the surveillance drones flew out.

He'd waited, watched, and waited some more. Gwen gave him images from the various drones in his goggles so he was aware of what the others saw. His role wasn't to find the enemy, however. It involved something much more fun than that.

When Diana identified the football stadium as the objective, Rath's time had come. "Gwen, current map."

"Acknowledged." Air patterns drew themselves into his display—red for ones powerful enough to give him lift, yellow for those that would keep him aloft, and blue for any that would drag him down. He pivoted to face the center point of the target, leapt from the antenna, and pressed the center button on his harness to deploy the glide wings. They snapped into place behind and above him, and he caught an orange stream that led more or less toward his destination and soared along it.

Flying in the daylight proved to be very different than his normal nighttime glides. It was a little more nerve-wracking, being able to see exactly how far it was to the ground. He checked to ensure his grapnel was primed and ready, and of course, it was. *Gwen would have warned me if it wasn't.* The AI anticipated his needs more and more as their partnership continued to develop. She drew a circle on every potential destination for the safety line as he moved across the north side of the city.

Much sooner than expected, the football field loomed before him. A pulsing yellow target throbbed at the near-left corner of the space, and he saw Hank's truck below him with an electronic tag indicating it was an ARES unit in his display. He passed the marker and banked to kill his speed as he spiraled down toward it. At the optimal moment, Gwen gave him a signal, and he pushed the button to collapse the wings and descended the remaining feet to the roof of the facility. He ran to the edge and shrugged the long cable off—it was incredibly thin given its strength—and tied one end to a support for one of the flags that dotted the perimeter of the building.

He threw the other end down to Diana and watched as she latched a small wheeled handle onto the teeth set into the cable and used it to ascend. From his angle, she looked like a superhero with one hand held forward as she ascended rapidly. The device hauled her over the lip of the roof, and she gave him a mid-five. She had an extra harness on over her armor and carried a long black rope with length markings on it. Her expression solemn, she crouched beside him. "We don't know where they're headed yet. Once we're sure, it'll be Nakatomi Plaza time."

Rath laughed when he recalled the scene of John McClane jumping off the roof with a firehose wrapped around him. "Yippie Ki Yay."

Sarah heard distant explosions and screams as her under-lings and Marcus's people wreaked havoc in different areas throughout the stadium. The plan had worked so far as there'd been virtually no response to their initial incursion several minutes before. Only now, as they moved into their final positions, was the crowd starting to realize that an event other than the concert was underway. They headed in increasing numbers for the exits. *If only I'd managed to get Dreven here, it would have been perfect. Damned useless "leader."*

Her followers had already locked down the elevators that led from their target area and barricaded the entrances into the stairwells. As the people fled from their boxes into the large glassed-in luxury space that backed them, the doors would lock closed behind them, trapping them inside the long corridor.

She finished her slow climb up the single staircase that wasn't sealed and found herself in the center of a chaotic flow of people. Small groups rushed from one place to another, trying to leave the area and failing, then attempting another exit vacated by a previous group. She rolled her eyes at the pathetic display. *Sheep. Prey. Idiots.*

The witch spread her arms wide and spoke to her most valued underlings, who had followed her up the stairs. "Corral these fools on the far side. I wish to neither see nor hear them. Find our targets and bring them to me."

They moved past her and she strode to a bar that stood abandoned on the wall nearest the elevators and walked behind it. While her people shouted and cursed and cast spells to prod the livestock along, she reviewed the selection of wines. They proved iffy, at best, but one expensive-looking bottle in the back seemed to have potential—a pinot noir. She pulled the cork with a spell and poured herself a large glass.

As she sipped, the space around her cleared and the clamor dwindled to virtually nothing. The soundproofing that secured this area was very effective in keeping those wealthy or lucky enough to afford a seat up here away from the common rabble from experiencing the chaos out on the field. *Except those humans don't realize that they, too, are common rabble. But they will soon, one in particular.*

By the time she'd finished the glass and secured a refill, her targets had arrived, prodded on by a quartet of witches and wizards with their wands extended. Most of the humans wore their fear on their faces, except for a man who simply looked annoyed and inconvenienced. He was the president of one of the largest companies in the area and also happened to be publicly vocal about his dislike of the magicals "invading" his city, country, and the world. He had become a popular talking head on several networks when they addressed the topic. When they'd needed someone to endanger in order to draw the enemy into their trap, he had been too fantastic an opportunity to pass up when his name appeared on the guestlist for his company's box.

She smiled at him, hoping he would see his certain imminent death in her eyes. "Hello, Jeffrey. So nice to finally meet you." He opened his mouth to reply but a quick flick of her wand stilled the words in his throat as he choked. Once he'd collapsed and turned purple, she relented and he lay heaving, his expression half-murderous and half-panicked.

Sarah grinned and sipped her wine. "Now, we wait."

CHAPTER TEN

C ara led Anik, Tony, and Hank through the fleeing crowds, pushing and shoving to clear a path along the right-hand wall. They'd entered near the southwest rotunda and raced through the main hall above the first level of seats. Merchandise stands on either side had been vacated, and the fleeing people were too afraid even to take advantage of the potential freebies.

Two enemies had waited at the entrance—street soldiers with pistols concealed low against their legs—but hasty stun blasts had disabled them. The fact that they had been dressed normally increased the degree of difficulty of the op and Tony had immediately reported the information to the others over the comms. Kayleigh had tasked more drones, and when there was a gap in the throng, Cara could see the black devices whirling over the seats set up in front of the stage.

An explosion on the field inspired panic in the crowd. She pointed toward it, and the agents moved together, inserting themselves in the wave of people and pushing their way to an aisle leading down. There were two clusters of adversaries below, one who fired almost indiscriminately with a traditional weapon and the other who flung magic into pockets of civilians. She stared ahead, momentarily confused. "Quinn, are they actually hitting anyone?"

Her AI replied after a brief pause. "A minimal amount of the time. Mainly, they are simply creating noise and smoke. Idiots." One of the wizards in the magical group was outlined in yellow. "This person is responsible for the majority of the strikes that are connecting."

"Copy that to my team." She pushed another civilian out of the way and vaulted over the railing onto the field, the other agents right behind her. "Take down the marked target. Weapons free on him, stun on everyone else unless and until they start directly hurting people."

Despite the range, the man fell when Tony drew his pistol, paused to aim, and pulled the trigger. Quinn gave her a zoomed view that showed the wizard down and bleeding from his shoulder. "Nice shot, Stark."

He affected a gunslinger's drawl and replied "Ain't nothin' to it, Croft," as he shifted into motion toward the groups of terrorists. The Remembrance members appeared to have noticed them and raised weapons in their direction.

"Uh-oh. Evasive." She dodged to the right as her team broke in different directions. Quinn populated the combat display that ran along the top of her vision, adding tiny images of each of the enemies they faced, black boxes behind the humans, and blue boxes behind the magicals.

Any notables, like Sarah or Marcus, would have red boxes. With a word, she could apply those outlines to the people in her glasses as well. It was a new feature that she and the AI had built together, unknown to the others. She thought Kayleigh would appreciate the video game feel of it, though.

The urge to put civilians in the hostiles' lines of fire was a natural inclination since on some level they were simply ambulatory obstacles. She fought it as she advanced, remained in the open, but moved unpredictably. Weapons fired around her, and she had to roll out of the way of a lightning bolt from one of the witches that was quicker on the uptake than her partners. By the time they fully realized that their quarry had arrived, however, the ARES agents were in range to cause trouble.

Anik had loaded up with grenades and hurled flash-bangs into the humans first, following them with sonics at the wizards and witches before he ducked out of sight in front of the security barrier that protected the stage. A line of bullets stitched it an instant too late to catch him in the open, and she hoped they hadn't punched through to hit the demolitions expert.

Meanwhile, Tony and Hank ran in a wide curve and exchanged max-range fire with the humans, counting on the stun rifles' broader firing arc to overcome the lethal payloads from the opponents' weapons. They managed it for a short time, assisted by the detonations of the grenades, until Marcus appeared at the head of a group of reinforcements with a black-suited man beside him and another behind whom they immediately recognized.

"Asset in view," Quinn reported. She outlined Sloan in green, the standard display color for allies.

"Shit. Copy that to everyone. Hey, everyone, Face is here, and the bastard with the robot arm has come out to the field to play."

The others chimed in with various expressions of alarm and anger before Diana asked, "Do you need us?"

Cara gritted her teeth and shook her head. "Hell no. We've got them. They merely think they've turned the tables." She fired her stun weapon to snag a couple of witches at the periphery of the magical group, then discarded it as she was forced to dive into a somersault and roll to dodge a force blast that ripped the ground apart at her feet. Her angle took her toward the right half of the huddle, farthest away from Marcus and the other newcomers. She bolted up and removed a wizard from the battle with a triple burst of anti-magic rounds from her carbine that ignored his shield, staggered him with two successive strikes to his vest, and felled him with one in the shoulder.

A small smile crept onto her lips and she adjusted her aim, then had to bob and weave to avoid the flurry of folding chairs that some clever wizard threw at her. *Stupid concert.* "Glam, I'm reasonably sure they've shown their hole card down here. How about deploying ours?"

"Affirmative. Thirty seconds."

Deacon sounded like he was holding his laughter in check. "Did you tell them that you're using Roombas these days?"

Kayleigh growled. "Shut it, Warlock. Make yourself useful and take over at the ballpark."

"Got it. Taking control of the police drones now."

Cara managed to fire a few shots while she dodged. They forced the other magicals facing her to keep their heads down, although they continued to cast spells that her deflectors shunted away. Chatter over the comms suggested that the others were doing well against the non-magicals and had eliminated a few of the wizards and witches as well. The scoreboard still showed at least a dozen and a half up, including the newcomers when Kayleigh's drones entered the fray.

The heavy-duty devices were shaped like small aircraft with engines at the back and on the wings and antennae on the top. They took off and landed vertically as the thrust pods rotated. The tech had described a more optimal system that would launch the vehicles like rockets from a high point for faster acceleration but hadn't yet received the go-ahead for that experiment. *It's probably only a matter of time before there are missile and drone launchers on top of the mobile armory if Hank has his way. I've set a monster loose, there.*

Cara yelled "Cover," as six of them—two-thirds of Kayleigh's full complement—strafed the enemy with a barrage of stun blasts delivered as rapidly as the weapons could cycle. The ARES agents' gear contained transponders that would prevent the drones from aiming at them, but it still made sense to get as far out of the field of fire as possible. She ran in a wide circle toward where she'd last seen Marcus. *If the drones kill him, I'll rip that bloody arm off just because.*

One of the wizards saw the incoming aircraft and sent a wash of flame at the line of drones. They plowed through it but the first took the brunt of the blast and spiraled to careen into the stage and explode. The structure caught fire immediately when the fabrics and video screens were damaged by flaming pieces of the wreckage. The rest were successful and fired stun blasts into the crowded hostiles to fell most of them, including the quick-reacting mage. Smoke from the immolated stage was carried on the wind and swirled over her, and there was a thunderous crash as a vertical set of speakers fell from where it had been suspended. By the time she choked out, "Quinn," the AI had already shifted to other visual modes that allowed her to make out the people nearby. There were three near her, presumably Marcus and his flunky, plus Sloan.

She was about to order the others to flank them from the side, almost salivating at the opportunity to confront the enemy leader, when the scoreboard in her display started to populate again. "Where?" A map appeared to reveal two more groups of combatants running onto the turf from behind the stage. "Damn it. Khan, Hercules, Stark, incoming from the south. They're yours. Glam, bring the drones in again if you can."

"Currently making a pass at the nearest college field in support of the police since we stole theirs," Kayleigh replied. "They'll be back to you in about seventy seconds."

That was a veritable eternity in combat. Anik yelled, "Flash-bang out," followed quickly by, "Damn telekinesis—scatter!" She presumed that a witch or wizard had hurled the device back at them. *I wonder how much anti-magic grenades would cost. Probably a ton.*

Then, her enemies were ranged before her and there was no more time to worry about the others. Marcus grinned. "Well, well, well. How lovely to see you again."

"Do you want to surrender before you lose another arm?"

His grin widened. "Losing another arm would merely make me that much stronger. Allow me to demonstrate." He raised the limb, and she was instantly forced to one knee by a furious blast of lightning.

"What's the deal, Friday?" Diana's AI had been programmed to sound exactly like the character from the Marvel films, which made her smile every time she heard it. *Endgame* had broken her heart, so she'd only been able to watch it twice in the theater. The AI reminded her of happier moments in the series.

"There are many enemy targets gathered in the luxury box hall. Subject Sarah is among them." A three-dimensional rendering of the area developed in her glasses and the system gave her a virtual fly-through of the enemies and neutrals in the space. A distant part of her mind cataloged the goings-on below, and when Sarah's human partner appeared on the field, she considered abandoning the witch. Fortunately, Cara claimed to not need her. *Hopefully, she's not being overconfident.*

She gestured to Rath and led the way at a run. The roof that overhung the top seats on the northern end of the stadium provided a path to reach the space the enemy had invaded. When they arrived, she yanked the small but super-powerful magnet from her belt. It was about the size of a grenade and would stick to anything metal for a short time. She laid on her stomach and leaned over the edge so

Friday could verify the drop length and spooled the rope out accordingly. The carabiner at the end snapped onto the magnet and there was nothing more to delay her.

Diana threaded the rope through her harness and grasped it with both hands at the mark she'd made earlier. She walked to the edge and peered down again to ensure it was lined up. Everything looked right. According to the projections Friday had animated for her, she'd land at the middle of the section and to the side of the elevator lobby closer to the large mass of civilians. She'd considered entering close to the civilians but feared Sarah would have planned for that eventuality. *I'm sure she has something in mind for a direct attack too, but I can't think of a better way to thwart her plan than beating her into the ground.* She took a dozen steps back from the lip, then squared off to it.

"Ready, buddy?"

Rath nodded with a broad grin. "Welcome to the party, pal."

She frowned. "I'm sure you've used that one before."

He laughed and stuck his tongue out at her. "Oldie but goodie."

She held a fist out. He bumped it before he turned and raced to the edge. When he ran out of roof, he thrust forward and activated his wings, angling to the right to circle. She dashed forward as soon as he was clear of the surface and leapt and her legs continued to pump. She curved downward as she hurtled forward, then the drop increased and she felt a moment of fear at the speed with which the ground rushed at her.

Ahead and above, Rath banked left and dipped to curve toward the facility. Their AIs had timed everything to the second, and the jerk of her line happened exactly at the expected moment. It spun her, and she freed a hand long enough to telekinetically correct her trajectory until she aimed toward the large glass window that ran along the entire main hallway. Inside were smallish figures going about their nefarious business with weapons or wands in their hands. None had noticed her yet. She laughed. *That'll change quickly.*

The agent squeezed the line with her boots and thighs and released it with her right hand. She fired a pulsing cone of force at the higher of the two-story-high windows that fronted the hall, then shifted her aim to the lower one as it shattered and launched wicked shards into the nearby hostiles. Her path took her under the frame that separated the two, and her rope caught on it and threw her upward. She detached it with a slap and soared in a shallow arc toward the far wall, controlling her flight with magic to land in balance and facing the main lobby area.

She heard the sound of Rath's wings buffeting the air and then retracting, and the troll dropped into place beside her as if that was exactly how they'd planned it. In fact, the plan hadn't really accounted for landing, so it was an extra bonus that it worked out so well. *Too bad we only have criminal scumbags to impress with our amazing aerial acrobatics.*

Sarah's voice came from around the corner of a tall pillar ahead. "Ah, you've finally arrived. Good. These humans had begun to bore me." A loud snapping noise was followed by screams.

Dammit. "All the assholes go down, buddy, whatever it takes. It's time to finish these bastards once and for all." She hurtled forward, ready to pound the witch with every ounce of her power.

The innocent people who careened toward her—all airborne—as she rounded the column came as a total surprise.

CHAPTER ELEVEN

Cara growled and forced herself to her feet to the sound of the capacitors in her vest popping one after the other. The lightning still stabbed into her arms and legs but her heart was protected from the blast, which was the important part. She saw something protruding from Marcus' mechanical limb and yanked her carbine up to shoot it.

The move was barely in time to intercept the incoming barrage from his ally in black, who unloaded a gigantic revolver at her. The rifle caught all the rounds except one, which grazed her vest as it passed under her left arm. She growled and pressed the strap release before she threw the carbine aside and drew her pistol in a single motion. When she fired half a magazine of anti-magic bullets at the metal arm, the little compartment snapped closed.

Her adversary drew his own pistol and fired but she had already dodged to her right, which forced him to track the weapon across his body to aim at her. She yanked a flash-bang out and threw it at the man who had demolished her rifle, and Sloan dragged the man in black away as it detonated. The two fell together in a tangle of limbs.

Hank, Anik, and Tony yelled over the comm as they attacked the incoming group, and Kayleigh updated them on the time remaining until the drones returned. For Cara, it was all background noise to her fight with the human leader of the Remembrance. He'd had it out for her, and she for him, since the museum battle had brought them into conflict for the first time. *You'll not escape this time, asshole. There's not enough luck in the world to let you get away from me again.*

He pushed toward her, and each of them continued to fire until their weapons were empty. They ejected their magazines almost simultaneously. When she saw him holster his weapon, she mirrored the action and drew the knives sheathed on both sides of the small of her back. He now wielded two blades that were longer than hers and with a slight curve to them. They weren't quite swords but not daggers, either. They came together in an initial clash, his attacks intended to overpower met by her subtle blocks and simple redirections.

Angel spoke into her mind, validating her strategy. "He's stronger than you. Meeting force with force would be a bad choice." She spun out of the way of a vertical slash down her centerline and leaned back to avoid the diagonal cut at her head that followed. He grinned, and the damned panel on his arm opened again. Her brain froze for a moment before she did the only thing she could think of and stepped in against it. When the lightning fired, it was confined to her vest, which absorbed it again. *Damn, that trick probably won't work many more times.* She lashed out with her own swift strikes and tried to use the shorter weapons' speed to her advantage. He accepted the impacts readily on his metal limb, which seemed undamaged by the blows, and blocked the other attacks with his blades.

She growled. "You're a little dependent on your technology, there, aren't ya?" He met another attack with the robot arm and swung a punch. She took it on the shoulder, stabbed with the other hand, and managed to slice his flesh and bone forearm.

He hopped back with a curse. "I was better than you before, and I'm much better now."

She shook her head. "I'm not sure you know what that word means. I'd tell you to check a dictionary, but you probably don't know what that word means, either."

He twisted his arm, and another panel opened. Before she could react, a series of tiny spheres erupted from it and landed at her feet. She leapt back but not fast enough to avoid the explosions as the items detonated. They packed a punch far out of proportion to their size and catapulted her several feet to land flat on her back.

Demon's dark laughter was no help. "You seem to be trying to prolong the battle. Are you playing with him?"

She flipped to her feet with a growl. "No. He's merely full of surprises." He had his gun out again, and she flicked a finger at it as she ran in. A bullet struck her vest at the same moment that the single dart of fire she'd launched caught the weapon and thrust it out of his hand. She staggered, her momentum broken by the bullet's impact, then lurched forward again.

Marcus drew the blade he'd sheathed in favor of the gun and snarled at her. "Okay, wench, time to die."

She coughed against the pain in her chest and responded with a haughty grin intended to tick him off. "Bring it, metal man."

Diana grabbed the first flying person—a woman about her size—with her telekinesis and lowered her gently to the floor. Sarah threw other human projectiles at her, and it took most of her concentration to keep them from getting hurt. The remaining shred of her brain was barely functional enough to ready a shield for the moment when the witch attacked directly, and she was able to deflect the cone of fire her foe launched and directed it harmlessly through the window in the elevator lobby. *Well, mostly harmless,* she thought as the barrier shattered and glass rained down far below.

The attackers from behind would have had her while she dealt with Sarah's human missiles if not for Rath. The AIs had marked them but she hadn't anticipated needing to protect so many people so actively immediately upon arrival. She'd seen his POV in the corner of her glasses during her own actions and was, as always, amazed at the way he used the agility of his three-foot form to his advantage. He'd charged the enemy head-on and dodged the spells from several on his way in. A wizard shot him with a fireball while the troll was busy knocking a witch from her feet with a baton combination, but the anti-magic deflectors on his vest absorbed it. By the time the arrogant mage realized his attack had failed, Rath had spun and stabbed him with the shock batons, taking him out of the fight.

Then there was only one, and a jump-flip-strike combo felled him with ease.

Two of Sarah's cohorts joined her—a witch on her left and a wizard on her right—and their arrogant expressions matched their leader's. The attitude struck her as inappropriate, considering the numbers. *Rath and me versus three of them? Easy-peasy.* The next instant revealed why, as two more adversaries appeared from where they'd been hiding in the elevators, followed by another two from one of the luxury boxes.

Diana offered a wry grin as she used the glasses' eye-motion recognition functions to tag the trio in front of her, assigning the other four to her partner. "Only seven? How insulting. Rath had hoped for more." His laughter over the comms warmed her soul.

The lead witch rolled her eyes and shook her head in annoyance. "Enough nonsense. Kill them both."

The BAM agents had brainstormed together on how to best deal with a scenario like this, even though the expectation was always that she and Rath would be the ones to face it. Cara had used the opportunity to repeat her concern that they needed more people, but her protest had been summarily dismissed with a crisp, "Find us some, then," from Diana, who knew the other woman had no more time to do so than she did. In truth, Friday was working on the task, but their needs were unique enough that identifying potential recruits was difficult now that they'd run out of direct contacts.

All that aside, everyone had agreed on one thing— reduce the odds as quickly as possible was vital. To that end, Rath had brought only sonic grenades, and Diana had two as well. Within a second of the witch's command, the canisters were out and rolling, hers at the group nearest her and his at the two separate partnerships of new arrivals. He charged the luxury-box duo to the right, and she targeted the wizard on that side of Sarah.

The troll's detonated, and both sets of targets recoiled from the blasts. He drew a pair of throwing knives as he ran, the rib holsters a new addition to his equipment. They meant he could only carry four instead of the six his normal setup would allow because of the way the straps for the wings fitted around him. In this case, though, two were more than sufficient. He threw them both at once and the blades tumbled end over end across the distance to their destinations in the space of a few steps. His aim was true, and they punched deep into the arms that held wands. Both magicals clutched their damaged limbs rather than raise them to attack.

The click of his batons signaled that he would be finished with that duo in short order. Her own target was already lifting his wand, her sonic assault defeated by a cover that Sarah had summoned around her and her lackeys. *Damn. It sucks when they learn.* She'd left her M-4 in the truck, unhappy with the way it overlapped the climbing harness, so she drew her pistol and fired a quick triple-burst at the wizard.

The anti-magic rounds seared through his hasty shield, but he'd moved as she attacked and only one reached him, striking his chest and throwing him back. She shifted her aim left at Sarah but the weapon spun out of her hand. Diana was instantly irate at the way the witch had repurposed her own wand-grabbing tactic, drew her backup

Ruger, and pulled the trigger as she brought it around. Two bullets hurtled toward the witch on the left with four for Sarah. All were absorbed by the body that had been lying on the ground at their feet when the lead witch threw it in the way. The agent dropped and rolled forward to avoid it as it rocketed over her head and bounded to her feet a foot away from Sarah's remaining partner. "Surprise."

But it was she who got the surprise as a wave of force lifted her off her feet and hurled her toward the windows at the back of the elevator lobby.

Cara twirled the daggers in her hands as she and Marcus stalked in a small circle. She remained just outside the range of his longer blades. They had run out of taunts and arrived at a place where only action mattered. She kept a careful eye on his mechanical left arm, which might contain any number of surprises in addition to its apparent invulnerability to her weapons.

Angel and Demon whispered alternately inside her mind, warning her of impending attacks and offering suggestions to thwart them. She'd forestalled several by simple shifts of her weight that took a target point out of the line of attack, and they continued to circle while watching for the other to falter. A countdown clicked away in the corner of her vision, marking the time until the stun drones would be back to eliminate the rest of the insurgents. *I only have to keep him busy until then.* Figures fell off the scoreboard at the top of her view as Anik, Tony, and Hank dealt with the most recently arrived scumbags.

Both her daggers' personalities spoke at once. "Attack high left." She obeyed without thought, darted in, and stabbed her left-hand blade at his right shoulder. He'd taken a step that was slightly too long and compromised his balance, and the knife penetrated deep into his flesh, unhindered by the fabric of the bulletproof vest he wore. He swung the weapon in his metal arm toward her, but she blocked his blade with her own and delivered a kick to his knee.

Marcus turned his leg to avoid having the joint disabled and swung the new arm at her again as he dropped to one knee. She hopped back and kicked up like she was punting a football, and the steel toe in her boot launched the knife out of the metal hand with a clang. It careened backward, and as she watched it, she noticed that the man in black had risen and now staggered toward them. Sloan trailed a few steps behind.

The distraction proved costly as her foe discharged another lightning barrage at her. His previous attacks had blown all the capacitors on her vest, and since the assault wasn't magic, the deflectors let it pass. She arched involuntarily as the power wreaked havoc on her nerves. The countdown clock reached twenty as he stood above her with a victorious grin on his face. "You're fast, wench, but you're not good enough." He held his metal arm up and her eyes widened as the hand morphed into a blade with a vicious point on the end.

He raised it, and she let her head fall back on the turf. *Dammit. Ten more seconds and I would have had him stunned and captured.* Using the mental techniques she'd learned from Nylotte and Diana, she segmented a part of her mind away from the power that licked and bit at her. She forced both arms to full extension and released her magic in a savage explosion of fire, expending all her energy in a series of flaming darts that struck him everywhere to drive him back and burn into his flesh. The initial blast was aimed at his face, and she raked the attack down his body, ignoring his metal arm.

He screamed and staggered and the blow he had begun slammed into the ground half a foot away from her cheek. She ignored it and maintained the assault as he forced himself to his feet and repositioned for another strike. Then Sloan and the man in black were there and dragged him away as he fought them, determined to kill her. In her mind, she screamed with rage at the sight of him escaping again, but she had nothing left. *Except this.* She raised a hand, pointed it at her foe, and Quinn triggered the launcher. One of Rath's markers sped at her enemy as her head and arm collapsed, exhausted.

She only dimly felt the pain of the electrical burns that covered her as the AI summoned Anik. Quinn's voice sounded worried, she thought, as if a computer program could have such emotions. Her mind slipped as the drones reappeared and flashed over her like avenging angels pursuing fleeing demons. She laughed at the paired groans from her daggers in response to the imagery as her eyes closed and she fell away.

Diana had a moment to wonder how the hell they'd managed to smack her quite so hard and quite so far when she broke the windows and sailed out of the building. Instinct took over and she reached out with a line of force, imagining it to be a large bungee cord, and used it to yank herself back into the room. She landed in a skid on the tiled floor of the elevator lobby with a grin. *So, I can fly or I have a web shooter. Either way, I'll take it.*

Rath stormed past her on his path toward the attackers beside her, who staggered to their feet after shaking off the effects of the sonic grenade. She was shocked to see him in his eight-foot form but assumed that maybe seeing her thrown out the window had triggered it. As he grasped the two wizards and pounded them together, she changed her mind and decided he'd probably done it mainly for fun.

My turn. She pointed a finger at the witch beside Sarah and targeted her with a slab of force that careened her across the room and into the back wall. Diana grinned when she fell senseless onto her face, then turned to regard Sarah, who had also watched the woman's flight and fall.

Her foe raised an eyebrow. "Simple but effective. It describes you and your people fairly well so far."

She shook her head. "Not as effective as we need to be since you and your boyfriend are still in the game."

The witch snorted. "Boyfriend? Hardly. Nothing would please me more than if you killed him. It might even be enough to buy you a few more days of life. Have you?"

"You can find out later when you're in prison together." She was stalling, counting on Rath to circle behind the woman.

Sarah grinned. "If that ever happens, you won't be around to see it."

Diana thrust into a charge, leading with cones of fire

from both hands. Suddenly, the air in front of her changed and became a rift in space with a dark room on the other side. She skidded to a stop to avoid the portal, but it swooped toward her and she was teleported away.

Rath watched Diana vanish and bolted at the witch with a loud cry, ready to crush individual pieces of her into tiny bits until she revealed where she'd sent his human. But Sarah summoned another circle and stepped into it before he reached her, departing with an arrogant grin that mocked his efforts. He went momentarily crazy, first lashing a punch into the face of the wounded wizard who'd staggered to his feet a moment before and then smashing everything near him until he ran out of non-living breakables. The troll sank to his knees and shrank to his three-foot size before he spoke quietly to Gwen, instructing her to share the news with the others.

He didn't know where Diana was, but there was not a single doubt in his mind that he would find her or that she would find him. When their end came, whether sooner or far, far, later, there was no question that they would face it together.

CHAPTER TWELVE

Diana hadn't realized that it was possible to send a portal over a person, rather than a person into a portal. *Something to file away for the future, I guess.* The surrounding room was dark, and as the rift closed and extinguished the small amount of light coming in before she could dive back through it, she was effectively blind. She crouched defensively, on guard against an attack that failed to materialize. She released a trickle of magic to summon a flickering flame along each fingertip of her left hand.

The place resembled Nehlan's receiving room—basically a blank space with a single door leading out. Although she was curious as to what might lie beyond that barrier, she was more than willing to leave it unexplored. She waved her other hand to summon a portal to her bedroom, but despite a few sparks in the air that trailed behind the gesture, the circle refused to hold itself together long enough to reach completion.

What the hell is this now? She frowned, concentrated

harder, and attempted to cast again. This time, she managed to get the oval about three-quarters of the way around before it collapsed into nothingness. She stubbornly tried one last time, expanding her senses as Nylotte had taught her to investigate the magic she created. Another presence was noticeable on the periphery of the spell, sensed almost like a subtle spice that clashed with her own power. *So, something is blocking me. But it can't be anti-magic since my improvised candle works.* She shrugged. *Okay then, I guess it's time to explore.*

She crossed to stand before the door, then thought better of it, backed up, and took a step to the side. Her telekinesis reached out and yanked on the handle, and the barrier swung open without a hint of anything untoward. She stuck her head around the corner and whipped it back scant inches ahead of a hail of spikes that hurtled directly toward her. *Oh, so that's how it is, is it?* After her indecisive battle against Sarah, she was more than ready to mix it up. Plus, she didn't fancy hanging out in the entry room for the rest of her life.

Diana crafted a tall shield of force, entered the doorway at a run, and turned toward her adversary. Another volley of spikes rocketed toward her from another wizard she hadn't seen at the opposite end of the corridor, and she hid behind the magical barrier as she raced forward. The projectiles hammered into it but failed to penetrate and simply quivered and remained stuck in the shield. They resembled long nails with a flattened end opposite a wicked point. Her danger sense activated, and time slowed. Since no other threats were visible ahead to cause it, she flung herself forward in a somersault to the left.

Fire washed through the area she'd occupied, bathing her in its heat but vanishing before it reached the wizard at the far end. She glanced at the witch she hadn't seen previously at the opposite end of the corridor. *Clever. Delaying until I was distracted.* She rose and put her back against the near wall, summoned a buckler of flame with her right hand, and maintained the force shield with her left. Attacks came from each direction and she weathered them easily, siphoning some of the incoming fire to power her defense. She noticed that she didn't seem to be draining as quickly as usual.

Damn. I must be on Oriceran or in a kemana or something. At that moment, though, more power seemed like a good thing. When the hail of projectiles paused as the wizard retrieved another round of ammunition, she dispelled the force shield and scuttled forward. She kept her attention divided between her two opponents and maintained her fire buckler, which had grown in size to accommodate the multiple streams of flame her opponent now directed at her. The mage launched his nails again, and she reached out with her telekinesis, located each one, and guided them past her, then gave them an extra push with her own magic. The fire-casting witch at the end of the hall yelped when she realized what was happening but had no time to marshal a defense before the tiny spikes pinioned her, liberally covering the front of her body. She fell back with a moan and the flames vanished.

Diana felt suffused with fire and decided to share her good fortune. She gathered a ball of flame in her hand and hurled it at the wizard. He intercepted it with a sphere of ice, and they exploded when they collided. She threw another, followed by another, and stalked forward as she continued to lob them at her foe and intercept the extras he whipped at her in reply. He started to retreat a step at a time, and a sneer curled her lip. "Oh, you're fine with attacking an unsuspecting opponent, but you run from a real fight? I don't think so."

She envisioned her force rope and threw it past him, then snatched it back to slam into his feet. At the same time, she gave him a telekinetic push on his forehead, and none of his magical powers could keep him from toppling. The sound his skull made as it cracked on the stone floor was deeply satisfying, and she saw that he was clearly out of the fight when she arrived at his side. She summoned a wave of force to hurl his unconscious form down the hallway to join the witch at the far end. *That'll keep them both out of my hair.*

A nod sent a piece of something dark floating in the air, and as she spun toward it, fearing another attack, her hair whipped in front of her face to reveal that a large section of it had been burned away. She growled. *Now you've done it. Trying to kill me is one thing, but wrecking my hair is mean.* She snorted at the stupidity of the thought as she reached the end of the hallway and turned the corner cautiously. There was a room ahead, a combination of living and dining areas to judge by the furniture. It was all attractive but not fancy, made of woods she didn't recognize and fabrics that looked like satin but probably weren't. There was no one present, so she continued. She tapped her glasses to activate the infrared overlay and saw nothing nearby. The range seemed to be minimal, which was logical since the technology no doubt relied on or at least accessed other technological networks that didn't exist on the magical planet.

She cleared several more vacant rooms before she found a door that exited the apparent living quarters into a work area. It was an anteroom with seats around the edges, presumably for those waiting to meet with someone important behind one of the three doors that led from the space. The trio of wizards who had waited in ambush attacked as soon as she crossed the threshold. She rolled to the right and reached for her pistol, ready to swap out the empty magazine and ram in another and berating herself for not having done so already, then remembered only when her hand found air that Sarah had stolen it from her. *Damn her to hell.*

Diana regained her feet and activated one of the experimental charms Nylotte had bestowed upon her. Three identical images of her appeared and ran a crisscross path around her. She moved with the illusions, and all of them turned together to attack the wizards. Their faces registered shock, but they rallied quickly and their leader released a horizontal fan of fire to intersect all the versions of her.

However, Nylotte was not simply an everyday magic user but a Dark Elf with decades, if not centuries, of experience. Two of the illusions went high and leapt upward to flip over the assault, while Diana and one of the others slid beneath it. She crossed behind the illusion and fired a beam of force at the wizard who'd been the first to attack, then bolted away as he staggered back and launched a cone of flame at the illusion. Her copy vanished, but she had used the moment of distraction to close with another of the enemy.

He started to wave his wand in a slashing motion across her, but she darted inside his guard and caught his hand, turned to put her spine against his stomach, and hammered the back of her head into his mouth. Her left elbow continued the momentum of her turn and impacted with his face, and he made a pained grunt through teeth broken by the two attacks. She spun under the arm, maintained her grip, and snapped the joint that connected his upper and lower arms with a palm strike that sent his wand clattering onto the floor and pulled a scream from deep inside him.

Then, borrowing a page from her enemies' playbook again, she used her telekinesis to throw him toward the other two wizards. The middle one waved him aside using his own magic, but her projectile's outstretched leg caught the first wizard she'd hit and he spun away. Diana glanced up at a series of chandeliers hanging in the room and reached out with a telekinetic fist to yank the nearest down on her reeling foe. The crash of metal and stone signaled his exit from the battle.

The remaining wizard took several steps back and nodded in appreciation of her skills. "You are as good as we were led to believe. I suppose I must thank you for elevating me to the top of the heap by virtue of demolishing my allies."

Her eyes narrowed. "Should I know you? Are you someone important?"

He chuckled. "No, you need not think of me in any way other than the wizard who defeated you and presented your corpse to his master." He thrust his wand forward and a storm of shadow washed over her, feeling like a blizzard of blades and despair. Diana realized she was creating those feelings internally as her anti-magic deflectors encased her in a protective oval that stopped the assault from reaching her. Her opponent's face registered surprise, and she laughed. "The fancy magician forgot that technology is a thing."

She darted in and ducked under the shadow blade he slashed over her head. The absence of the sound to indicate the deflectors activating revealed that they'd been consumed far quicker than she was used to. She kicked him low and pounded her shin armor plate against the nerve bundle in his upper thigh. He swiped down diagonally with the blade as the limb collapsed. She stepped back to let it pass in front of her, then swung in to deliver a triple punch combination to his head, each blow punctuated by a snap from her shock gloves. He was unconscious before he tumbled. She picked her way through the debris to the one she'd hurled across the room and tapped him on the temple as well to ensure that he couldn't follow her. The enemy mage buried under metal and stone wasn't a cause for concern.

Diana straightened and took stock of her situation. Her first priority was to check herself for damage, but other than her crisped hair, all she felt was a little tiredness from the energy expenditures. She said a silent thank you to Nylotte for her clever experimentation and ongoing enthusiasm for using her student as a guinea pig. A tap on her glasses revealed two warm bodies on the other side of a door and no others nearby. She tried to cast a portal again but was blocked by the same interference before the oval was a quarter complete. *It's probably one of those two. Or at least I hope so.*

She moved to the center of the chamber and faced the door, gathering her force power and letting it build around her fists. When they reached full capacity, she thrust them both forward and the door exploded off its hinges and rocketed into the room beyond. It veered to the right to reveal a grinning wizard in a set of ancient-looking leather and chain armor. She was reflexively worried that it was Rhazdon's Defense, but from what she recalled, those pieces were a different style. *So, merely a garden-variety asshole, then.* He beckoned her ahead, and she sighed. *One of these days, I'll be the person on the home turf.* Her mental voice, which had remained pleasantly quiet through the whole experience, suggested, *"Maybe you ought to think that through a little better. Do you really want enemies in your base? Or in your house again?"*

Irritated, she shook her head and stalked forward into the room, her fists clenched. She pushed on her magical sense, seeking any obvious danger, but none registered. Clearly, the closest of the two figures was a threat, and the one in the back seemed unaware that she was there, locked in a trance of some kind. *He must be the jerk blocking me from portaling out of here.* She snapped a bolt of flame at him as a test, but the wizard before her flicked his fingers to nudge it away from its target. It splashed harmlessly off a wall as he broke the silence in a voice that dripped with conde-scension. "It is a true pleasure to see you again, Agent Diana Sheen."

She frowned. "Do I know you? I thought I had a fairly solid handle on all you Remembrance assholes."

He laughed. "Last time we met, I was stealing your quarry from you in the prison."

Dianna stared in surprise, having mostly forgotten about the man who appeared at the end to thwart their capture of the witch. "Good. I've been looking forward to repaying you for that."

The man shook his head slowly. "The only payment will be your death. When you arrive in whatever hell your kind believes in, be sure to tell them Dreven sent you." He swept his arms wide and a hail of tiny shadow orbs flew at her.

Dammit, why did it have to be shadow? She summoned a force shield, but he waved his hands and they evaded the barrier and curled toward her back. Hastily, she created more slabs to cover herself and they connected violently with it and drained her power. Even the ubiquity of magic couldn't compensate for defending against such a strong barrage. The stream didn't decrease, and she felt herself weakening. She tried to investigate the shadow, to siphon from it despite using a different form of power as a defense, but the effort failed.

Knowing that to stay in place was to eventually lose, she dropped the shields and used her magic to launch herself upward, accepting some shadow hits in return, and somersaulted in midair to hurtle down at her enemy. He gestured and thrust her to the side with a blast of force, but she controlled her flight with her own power and settled herself onto the ground. As he turned to face her, she threw darts of fire at him, an attack she'd learned while Nylotte trained

Cara. He was forced to defend against the tiny shards of flame with sweeping motions that interposed barriers of solidified darkness, but the assault kept him from attacking.

She closed the distance while he battled her magic. When she was finally near enough to act, she let the fire attack fall, summoned a force blade in her left hand, and darted into close range. He swung at her with a shadow blade that appeared instantly in his hand, and she caught it on her own magical weapon. His other hand stabbed at her with another, but she blocked the arm with a raised knee and levered a punch into his chest. The snapping shock was dissipated by his armor, but the force-assisted blow drove him stumbling back.

Wasting no time, she pressed her advantage, but he recovered quickly and fired a needle-thin blast of flame at her face. It was so small it was barely visible, and only the slow-motion provided by her magical warning sense allowed her to fall out of its path. She landed hard and rolled immediately to the side, fearing his follow-up attack, but wasn't fast enough. The onslaught struck her shoulder blade and burned through her armor to her flesh in an instant. She flipped and conjured a shield, and he began to pepper it with multiple attacks. Her wound throbbed, and the weakening sensation she felt told her she was bleeding.

Diana huddled under the shield and covered herself with it while he continued the barrage. He stared relentlessly at her with a smug smile on his face, knowing that she would weaken and he would win. As her back arched involuntarily from the pain of the wound, the upside-down man in the corner behind her came into view. She stretched with her right hand, snatched the Bowie knife from her vest, and hurled it at the entranced mage. It struck him in the chest, and his eyes flew open as he uttered a choking gasp. She cast a portal beneath her, dropped through it, and yanked it closed before the enemy could pursue. Her descent continued for several feet until she landed hard on a stone floor.

She rolled over with a groan as Nylotte pounded down the stairs of her shop into the training area. The Drow gave her a glare that was part worry but mostly annoyance. Diana laughed painfully. "Hey, teach. Thanks for the charms." She put her forehead down on the ground and sobbed at the pain as her teacher hurried forward to assist her damaged and ever-disappointing student.

CHAPTER THIRTEEN

Tony groaned as he climbed the final stairs to the roof of the tall building. Even though the elevator had carried them most of the way to their objective, the top several floors were only serviced by a freight elevator, and the illusions they wore didn't give them access to it. They'd tried unsuccessfully to entice the company to sign on with Two Worlds Security Consulting, and the stairs provided the only remaining option.

His partner's laugh settled into a broad grin. Anik looked completely comfortable in his coveralls and large backpack. "Come on, old man. You gotta get that cardio in."

The investigator wiped his face as they broke out into the sunlight. "Bite me, Anik. You suck. Some of us have big brains to carry around."

The demolitions expert nodded sagely. "Yeah, it's your brain that's causing the problem. Sure." He gazed pointedly at the place where Tony's midsection pushed against the seals of his coverall. "You keep it in your stomach, then?"

Tony flipped him off amiably as they walked in step to the corner of the roof. He tapped his glasses to activate his comms, which he'd disabled to avoid detection inside the building. "Glam, how do we look?"

Kayleigh's voice was amused, which suggested that she'd listened in somehow. *Anik's doing, probably. Jerk.* "You have a perfect line of sight on her apartment. Go to work."

He shook his head. Even though the idea was his, he hadn't really considered the possibility that he'd actually have to carry and install the equipment himself. *I really am more of an ideas man.* He chuckled inwardly, set his toolbox down beside the backpack Anik had dropped on the graveled rooftop, and shrugged out of the bag he carried crosswise on his back. From the latter, he withdrew a stubby tripod. It was a moment's work to extend the legs, withdraw the motor from his box and attach it, and flip the switch on the device that controlled the elevation of the central pole. The tiny black rectangle ran through its diagnostics and returned a green signal. *All good.*

Meanwhile, Anik had pulled out the sensor unit itself, which had a large lens for visuals plus a powerful microphone that would be able to read sound vibrations from her windows. Kayleigh said it would be sensitive enough to hear her snoring, whispering, or talking to herself, whichever the case may be. After a demonstration of the setup during which they listened in on a couple arguing inside a restaurant across the river, his estimate of the amount of direct human effort it would take to monitor the woman had changed. Once the device was in place and locked on to her lair, the systems would handle the majority of the work going forward.

While Hank, Anik, and Tony had followed her, she never directly entered or exited the building across the street. Her tradecraft was strong and she used portals to move around that vanished too quickly to trace. They'd attempted to tag her with one of Rath's slightly radioactive targets but had failed miserably as she seemed to maintain a defensive field to protect herself at all times. Diana had promised to discuss how such a thing was possible with Nylotte because none of the magicals on the team—or any other they knew—could do it. Kayleigh couldn't even determine how to mimic the personal shield technologically, which was a source of significant frustration for her.

They'd received a lucky break when the person they did manage to tag took up a position outside her building. Cara's attempt to tag the man with the metal arm with a tracker had missed, and he'd disappeared entirely from their radar. But her bug had managed to catch the man in black, and he'd been traced to the location too many times for it to be anything but intentional. The three agents had watched the building from multiple angles around the clock whenever Sloan indicated her departure from the warehouse, and it had been the newest member of their team who'd finally saw her through the condo's window.

Tony wiped his brow again and turned to watch the demolitions expert set up the sensor box, attach it to the tripod, and run a cable down to the motor. The system began to move up and down and spin the camera left and right as it warmed up. "Alfred says we're all good," Kayleigh reported. "But at least one of you should stay up there until we know for sure that everything's working properly."

He groaned, and Anik laughed. "We'll both do it,

brother. Let's go into the stairwell where there's some shade." Tony followed him over, and they found places to sit. A lens of their glasses showed the feed from the camera, and they settled in to wait for developments. Tony watched a Philip Marlowe film in the other lens, while Anik's light snoring suggested that he trusted the systems to alert him to any activity.

It was several hours before anything happened, but when it did, it was good. First, the system beeped rhythmically to signal that it had detected noise. They straightened and their glasses shifted into VR mode, which displayed the scene as if they were looking through the camera's lens. Tony tapped the icon to slave the sensor box to his glasses so it would move with him. The witch walked into view, threw her bag onto the couch, and crossed into a hallway out of sight. He turned his head and reacquired her when she entered the bedroom. She disappeared into what they knew was a closet, thanks to the blueprints they'd found of the building, and emerged wearing comfortable clothes. He nudged Anik. "Try to keep your mind on the game. I know you're not used to seeing attractive women in any stage of undress."

His partner snorted. "Do you want to compare notes? You'll probably have to dust yours off, they're so old."

Tony flicked a hand out to smack him, and it was easily blocked by the demolitions expert. The witch started to move again, and he tracked her down the hallway and had her perfectly centered when she stepped into view again in the living room. She crossed to the table and set a statue on the table, then fumbled with something at her neck. The camera couldn't quite focus in far enough to see what it was, but he was sure that the techs could blow it up or do whatever other technical wizardry was required to reveal it. A blue glow emerged above the statue, and a figure appeared. He chuckled. "It's like Star Wars, only Emperor Palpatine instead of Princess Leia."

Anik laughed as well. "Help me, Sarah you evil witch. You're my only hope."

The microphone picked up her side of the conversation only, which was strange. She seemed to be receiving orders from the man, based on the shortness of her answers, which mainly alternated between yes and no. At one point, she asked if they could simply blow it up—with no clear indication of what "it" was—and appeared to receive a reply that pleased her. The image disappeared, and she sighed loudly. Her voice lost its subservient edge. "Idiot. I will enjoy watching you die."

She sat up suddenly as if startled and her hands jerked to her neck. She picked up the wand from where it lay on the table and waved it around her. The visual feed turned to static and the sounds vanished. Tony tapped his comm. "Uh, Kayleigh?"

He could picture the scowl he heard in her voice. "It's not technological. Damn magic. She must have activated some kind of defense we aren't prepared for."

Anik sighed, and Tony echoed it. "Right when we thought we had her, it turns out we don't. Why are we surprised? So now what?"

She replied, "I'll consult with Deacon. We'll think of something. The system works fine, though, so you guys come on back."

Kayleigh moved to where her colleague sat behind his computers. She pulled the earphone off the side of his head and asked, "Have you been listening?"

"Nope. Working." He nodded at the screen in front of him. "I'm going to try to weave some magic into the virus. That might help it slide through defenses a little better, especially if they're smart enough to use computer magic too."

She yanked the headphones the rest of the way off as she sat beside him. "You can get back to that in a second. I need some thoughts on how to pierce the wards around the witch's condo."

He frowned. "I guess it's too much to hope that our enemies will always be stupid, huh?"

Kayleigh shrugged. "So far, at least."

Deacon tapped his chin thoughtfully. "And we want to do it without her noticing, right? This isn't a smash and grab but long-term surveillance?" She nodded, and he sighed. "There's only one answer, then. In order to do it in a way she won't detect as enemy magic, we'll have to get some drone bugs from Oriceran."

"What the hell are you talking about?"

He laughed. "You're such a magical Luddite. You are aware that people in Oriceran have managed to combine magic and technology in useful ways, right?"

She raised an eyebrow. "I'm not an idiot, you know."

"Could've fooled me." He stuck his tongue out at her. Her ensuing smack made him yelp and rub his upper arm. "Anyway, they have these things that look like bugs but are actually surveillance devices. If she's searching for hostile magic or for hostile technology, they shouldn't be detected because they're not really either."

"Wouldn't they register as both?"

He shook his head. "Intent matters. Unless the witch is specifically thinking about a hybrid, they should remain unnoticed."

She nodded. "All right. How do we get some?"

Deacon grimaced. "That's the hard part. How many arms and legs do you have to sell?"

CHAPTER FOURTEEN

Since taking over for Taggart as the acting head of ARES, Bryant had grown increasingly uncomfortable with the members of the oversight committee. The revelations from Diana's team about possible Chinese and Oriceran influence on them was merely the distasteful icing on a cake he'd already baked. As such, he found it difficult to be appropriately subservient and respectful.

At the appointed time for the meeting, he was still in Taggart's office. He finished the piece of paperwork he was working on before he rose from the chair, drew his wand from its holster under his right arm, and waved it in a circle to summon a portal. His research into the locations of the anti-magic emitters that served the buildings Congress inhabited had identified a hole he could exploit. His first inclination had been to quietly alert the building's authorities but instead, he had decided the possibility that it could be a tool for enemy agents might prove to be a source of useful information. He stepped through and closed the rift behind him, then placed the tiny bug—half magic and half tech—in a darkened corner of the ceiling with a gentle telekinetic burst. He straightened his dark pinstriped suit, ran a hand through his hair, and stalked down the hallway to the meeting room.

When he entered, the full oversight committee was already assembled as he had requested. They had arranged themselves along opposing sides of the table. Finley had chosen the chair at the far end as the designated intermediary, and the other end had been left vacant for him. He went first to the credenza and busied himself with a mug of coffee, feeling the irritation on one side of the room grow palpable behind him. When he turned to take his seat, he also noted the stifled grins of the two on the opposite side.

Finley sounded like he was trying to hide his own amusement. "Special Agent in Charge Bates, thank you for joining us."

He nodded. "Thank you all for agreeing to my request for this meeting."

Cyphret, closest to Finley on the "anti" side of the table, barked a laugh. "Rest assured, Agent, we would have summoned you shortly in any case. Your leadership has not exactly been stellar, thus far."

He shrugged and took a slow sip of his coffee, holding the mug in his left hand, and slurped it deliberately, both as a generalized sign of disrespect and as an act of misdirection. His right hand slid into his pocket and tapped a sequence of beats on the face of his phone. A gentle vibration let him know it was doing its work. He lowered the mug with a nod. "Well, Senator, it's true that it has not been without its challenges. I would not call it a failure of any kind, however."

Beside her, Winston Tomassi shook his head. Bryant narrowed his eyes at the hypocrite who routinely made principled stands against vices of all kinds but was secretly an inveterate gambler knowingly or unknowingly in the pocket of the Chinese. *And maybe in our enemies' pockets, as well.* "It is necessary—and long overdue—that we consider a more permanent replacement for Special Agent in Charge Taggart," the senator stated coldly.

The third person on that side of the table was one Bryant had never met in the flesh before. Zachariah Clarke kept a low profile and maneuvered behind the scenes, mainly to his own benefit but also that of the state he represented and—as they now knew—on behalf of Chinese Intelligence. Bryant was sure this man was fully aware of his espionage, unlike Tomassi, and likely reveled in it. His voice was slow and arrogant. "Perhaps it is a broader question we need to consider—whether ARES should continue in its current form at all. I am of the opinion that we should disband it and reassign its personnel to bolster the FBI, which has a more appropriate and effective chain of command to provide proper ongoing oversight and intervention."

He gave the man a nod full of false respect and turned to Finley, who seemed about to speak. The senator was cut off by Sam Somers, whose white mustache and close-trimmed beard offered a gentleness that offset the fiery look in his eyes. He immediately pictured a fun grandfather retrieving a belt to administer a beating. "While my distinguished colleagues are rightfully concerned about the challenges the organization faces, that particular suggestion is, pardon my language, pure bullshit. We need the special talents offered by ARES, and we need the ability to work around existing bureaucracies. Especially those who would suddenly be in the know if ARES was reintegrated into the FBI."

Bryant nodded again, this time with actual respect. The current arrangement kept the president out of the loop and allowed whoever held the office to claim full deniability. While the vice president was aware by virtue of being a member of the committee, the likelihood of that individual being asked about the agency was small. And, if they happened to ascend to the Oval Office, they would quickly receive official word that ARES had been disbanded. Simultaneously, an identical organization with a different name would rise in its place, drawing the new vice president into its oversight committee.

The other senator on the pro side, Ellyn Hughes, was also a new face to Bryant. She was an older African-American woman, not as old as Clarke or Somers but not as young as the rest. Her black and grey hair rose in tight curls a couple of inches off her head. Bryant was struck by her eyes, which were piercing, and her model-perfect lips and teeth. She sliced her hand through the air as if chopping through an enemy combatant with a sword. Her voice was no-nonsense and permitted no argument. "Cut the posturing, people. We won't eliminate ARES when so many important issues are in play. Save the politicking for the campaign trail and focus on business. Special

Agent in Charge Bates, why did you request this meeting?"

So I could download Deacon's virus into every electronic device you all are carrying, of course. He smiled and inclined his head toward his counterpart at the table's other pole. "Senator Finley and I have had preliminary conversations about this, but one of my agents uncovered evidence of information leaks about ARES to our enemies that seemed to justify an immediate discussion with the entire committee." He paused and deliberately didn't look at anyone in particular and was impressed by the way the opposition side of the table continued to look haughty and judgmental. "We have discovered that someone—likely inside the pool of assistants, technicians, and aides associated with your side of the operation—has shared secrets with a person or persons on Oriceran."

Clarke was the first to reply and almost choked on his theatrical outrage. "Preposterous. What evidence do you have?"

Bryant spread his hands in a gesture of innocence. "Only that information the enemy should not have regarding the internal operations of ARES reached an Oriceran named Nehlan."

Somers's face took on a frown. "Where have I heard that name before?"

Finley explained, "He abducted a person of interest to one of our agents and transported her to Oriceran. He died in the rescue operation."

Tomassi rolled his eyes. "So this being is off the board. It seems like the danger has passed."

The woman on the pro side of the table shook her head.

"Even if the target is now gone, the fact that someone is apparently speaking to people they shouldn't is an issue. We must implement a scan of those Special Agent in Charge Bates mentioned as soon as possible." Diana and Bryant had agreed that giving the senators a potential scapegoat was the right move to keep them confident in their security. She wasn't in on the plan, but Hughes played her part well by honestly living up to the responsibilities of her position.

Cyphret shook her head. "Agent Bates, I feel I can speak for the table at large when I say that you stand on the very thinnest of ice. If there are any more failures by your organization, big or small, I will not hesitate to call for its elimination. ARES has done good work in the past, but it increasingly appears that current events have outstripped your ability to cope with them, especially without the leadership of Special Agent in Charge Taggart."

Janet. I'm hurt. How could you? He nodded and forced appropriate seriousness into his expression. "I understand, Senator."

Clarke slapped his palms down on the table. "I say they have had enough chances and *more* than enough. I propose we disband ARES immediately."

Before Bryant could protest, Tomassi chimed in, "Second."

Finley sounded tired as if they'd been down this road before. "Discussion? Hearing none, move to a vote. Those in favor?"

Three hands raised instantly on one side of the table. "Opposed?" The other trio of hands rose. "Tie vote, no action at this time."

He turned to face Bryant. "Do you have anything further, Special Agent in Charge Bates?"

Bryant had received the pulse indicating the successful transmission of the computer virus while the senators were voting. He smiled. "Nothing at the moment, Senator."

With a disgusted shake of his head, Finley said, "We are adjourned." The other politicians flowed out of the room, arguing with one another. Bryant watched them go, sipping his coffee, and turned to Finley with a smile when they had departed. "Are they always like this, Aaron?"

The other man laughed and rose to fill his own cup. He took a few sips before answering, then sighed. "They were actually on fairly good behavior today. No one fired any direct potshots at anyone else." He sat in the chair nearest the agent and leaned forward. "There's something you're not saying. You don't have to tell me what it is—in fact, it's probably better if I remain unaware. But I do need to know one thing in order to do my job properly. Are any of the Senators in immediate danger, either from one another or from an external party?"

The question set him back on his heels. He honestly hadn't contemplated that their arguments over the fate of ARES could ever extend beyond the confines of whatever room they were arguing in. Certainly, the idea that there might be physical danger had never crossed his mind. He thought about it for a second and, unhappy about doing so even though he knew he had to, considered the political implications of his conclusion before he shared it. Fortunately, the actual and political answers were the same. "I can't imagine so. Whoever is receiving any information would be unlikely to act in a way that might cut the flow off. I would expect the status quo to be maintained until something interrupts the supply of secrets."

Finley nodded. "If that changes, please inform me immediately. They're annoying, but it's my responsibility to keep the oversight committee functional—and that certainly includes making sure the members stay safe."

Bryant nodded, and their conversation turned to more pleasant affairs for a few moments before the senator departed for his next meeting. Bryant noted him checking his smartwatch as he left—a disguised ARES model—and made a small request to the universe. *Please don't let Finley be implicated.* He rose with a sigh and set his cup on the tray provided for used crockery. He took the long way out of the building, strolled through the public spaces, and admired the hustle and bustle of the government at work. Once outside, he tapped his comms and called Diana.

She sounded harried. "Hey, Bryant. You just caught me. I was on my way out. What's up?"

He couldn't resist. "Do you have a hot date?"

She laughed and a little of the tension he'd heard evaporating with the sound. She deadpanned her reply. "Yes. With Nylotte. She and I are a couple now. Didn't I tell you?"

He grinned and failed to keep the laughter from his voice. "Well, then, in fear for my life, I will nobly step aside. I wish you two only the best. But if you'd pass on a message to your roomie for me, that would be great. Let her know we're on for the game." It was the code phrase they'd agreed upon to indicate successful delivery of the virus.

Diana laughed again, but it was forced. "She'll be so glad

to hear that. When she gets her teeth into a deathmatch, she's beyond fierce. I wouldn't want to go up against her."

"We can only hope she does us proud." The line dropped, and he sighed. *And that the traitors we discover on the committee are the ones we already know about.*

CHAPTER FIFTEEN

Diana stepped out of the corner of her bedroom at home and into the corner of the bedroom in her stronghold on Oriceran. She and Nylotte had worked to fortify its defenses and to stock it with supplies against the need to spend significant amounts of time there during their pursuit of the last missing part of Rhazdon's Vengeance, the sword Fury. The Drow had also taken great pains to scrub away the stench of the place's previous occupant with liberal applications of magic. The torture and research rooms had been cleared, as had almost all the furniture except for a few bookshelves, the dining table—which was a truly gorgeous piece crafted from a single large slab of wood—and the desk made from the madness-inducing trees of the forest.

The agent had procured and delivered enough gear to fully outfit any four agents and was diligent about keeping the supplies fully stocked. Unlike the metal lockers at the base, however, the weapons and defensive pieces rested on armor dummies and in opulent display cases. When she'd asked Nylotte why she'd selected those items, the Drow had shrugged. "Part of your heritage is an appreciation of beauty. There's no time to start embracing that like the present." The Dark Elf had laughed and gestured at her hair. "You can begin there. It's all lopsided."

She had frowned and retorted, "Okay, next time, you fight the crazy wizard and his henchmen, and I'll set up an appointment at the salon." Her teacher hadn't been impressed.

The bedroom was empty, and she gazed with true longing at the heavy blankets and plump pillows on the bed. It was always cold in the bunker, exactly the way she liked it best. A small, carefully hidden part of her looked forward to when she would be able to share the renewed space with Rath, Cara, and the rest of the team. *But things will need to be much more stable than they are now for that to happen. At the moment, anyone here is a target.* While she was comfortable wearing a figurative giant X on her chest, she wasn't about to risk others in her pursuit of the sword if she could avoid it, given the destruction they'd narrowly avoided in the cavern that had been home to the daggers.

The agent wandered the halls, threading a path toward the office that took her through the other rooms. She had to admit, the Drow's sense of style matched her own very well. *Or maybe she chooses the items based on my tastes specifically. Either way works.* Nylotte's mentorship, however acerbic and annoying it might be at times—which was very acerbic and annoying—had become a true gift and was now one of the pillars that her personal foundation of being rested upon. Her happy thoughts were invaded by the object of her thoughts, whose sarcastic welcome greeted her as she stepped into the armory area. "Oh, you're finally here. How wonderful. Waiting for you was not boring at all." The Dark Elf reclined on the elegant wingback leather chair she had placed in the room so she could harangue her student as she prepared.

"It's lovely to see you too, most honored teacher." She set her backpack, filled with supplies, carefully to the side to unpack later. There was little preparation needed aside from her armor. She already wore her tactical pants, boots, and under tunic, plus the necklace that kept her connected to Lisa and the charm bracelet around her right wrist. The illusion detection band rested above the watch on her other hand. She wore her comm, but only for its enhanced sensing capabilities. She couldn't connect electronically with the other planet, and since Nylotte was able to speak into her mind, there was no need for her to wear one. Diana had made the offer on Earth, and the Dark Elf had merely raised an eyebrow and stared, which had effectively conveyed her opinion of that particular notion.

She shook her head at the memory and started to pull the armor pieces from the nearest full-body mannequin. "So, where are we off to today?"

The Drow straightened and pointed. "Your buckle is twisted." Diana rolled her eyes and the other woman smiled. "Not too far, actually. There is a keep nearby that was once the home of someone high up in Rhazdon's hierarchy. It's the next most likely holding place for artifacts from the time before the war."

She frowned as she strapped her arm guards on. "It hasn't already been ransacked? It seems an obvious location."

Her teacher nodded. "True. But I came across a well-hidden reference that suggests a cavern under the dungeons that may still lie undiscovered."

Diana lowered her vest over her shoulders and secured the straps to tighten it in place. This version was a little heavier than normal as it had an undercoating of tiny chain links made of titanium. The likelihood of blade combat was increased on Oriceran, based upon her experiences with the planet so far, and the addition might at least give her an edge. She checked her Ruger to verify its load and the cylinder's action and slipped it into its holster. Her Glock slid into position at her hip, and she draped her carbine across her chest, the barrel pointing down to the left. She turned to Nylotte. "How do I look?"

The Drow snorted as she rose to her feet. "Like…what's his name? Rambo, only less attractive."

"Cold. Really cold." Her teacher was dressed in her own battle attire, and Diana had to admit it was more stylish than her own. Leather straps covered her legs and arms, and a long chest piece of chainmail and more leather split into a skirt at her waist that reached to above her knees. She wore a belt over it with pouches similar to hers but it, too, was much more attractive. Her mane of white hair was bound in two ponytails. One pulled the top and sides together high on the back of her skull, and the other gathered the remainder at the nape of her neck. *She looks like an illustration from a book about gods and goddesses.* Her internal voice poked her. *"Jealous?"* Diana took another look and nodded. *Yeah, actually.* Her internal voice replied with something like a sigh, *"Me too."*

Nylotte gestured with her arms and twitched her long

fingers to summon a portal. When it was complete, the illumination spilling into it revealed a creepy looking corridor of roughhewn rock. The agent frowned. "So, straight into the dungeon, then?" The Dark Elf gestured her forward. She tapped her glasses to switch them to low light and stepped through.

The place smelled as old as it looked with decaying vegetation seemingly crushed where it poked through cracks in the rough-hewn blocks to either side. It proved to be barely taller than the elf as she followed and dispelled the rift behind them. The narrow space felt claustrophobic in the extreme. They traveled only a short distance before they entered a large room with stone tables set in a triangle in the center. As a gesture from the Drow, long extinguished torches flared to life to reveal the room's low ceiling and rocky walls—and the bloodstains that covered each of the large gray slabs. Diana sighed. "You always bring me to the nicest places. Was this guy an asshole torturer, too?"

Her companion laughed. "It was a woman, actually, and the record suggests she mainly worked with cadavers— admittedly, very recently dead cadavers. The book makes no mention of her creating her own, however."

Looking around the room at the various weapons that hung from the walls and surgical instruments that lay on trays along one side, Diana concluded that history had probably treated the woman too kindly. She was distracted from the thought by the sight of Nylotte near the far wall where she crouched to touch the ground. She crossed to kneel beside her teacher. "What is it?"

The Dark Elf waved a hand parallel to the floor, and a

set of runes materialized to outline a small circle. "This appears to be the trigger for something, but I can't sense what it's connected to."

"Is that normal?"

Her teacher nodded. "For something this ancient, yes. But it does increase the degree of danger considerably if it's a trap."

Diana sighed and stood. "Tell me what I need to say." It was her quest, after all, and the risks should be hers. Nylotte rose as well and pushed her away from the circle with a grim shake of her head. "I am better equipped to deal with the assorted magics that might be involved with such a trap." She paced the perimeter of the circle and stared at it before she gave a decisive nod. "I think it is simply the lock to a hidden door. I want you to cast force barriers around and above me as soon as I cross the boundary."

She nodded and created force walls on all sides, as well as one overhead. The Dark Elf chuckled. "Remind me, assuming we survive, to teach you that circles are far stronger than angles." Without another word, she stepped onto the circle and spoke a command in a language Diana didn't understand. The area within the force box began to glow, occluding the sight of her, and the agent stared into it, hoped the woman was okay, and feared the result if she was not. In only a few moments, the light diminished and a grinding sound emanated from within the triangle demarcated by the slabs.

Nylotte dismissed the force barriers and stepped free. "As I thought. It's simply a lock. It took a few moments to divine the right key." Diana nodded and followed her teacher as she crossed to the hole in the floor. The Drow summoned a ball of flame and cast it inside to reveal the rock of the promised cavern far below. Low moans rose from the room, sounding like beings in pain. They were interspersed with snarls and the sounds of movement. She looked at her companion with a half-grin. "How unexpected. It appears things are alive down there after all this time. Or perhaps the fire woke them."

Diana leaned gingerly over the opening and peered down. Below, the ground itself seemed to writhe and move. She backed away a step with a sigh. "Snakes. Why did it have to be snakes?"

The other woman shrugged. "So, it's more dangerous than we expected. Are you willing to give up the pursuit of the sword?"

"Absolutely not. I have one related question before we go, though. Do healing potions work as anti-venom?"

Her teacher rewarded the inquiry with a wicked grin. "I have no idea. Let's find out." She hurled several fireballs through the opening, leapt in behind them, and vanished instantly from view.

The agent shook her head. "I have a bad feeling about this." She stepped over the edge before she could reconsider.

CHAPTER SIXTEEN

The pillar of energy she summoned to control her descent created a wave and she rode it down and pushed the teeming mass of creatures on the floor away. They seemed to be a combination of bugs, rodents, and snakes, all of which displayed irritation at their presence. The Drow was already waiting on the bottom and tapped her foot impatiently. A force shield covered her skin in a mostly transparent barrier.

Diana landed in balance and raised her carbine. Nylotte summoned another pair of fireballs and made them hover to provide light in overlapping circles to either side of them. A rat-like creature about as large as a wolf appeared to the left, and the agent dispatched it with several rapid shots. Her teacher stared at her and she shrugged. "Rodents of unusual size are never friendly. Don't you ever watch movies?"

The Dark Elf shook her head, clearly despairing of her student's sanity, and led the way forward. Force and fire cleared the path, but the sense of being surrounded was constant and disconcerting. Occasionally, something large enough to be threatening would appear, and she would kill it or send it scurrying away with a few rounds from the carbine. By the time she'd emptied the first magazine, they still hadn't seen a sign of anything useful in the cavern.

The moaning noises drew closer—or, more accurately, they moved closer to the sounds. After another couple of dozen feet, her teacher nodded to gesture ahead. The far wall was finally visible. A tunnel led through it away from the teeming vermin but toward the moans and growls. Diana sighed. "Why does it seem we're always moving toward areas of more danger? Wouldn't intelligent beings choose differently?"

Nylotte's ponytails bounced as she shook her head. "Not intelligent beings with a purpose. And, really, a being without a purpose can hardly be called intelligent."

"What's your purpose, then?" The question was flippant but also sincere. She always wondered about the other woman's motivations.

The Drow laughed. "To see what you are capable of becoming, of course. After all, you are an evolutionary branch of my species. All Drow are related. Although your ongoing fascination with mundane weapons will probably stunt your growth."

"Shut up or I'll shoot you." She followed her into the narrow tunnel. Her teacher paused and cast a wall of force over the entrance behind them, then moved ahead again. *Damn. Managing to keep that up while also being ready for the next fight is impressive. Especially since it's out of her line of sight.*

As if she'd heard the thought, Nylotte explained, "You

will learn to see differently. It is simply a matter of using other senses and separating a portion of your mind to focus on an existing spell. It's not hard." She snorted inwardly. What the Drow considered simple was often still beyond Diana's best efforts.

Her partner came to a sudden stop, and she crouched and sighted along the barrel of her M4. There was a glow up ahead that didn't come from the fiery spheres floating nearby. A wave of her teacher's hand dismissed the orbs, and the duo moved forward cautiously. The tunnel opened into a wide, meandering hallway large enough to fit four people walking side by side. Torches flickered at intervals on both walls, disturbingly asymmetrical. Nylotte growled. "So the arrogant bastards wanted us to know they were here first?"

"What?"

With an exasperated sigh, she gestured at the torches. "They're burning. Obviously, since we haven't seen any others alight, they had the ability to deal with the darkness without them. So they lit them as a message that this place was not as secret as we thought."

"Do we turn back then?"

"Hardly. We have no way to know how long ago they were here, or whether they were successful. It could be those moaning sounds are animals feasting on their remains."

Diana shuddered. "That's a pleasant image. Thanks. Much appreciated."

A ghost of a smile flickered at the corners of her teacher's lips. "Forward, protégé."

Two turns later, they discovered what the moaning

sounds were. Half-decomposed corpses shambled around, generally limping and universally hideous. The smell they gave off was disgusting, and Diana covered her mouth and nose with a sleeve. She hissed, "What the hell are those?"

"Necromancy. It's not usually considered a polite form of magic. These were probably animated long ago—and imperfectly, to judge by the level of decay." She sounded professionally disappointed at the use of imperfect magic. It was a sound the agent had heard in her voice a seemingly endless number of times. "Our predecessors appear to have avoided them, rather than engaged with them."

"So what's the plan?"

The Dark Elf turned to her with a grin. "I hear burning is an appropriate method for dealing with such leftovers." She gestured at the shambling crowd. "Make it so."

She let her carbine fall on its strap and concentrated to calculate the right balance between power preservation and expenditure. When ready, she raised her hands and summoned her will, and washes of fire that mimicked the output of a flamethrower erupted from each. She tracked the blazes over the hallway to ensure that all the disgusting vestiges of life were targeted. The screams were horrifying, but her mind put an edge of gratefulness or resignation into them, as she definitely wouldn't want to spend eternity working for some evil wizard or witch. When the flames burned down, the corridor had been swept clean and even the ash reduced to nothing. A heavy door was now visible at the end of it.

Nylotte led the way as they hurried forward to flank the wooden barrier. She closed her eyes and seemed to be concentrating, so Diana did the same, trying to extend her senses through the wall. She heard some muffled sounds but couldn't make out what they were. When she opened her eyes, her teacher stared at her with an amused expression that carried into her voice. "Did you hear anything?"

She shrugged. "Something's on the other side, but I can't tell what."

"That's something, at least, although probably on the level of an Oriceran five-year-old."

"Bite me."

Her laugh was quiet. "Such sophisticated banter. I've identified at least five different sources of sound in the next room, which appears to be fairly large based on their spacing. I also detected something that sounded like scraping, which might be anything from weapons being dragged on the floor to large-scale magic moving blocks around."

Diana shook her head. "Your magical super senses aren't all that helpful, are they?"

"More helpful than yours. I'll get the door. You lead the way. Head toward the smallest threat you see, I'll take on the largest."

She nodded. There was no need for pretense with her teacher, as she was still far more powerful where magic was concerned. *But the distance is narrowing, every day.* Her inner voice laughed at her optimism, but before she could muster a thought in response, the door was open and her body darted across the threshold into the dangerous space beyond.

There were considerably more than five beings. The room was crammed with dwarves in one corner and Kilomea in the other, each group focused on disassembling their own trio of large ornamental columns. Two of the four corners were already covered in rubble, which suggested that they had been occupied with the task for some time. Diana froze at the unexpected sight, and Nylotte stepped up beside her. The Drow whispered, "This is not good. The Dwarves are mine."

"I thought you said you'd take the more powerful ones."

Her teacher chuckled and shook her head. "Trust me, I am. Dwarves can be wicked with magic. Kilomea, mostly, are focused on physical attacks."

She grumbled under her breath, then gestured at a high spot in the room in the middle of the far wall, where short staircases led up to a throne of some kind. On one side of it stood a dwarf and on the other, a Kilomea. They appeared to be overseeing the work below. "I assume those are the ones in charge. Should we kill them first?"

Nylotte shook her head. "They're defended by a shield that follows the lip of the raised area."

Diana cursed softly and wished once again that she had the sort of natural affinity for magic that her teacher did. The one time she'd mentioned it aloud, the other woman had offered a simple reply. "Patience. It's there, waiting to be discovered." So far, she hadn't found it and was increasingly convinced that she never would. *So, I guess I'll go with the skills I do have a natural affinity for.*

She rushed forward toward the pack of Kilomea. "On the ground, scumbags." Some part of her required that she give them the opportunity to end the situation peacefully, even though she knew there was no chance of success. The way they turned and brandished the hammers and axes they'd used to demolish the structure confirmed her belief. The sounds of a magical battle resounded from across the room as Nylotte confronted the dwarves.

There were eight Kilomea, far more than she'd ever imagined facing alone. She skidded to a halt as they began to move toward her and fired. Two bullets each thudded into the chests of the front-rank duo, but they seemed to not notice. *Armor. Hide. Whatever. Damn.* She lowered the barrel and sighted carefully to fire at their knees. The joints were less well protected, and she managed to bring them down. Even wounded, they continued to crawl in her direction.

Double Damn. Another two pressed toward her, and she sensed movement to the left and right. She fired at the ones ahead and they dodged. When her magazine clicked empty, she drew her pistol and fired every round in rapid succession. She managed to eliminate one of them completely and slow the other before she had to abandon ranged weapons. A hasty scramble took her under the swipe of a pickax from the left. She blocked an overhead strike from the right with a shuffle inside the attacker's guard and a raised forearm armor plate to catch the blow. The headbutt she'd normally throw would have landed on his breastbone, given their differences in height, so she kicked at his groin instead and connected hard enough to drive him back a few steps.

She couldn't follow up, though, because the other two who had circled from the sides were suddenly on her, melting out of the shadows. Diana managed to roll with the hammer blow as it struck her ribs and the motion and the armor mitigated most of the damage. She landed painfully, bounded back to her feet, and tried to bolt to the side. One of the bastards she'd kneecapped grasped her shin and threw a punch at her knee.

Her reaction was instinctive and the force blast hurled her back. She used her magic to hover and cast about for a safe space to land. One of the other Kilomea had outdistanced the others in its pursuit. She dropped the magic and plummeted at an angle and her heavy boots connected with his shoulders and shattered his collarbone with a loud crack. *Three all the way out, one still crawling, and four at full strength.*

When the next adversary appeared from around a corner, she had the time to draw the Ruger and pepper his legs with bullet wounds. She wasn't sure she'd caught the knee, but at a minimum, he wouldn't be able to move very fast. That left three whole and hearty. She discovered the rest had encircled her while the other had played prey as a distraction. *Dammit. They're hunters, right. Get your head in the game, Diana.* She considered and discarded grenades as an option, afraid that she'd bring the place down on them. A loud noise from across the room was followed by a flaming dwarf hurtling into the barrier that protected the two near the throne. *At least Nylotte has her end handled.*

She summoned a sword in her right hand and a shield in her left and for a brief moment felt like a combination of Ronin and Captain America. Both were made of force, and she applied another surge of power to light the sword aflame. Her attackers recoiled momentarily as she turned in a slow circle with the weapon extended. "Last chance, scumbags." She growled with as much menace as she could to emphasize her intent. "Get the fuck out or die."

The lead Kilomea, a female, laughed at her. "Come along, little human, let's see what you have."

"Fine. It's your funeral. I'll kill you last." She delivered the line in its appropriate Austrian accent. *Rath would be proud.* She charged the one to the female's left, a large male who seemed to be the least agile of the trio. He spun aside from her blow and turned the motion into a foot sweep that she had to leap to avoid. *He's still damn agile, though.* His eyes tracked the sword, which left him unprepared for the shield she smashed into his face with a surge forward and a shout. He stumbled away, his arms flailing, and she stabbed the blade deep into his stomach, then yanked it to the side to widen the wound as she wrenched it free.

Diana raised it again barely in time to catch the head of a hammer before it pounded into her skull, courtesy of the other male. The female aimed a kick at her a moment after and she caught it on her shield. She realized she was trapped and dismissed her weapons, replacing them with an instant force blast that hurled her enemies away and launched her upward again. Her telekinesis effectively adjusted her trajectory and she landed behind the male as he struggled to his feet. She delivered four punches to his body before he regained his balance and a kick to the back of his leg forced him to one knee. With his head finally at a height she could reach, she lunged into a spinning hook kick and drove her heel into his skull. He teetered for a moment before he fell. The blow would most likely have killed a human, so she hoped it would keep him out of the fight for a while, at least.

The agent straightened and faced the female, who was the only one left standing among her enemies. The sounds of battle from the far side of the room had ceased and for a moment, she feared Nylotte had been defeated. She'd no sooner considered that when the Drow appeared, striding toward the duo near the throne with her hands in guard position. Diana shook her head and looked at her opponent. "It appears I need to finish this so my partner doesn't have to fight your bosses alone."

The Kilomea spat to the side. "Only Pesharn is my superior. I hope your partner kills the dwarf before she dies."

She shrugged. "Whatever. Bring it, sister."

The massive combatant attacked, leading with one of the wicked pickaxes. Diana ducked the blow and landed two force-assisted punches before her foe whipped the ax in her direction and released it. She threw herself onto her back and triggered a panicked blast to deflect it, but it still managed to clip her ear as it spun past. She grimaced as warm blood flowed and flipped to her feet in a rage. Her enemy had closed while she was down, and the kick struck home before she even saw it. She careened away to land heavily and slide until her spinning form impacted with one of the columns and stopped abruptly.

She focused on the Kilomea through the stars that filled her vision as her foe barreled in for a final kick and lobbed a fireball at the aggressor's head. Her target shrieked and fell, keening as she rolled blindly with her hands pressed over her face. Diana used the column as support to climb to her feet and crossed to the wounded creature, then used the last charge in her shock gloves to knock her unconscious.

Each step was accompanied with a flare of pain that

stole her breath, and she knew she'd broken at least one rib, probably several. She took the healing potion flask from her belt and downed it, then followed it with the vial of energy magic. Diana was grinning and feeling fantastic by the time she reached Nylotte's side. The Dark Elf stared at the two remaining adversaries near the throne. Diana clapped her teacher on the back, which earned her a withering glare before the Drow returned her attention to the others.

Her voice was filled with scorn, an enraging technique the Dark Elf had used on her many times. "Two of us, two of you. Don't tell me you're afraid."

The dwarf laughed. "Of you, outcast? Hardly. Of your pet? Impossible."

The agent bristled. "Who are you calling pet, short stuff?"

"Who are you calling *short*, human?" He laughed again.

She turned to whisper to her teacher. "Okay, he has to die now. Who are these pricks?"

Nylotte spoke loudly so their enemies would hear. "The one on the left is Pesharn. She is a leader among the Kilomea. The one on the right is Jakko, an otherwise undistinguished dwarf."

The Kilomea laughed and drew a dirty look from her partner. "In any case, you are too late. We have finished our search and discovered nothing worth keeping, including you."

She nodded and the dwarf raised his bare arms. Glyphs or runes of some kind—different than her own—glowed as he cast a spell, and the ceiling above began to shake. Nylotte grabbed her arm. "It's time to go." The Drow created a portal under their feet and they dropped through it. She saw rocks plummeting toward them and scrambled out of the way, but her teacher closed the rift before they could come through.

Diana leaned back on her elbows and looked at the ceiling of her arming room, which had apparently become Nylotte's preferred portal home in the bunker. "Remind me again why I don't have healing and energy potions every day?"

The Drow chuckled in amused disbelief. "Let's get you back to your house before all this wonderfulness leaves you and you sleep for two days." She frowned. "Did you drink all of both?"

She laughed. "Yep."

"Okay." Her teacher sighed. Three days. Let's go, giggly-face."

The moniker only made her laugh more, and the Dark Elf had no sooner dumped her in bed at home than the good feelings vanished under a wave of exhaustion so profound she couldn't imagine ever surfacing from beneath it.

CHAPTER SEVENTEEN

The coin had grown warm around her neck some hours before, but Sarah had been at the office and was unwilling to communicate from there. Her enemies had done her an unwitting service by bugging the warehouse. The security threat compelled her to return home before speaking with Dreven, which in turn, allowed her to delay the effort as long as desired.

She'd finally accomplished virtually everything she could at the base, however, and surrendered to the fact that she couldn't delay it any longer. With one last look around, she locked the office door from the inside and created a portal to an alley behind a south side coffeehouse. After securing her favorite drink of the moment—a flat white with vanilla—she used the secluded passage between the buildings to magically relocate to the parking garage beneath her condo.

Sarah sipped her coffee appreciatively during the elevator ride up and nodded to the other residents of the building as they entered and exited. During the week since the event, she'd reveled in a bout of positivity. The last attack had gone well, even though it had not resulted in a clear victory. The annoying human who liked to speak out against Oricerans was dead at her hands, and she still remembered the sound of all his bones breaking at once with deep satisfaction. They'd winnowed the numbers of the police a little and struck fear into the populace, who would now put pressure on the politicians and thus create additional chaos.

Better still, she'd defeated the leader of the enemy forces and dispatched her to a trap on Oriceran. *The World in Between would have been my preferred place to banish her, but it's something, at least.* The stunned expression on her face as the portal swept over her had become an often-visited memory of the event. Her people told her that the troll had been inconsolable and destroyed everything in sight, which was another mental image she enjoyed.

The silence from Dreven was worrying at first, but she'd put it down to the man's arrogance. She would surely have heard from Iressa if the wizard had fallen to the woman, which was unlikely, in any case. The lack of communication from her new patron had also been a source of concern, but it was in keeping with the dark witch's style to thwart her expectations.

She set the drink down on her coffee table. The statue's resting place was on a thin pedestal in the hallway that connected the living room to the bedroom, and she retrieved it before she returned to sit on the white leather couch. She paused for a moment to soak in the quiet and stillness around her. It had been a day's work to add spells to improve the soundproofing in the apartment and the precautions used only a small daily expenditure of power to keep the improvement active. Now, only the loudest noises of the city far below signaled the existence of a world beyond her windows unless she sought it out. The condo truly had become a sanctuary for her.

One interrupted every so often by an idiot mage from another planet. She withdrew the coin and set it in place, and the hovering blue image of her irritating superior appeared. He did not look happy. "The bitch escaped. She killed several of my assistants and bolted when I was about to eliminate her."

Sarah scowled and shook her head in what she hoped was an appropriate response. Inside, she was half-laughing and half-annoyed. *Now, I have two unknowns running around my city—Diana Sheen and that moron Marcus, who I'm sure hasn't done me the favor of dying during his disappearance.* Neither had been seen by anyone from the Remembrance since the night of the battle. She'd considered torturing Marcus's two little friends, the henchman and the hanger-on, but hadn't wanted to expose her interest. *And killing them would be inappropriate. For now.*

Dreven's ire was obvious as his small avatar paced restlessly, its hood pulled back to reveal disheveled hair and a furious glare. He seemed to be having an internal conversation and only occasionally remembered she was there. Finally, he turned to face her. "You and your people need to make killing that woman your top priority. Everything else is secondary. If she's not dead in a week, I'll have to come there and take care of it personally. Believe me when I say that if I have to do so, you will not enjoy it."

He killed the connection quickly, fortunately, so the

laugh that escaped at his threat didn't cause her further trouble. *As if having you on the planet could* ever *be enjoyable, you pretentious scumbag.* She sighed at the complication of Sheen's continued existence and walked down the hallway, through the bedroom, and into her closet.

It was a large walk-in, and one side was home to clothing and accessories, with a special section reserved for the most expensive and most loved items. She trailed her fingers across a tight black dress that resembled the ones Iressa wore. She was saving it for exactly the right moment, not sure what that might be but confident she'd know it when it arrived. The other side of the closet was her current focus, however.

It was filled with shelves of varying heights displaying the implements of her trade. Extra wands stood in a shallow holder on the far end, and an assortment of investigative tools—including a fake crystal ball and an actual scrying bowl—rested on the surfaces closest to the entrance. It was the small set of miniature apothecary drawers that drew her attention now. The large box that held the smaller containers was aged wood, and the antique shop she'd stolen it from had dated it as coming from the 1800s. She'd cleaned it thoroughly and put magical seals in place in each drawer to avoid contamination. Another witch might contend that it was wasted time when there were other choices to accomplish the same goal, but the sight of the object gave her pleasure, and that was reason enough for her.

One of the drawers had the letter S written on the ivory card in front, and she removed several strands of hair that lay inside. During their last battle, her foe had been less agile than she'd thought and her re-entry through the shat-tered window Sarah had hurled her out of had clipped these threads from the dark mess on top of her head. To a magic-user, such items were invaluable. She snagged the magical compass she'd purchased from a black-market mage in a nearby city and carried it out to her table to work.

The device was a combination of magic and human science, albeit an old technology since replaced by satel-lites. She lifted the part with the dial and arrow from its container and set the pieces of hair inside before she placed it back in its home. With a tap of her wand, she released a thread of magic into it and spoke the word of activation. The arrow spun as she maintained the flow of power into the item. There was no telling how long it would take to attune the device to the woman who'd invol-untarily donated the hair, so she used the time to consider her next moves. Eliminating her foe would require the right battlefield, and with a grin, she realized she could merge two of her objectives together.

The arrow slowed, then stopped pointing to the large "E" on the compass. She walked around the condo with the object in her hand, but the indication didn't change. Sheen was currently to the east. It would be a simple matter to triangulate her exact location when needed. She grinned and spoke to the empty space. "Now I have you, and you won't get away again."

She retrieved her wand from where it had fallen between two cushions and waved it in a large circle to acti-vate the protective wards that permeated the walls, windows, ceiling, and floor. The remaining trace of noise from the city subsided, and the unreality of the space unnerved her a little, as it always did. The necklace had signaled her true superior's desire for communication for about half an hour, but once she'd started the activation of the compass, she had to either complete it or lose the power of the source material to track her foe.

The witch leaned back, put her fingers on the jewelry, and was mentally transported to a different place. This time, it seemed to be a living room. Her virtual body was locked and stood rigidly in the center, unable to move. The black-clad witch who'd summoned her sat in a chair near a flickering fireplace and idly casting spurts of flame into the wood from her wand. She didn't look up as she spoke. "Report."

"Dreven failed. The woman still lives."

Iressa gave a snort, followed by a slow laugh. "Of course she does. Dreven is an idiot. Did she manage to kill him?"

Sarah tried instinctively to shake her head, but it refused to budge. Only her mouth worked, it seemed. "No, he appears to be unharmed. He said that she killed several of his assistants, however."

The witch sighed. "Well, that's something at least. What are your plans now?"

She wasn't sure if the woman was referring to plans for Sheen, for Marcus, or for Dreven, so she covered all the possibilities. "I have devised a way to track Sheen. We will isolate her and kill her. As far as Marcus is concerned, as long as Dreven is still around I cannot act against the half-man without risking my superior's displeasure." She injected sarcasm into the final words and coaxed a small smile from her patron.

"And, finally, I await your instructions where Dreven is concerned. You have only to tell me what you wish, and it will be done."

Iressa nodded. "Very good. Matters seem well in hand. Let us discuss your plan to eliminate the vexing woman who constantly interferes with our plans."

CHAPTER EIGHTEEN

K ayleigh frowned at the playback of the witch's words. Alfred had alerted her to the recording in real-time, but she hadn't been able to break free of the conference call with the techs at ARES DC. They were working on new drone models that would offer greater flexibility in combat situations, and she was committed to ensuring proper safeguards at every step of the process. *Whether they like it or not. It's good having Emerson's support, even though he's not part of this particular project.*

As usual, only Sarah's side of the conversation had been recorded. The team was divided on the reason. Half believed it was something to do with passive wards placed around the condo, and the other half assumed that he simply spoke into her mind with magic. The tech didn't particularly care. Neither argument precluded the need to get more intel.

The previous day had been spent with Deacon on a quick road trip to the nearby city of Youngstown, about halfway between Pittsburgh and Cleveland. Diana had let them borrow her Mustang, and between the music and the speed, it had been a great way to release tension. She'd been surprised when he'd led her into a small magic shop—the human misdirection type—but it made sense to hide real magic under the cover of skill in illusion. The proprietor was a tall, thin man with a goatee who was as enthusiastic as could be about the magic kits and items for sale in the front of the shop. She remembered the details of the visit fondly.

When her colleague provided the code word and they entered the rear of the building, the illusion fell away to reveal the elf's pointed ears and more finely sculpted cheekbones. He'd explained that he had been born on Earth but had been one of the first to return to the magical planet when the opportunity had presented itself. His thirst for knowledge had driven him to make connections with anyone who could provide information. That inevitably led to trades of items, rather than merely concepts, and he had become an in-demand black market supplier on both worlds.

His voice was joyful and filled with self-deprecating humor. "Yep, we close here on Mondays through Wednesdays so I can spend time at my other shop. It's busy, but it's a living." The rear room was a luxurious space with two dark leather-and-wood couches facing one another over a low ebony coffee table. Every wall was filled with cabinets containing items that she mostly couldn't recognize. The elf, Santith, gestured them to one couch and he sat on the other. He waved an arm and one of the cabinet doors opened to reveal itself as a refrigerator. Three bottles of Great Lakes beer floated into their waiting hands, and a second gesture popped the tops and rocketed the caps into a corner wastebasket. He leaned back and took a long sip, then sighed. "What can I do for you two?"

Deacon was their spokesperson for the trip. "I got your name from a mutual acquaintance. She said that you would have access to hybrid magic tech."

Santith nodded. "Indeed, I do, and she warned me you would come, so we can both be reassured of the loyalty of our friend."

He grinned. "Perfect. Did she tell you what I am looking for?"

The elf stretched a hand out and a thin case soared across the room to land in his grasp. He set the wooden box on the table, and Kayleigh was struck by how much it resembled a silverware container, only not quite as large. He released the latch and folded it open to reveal several items that looked like small locusts.

Her partner leaned forward with an eager, "Sweeeet," and held one of them up to the light. Having ruined their negotiating position with his enthusiasm, he agreed to the elf's price, which wasn't all that exorbitant—an arm and part of a leg, at most. They'd brought a few items that Diana and Cara had snagged on their various adventures and closed the deal with a top-up of actual cash—in a briefcase and everything. She couldn't help but smile at the corny reality.

They'd parted with promises of future collaboration, and the objects now sat on the corner of the worktable before her. She'd keep one for deep analysis and decon-struction, which Deacon had promised to assist with. The rest would somehow go into Sarah's fancy living space.

Exactly how to accomplish that was still an open question. The only surety was that it would involve Rath, and she smiled as the troll bounded into the room, followed by his loyal mount, Max. With a soft bark, the dog stretched beside her and demanded petting, which she provided and received several wet licks in return. The three-foot bundle of trouble vaulted onto her table and sat cross-legged near the wall.

She grinned. "Hi, Rath."

He returned the smile. "Hi, Kayleigh. Long time no see." They both laughed as they'd had breakfast together only a few hours before. It was one of many standing roommate-related jokes they shared.

Deacon joined them for a moment to ensure the troll understood how the bugs worked. He repeated the instructions he'd been given, and the other tech gave him a high five before departing back to his computer setup. Now, it was up to her and Rath to decide the way forward. "So, did you do some recon?"

He nodded. "Flew over with Gwen while the witch was away." Sloan kept them all apprised of her movements whenever he could. "Mapped the building services. Air vents are best option." The ages-old trope of people clambering through ductwork had been their inspiration for that particular possibility, even though they all knew it wasn't really possible. A troll, however, could make the passage by shrinking if the space grew too small.

Kayleigh had concerns. "What if there are magical wards?"

"Danger is my middle name." Rath shrugged.

She groaned and shook her head. "Okay, if you say so,

International Troll of Mystery." He laughed, clearly unconcerned about the task ahead, so she pushed her own anxiety aside. "Do you think you'll be able to do the whole thing at this size?"

"Maybe. But will shrink if necessary."

"But that changes the equipment I can send you in with." He nodded, and she drummed her fingers on the table, then sighed. "Okay, let's see what we can come up with. There's no time like the present, right?"

They'd received the signal that Sarah was spending the evening at the warehouse, working with the witches and wizards on some future operation. Sloan wasn't able to share more than that because the humans weren't part of it. After Diana's mercifully short disappearance, the entire team was on edge about the prospective plans of the Remembrance, Rath triply so. The troll gave a soft sigh. *Which is why I need to get these planted so we know what the evil witch is up to.*

He was perched on top of the building with the surveillance equipment, waiting for night to descend fully. The city lights below precluded real darkness, but he wasn't about to jeopardize the mission by leaping over the street, only to become a spectacle triggered by an errant glance upward. Gwen chimed in his ear when it was time, and he launched himself forward and snapped his glide wings out. They carried him across to the other building in silence, and he landed carefully, pulled up to slow his velocity, and touched down with barely a slide. He removed all his gear, bundled it together, and secured it with a magnet to the side of the air vent. All that remained was a small but powerful drill with multiple tips attached to the strap of leather he would carry or drag through the ductwork.

It was quick work to use the tool to remove the exterior grate, and he peered in to confirm a drop that ran the full height of the structure to allow return air to escape. He'd reviewed the plans with Gwen a dozen times while he waited and knew he would have to exit the shaft two levels down, then crawl halfway around the building before he would have access to the witch's apartment. He was without communication on this run, as he needed to be bigger than the smallest comms but prepared to grow smaller than the regular ones. Kayleigh had offered to make a custom version in a middle size, but neither had welcomed the delay and he was on his own. *Noble loner troll infiltrates the enemy stronghold.* Action movie music played in a quiet corner of his mind as he worked.

He retrieved the line he'd pooled beside the vent and attached its carabiner to the magnet, then threw the rest of the rope into the shaft. A weight at the bottom kept it from flapping too much in the breeze. Rath took one more look around, shrank to about two feet, caught the strap holding the drone bugs and his screwdriver-drill combo, and climbed onto the lip of the vent. He made himself even smaller, secured the leather around his waist for the descent, and lowered himself hand over hand to the target level.

Here, the line moved with the air currents, and he had to swing to the far side and push off to lock his fingers into the grate separating the horizontal section of ductwork from the vertical one. He hooked his legs around the line and used his free hand to retrieve the tool and remove three screws that held the barrier in place. The troll loosened the fourth almost completely, and the whole thing fell out of the way and swung gently from its remaining fastener. He scrambled out of the shaft, breathing heavily from the exertion required to clear the grate and avoid falling at the same time.

He grinned. *Daredevil troll has thwarted the initial defense. But will he be strong enough to overcome the long run?* The thoughts came in a movie narrator's voice and combined with the music, inspired a chuckle as he moved as quickly as caution allowed. They'd all agreed that silence was important as he'd move through other apartments and common spaces on the way to the witch's condo. Any noise might result in discovery, which would be awkward at best and potentially fatal at worst.

Finally, he turned the corner that marked the far end of the building. *Only another half to go, but it's the long half.* They hadn't been fortunate with the placement of the air vent as it was more or less exactly opposite the target. He left marks in the dust as he trudged along, the airflow in this portion of the path not strong enough to overcome the weight of all the debris inside it. *The movies always make this look clean. Ewww. I'll need two showers when this is over.*

He counted and looked through the grates into the apartments as he passed until finally, he reached the one that led to the witch's living room, which he recognized from the surveillance video. He slowly and carefully removed three of the four fasteners and pushed it out of the way enough that he could squeeze through. *Now comes the hard part.* The troll slid a hand into his tiny belt and withdrew the hand and foot grips Kayleigh had devised for the mission. They'd agreed that the witch stood a better chance of noticing the intrusion the further into her active space he went and decided to address the challenge by keeping him up high.

He'd requested web-shooters, but the tech hadn't been able to accomplish that in the allotted time either. Still, when he moved out onto the wall, the way the gloves and shoes allowed him to crawl along them was exactly like one of the superheroes he idolized. *Spider-troll, Spider-troll. Does whatever a...uh... Always in control. Crawls on walls, deposits bugs. Gets away, gets some hugs. Look out...* He laughed at himself again as he secured one of the little surveillance devices and crept along the top of the wall to the small kitchen.

A half-hour later, he had placed one of the devices everywhere except in the bedroom. When he discovered the closet, he knew the bug had to go there and hid it up at the top corner and furthest away from the overhead light on the clothing side of the room. He felt a sense of danger from the magical items arrayed on the far side, an almost palpable menace that filled the small space and made him want to gag. He retraced his steps into the vent and gave the apartment a final scrutiny after he'd secured the grate in place.

Okay, witch. Your secrets are now ours. Spider-troll out.

CHAPTER NINETEEN

S loan's new phone was an upgrade, an android device that appeared low-end despite being packed with all kinds of useful stuff inside. *Tommy Ketchum really is moving up in the world. First a beater car, now a phone that a teenager would be embarrassed to be seen with.* He shook his head and wished yet again that for once, he could have an undercover gig that required him to be a wealthy playboy. *Bond always seems to manage it.*

The text came from a number associated with a political action committee that the ARES team had spoofed. If asked, he had a great story about how he'd been trying to date one of the graduate students who canvassed door to door but had failed miserably. The others in the Remembrance group enjoyed hearing the tales that ended with Tommy losing.

What it really signified was far more interesting, however. It was Kayleigh's code name, which would only mean one of two things. If followed with any use of the word urgent, the contact meant he should disconnect from his cover immediately using an exit strategy they'd created at the start. The message lacked that, so it had to be the other option.

In simple terms, he had a present waiting for him at a dead drop. It didn't specify where, which was a second layer to the tradecraft. He'd have to make a circuit of them until a particular piece of graffiti appeared at one of the designated locations. The old tricks were the best tricks, even if they'd already been used in countless television shows and movies. *Hell, that makes them even better since they'd be discounted on that basis more often than not.*

He climbed into his beat-up Nissan Sentra—which was older than some of the previously imagined phone-rejecting teenagers—and turned the key. His faith was once again validated as the engine came to life without complaint. Hank had managed a surreptitious visit to where Sloan had left the vehicle in a parking garage and given it a once-over, leaving a pine air freshener behind as a sign of his intervention. Since then, the passenger door had broken and steadfastly refused to close, and he'd replaced it from a junkyard. The car was now mostly rust-brown with one dented white door. It was his goal to mix and match on the assumption that it played well with his cover.

Sloan pulled the sim chip out of his phone and powered the device down, then pushed on the accelerator and drove to the seedier side of the strip district, home to strip clubs and places of much more illicit activity. One of the drops was actually at the nicest of the clubs, but no marker was present, so he continued his journey. The next was in the alley beside a small Vietnamese restaurant that he adored, but that one lacked a sign as well. With a sigh, he wrenched the wheel to the left and headed to the bridge leading to the highway that ran north of the river.

The next two locations were also unmarked, so only one possibility remained. He pulled into the Zoo parking lot, made his way through the gates, and paid for a single visit. Rath had suggested this location as it was one of his favorite places in the city. Sloan wandered to the Red Panda enclosure and looked through the glass at the frolicking creatures who never failed to bring a smile. He sauntered up the hill toward the elephants and saw the marker ahead at the turn leading to the giraffe exhibit. With a confused expression on his face, he paused and retraced his steps, checking for tails, but he was confident that he would have seen anyone following him by now.

He entered the savannah restaurant and visited the restroom, selecting the stall furthest from the door. Touching his disguised ARES watch to the wall caused a hidden panel to slip aside, revealing a space about the size of a shoebox. In it lay a capsule and a tube that looked like a straw with a button on it. He retrieved the items and the small disc that rested under them, then sealed everything again and left the building.

It didn't take long to separate one of the guests seated in the food court area from their cell phone, although he'd had to pass several candidates before locating an Apple device. He activated the flashlight, which didn't require a password, and held it up to the disc. The object drew power from the specific frequency of the light, and a message scrolled across it in miniature glowing letters. **Subject always shielded outside. Hit with tracker inside.**

He scowled as the words repeated, then crushed the tiny disc between his fingertips. *Shoot the paranoid witch in front of a ton of potential witnesses. Awesome. Thanks, y'all.* He deposited the phone with its owner—and asked her and her friend for directions to the otters to distract her from his subterfuge—and returned to the parking lot.

The message waiting when he'd reactivated his phone had increased his worry all the more. Murray had sent him several texts and resorted to voice messages when they'd failed to connect. His presence was requested—meaning required—at a dinner for the human inner circle. He'd only had time to stash the straw and capsule in the hidden compartment Hank had added into the dashboard and speed through rush-hour traffic to reach the restaurant at the indicated hour.

It was a private room in a large bar-restaurant downtown that specifically didn't cater to the business crowd. The place was usually rowdy downstairs and always rowdier upstairs. They had the private bar at the back of the main floor to themselves, with permission to enter through the kitchen to avoid drawing attention. He was relieved to see he wasn't the last to arrive as he walked into the space. The broad rectangular table in the center was only half-filled, and Murray's black outfit made him seem quite natural in his position behind the bar.

The man slid a drink to him as soon as he approached. It turned out to be a perfectly mixed Manhattan, with exactly the right amount of Vermouth and a top-shelf bourbon. Sloan sipped it appreciatively and raised the glass in a toast. Mur gave him a half-smile, but there was a concerned edge to it. He pushed his magic but as usual, it failed to provide results on demand.

A seat sat empty at the head of the table, and a cluster of people was already seated near it. The arrangement pointed to something he'd anticipated—Marcus' return from his mysterious "business trip." Only Murray knew where he'd been, although Sloan had some suspicions. The other man remained extremely tight-lipped on the subject, however, and he'd quickly abandoned the attempt to get him to talk.

Their leader appeared through the rear door and looked much healthier than when they'd dragged him from the stadium field covered in burns. Marcus had ranted the whole way back to the humans' hideout and banished Sloan from his sight. He'd momentarily feared for his life but assumed that as long as Murray was around, there would be a voice of reason whispering in their leader's ear.

The human leader of the Remembrance wore black pants and a white dress shirt rolled up to the forearms. He called for the others to come to the table, including the small gaggle of henchmen who had followed him in, and they took their seats with him selecting the open one at the end. Huge plates of food arrived immediately, a family-style serving of pasta, a couple of varieties of chicken, and salads in addition to a bowl of Italian wedding soup for everyone.

The conversation remained light while they ate, but there was an edge in Marcus's eyes that inspired concern. *Shit. This isn't merely a social occasion. He has something planned.* None of the others seemed to pick up on it, though. His talent triggered when he glanced at Murray and revealed that he was filled with anxiety. Sloan had thought about what his being outed as a spy might invoke in the man who had looked out for him since the early days and decided it would involve regret and guilt, neither of which he felt emanating from him. *So it's not me. Probably.*

He did what he always did in such moments and ate a little extra and drank a little extra, deciding he deserved the luxury if he was about to die. Finally, after desserts were consumed and cappuccinos delivered, Marcus leaned back in his chair with a satisfied sigh. "It's good to be with you all again. The last week has been as boring as all hell." The remark drew a laugh, and smiles appeared on several faces, only to vanish with his next words. "For me, that is. For some of you, though, it appears that it's been very exciting indeed."

Sloan straightened involuntarily as that particular statement could refer to him. He covered it by leaning toward the man like a good soldier would to focus completely on what he was about to say. Marcus grinned, but it was a vicious thing that promised trouble rather than enjoyment. "It seems that there have been some...what might be called extra-curricular activities going on while I was away." He dragged his gaze over each person at the table, and the Face imagined the others might also feel concerned, even when they knew it couldn't be them. *Probably. That look and tone of voice should make everyone feel guilty about something.*

Marcus wiped his lips with a napkin and discarded it as he rose. "I don't ask for much, but I do demand absolute loyalty from those I run with. Sadly, two of you have chosen to freelance, which means you are no longer welcome at my table." He raised his hands and pointed at one person on each side. They scrambled up with protests of innocence that were quickly lost in the sound of the electricity that engulfed them and the screams it engendered. The attack ceased and they collapsed to moan pitifully on the floor as the pain overwhelmed them.

Their leader pointed at several of the men at the table. "Get them out of here. We'll give them a fighting chance and throw them in the river. If they survive, they'll hopefully be smart enough to stay in whatever downstream podunk town they wash up in." It was only when he followed the man out for a separate meeting—one with only him, Murray, and a couple of others—that what he'd seen registered in his brain.

Two fingers. Two hands. Two arms. Two mechanical arms. Holy shit, he got upgrades.

CHAPTER TWENTY

Cara cursed as her force shield failed under the barrage of shadow. She'd had a moment of warning and rolled aside to rise on one knee with a barrier of fire to block the continued attacks. Nylotte scowled and changed methods to deliver a rain of ice against it. The Drow had explained once before that it cost more energy to defend against an opposite and the difference was palpable.

Her teacher yelled, "Enough," and Cara rose warily to her feet. The Dark Elf paced and shook her head as she muttered to herself, which was never a good sign. Diana sat on a pile of crates outside the combat area of the basement and watched the white-haired woman with an amused twist to her lips.

Finally, Nylotte stopped pacing and turned to her first student. "Shut up, you." Then, she addressed Cara. "If I didn't know better, I would say that you want to fail at everything but fire. Do you?"

She was stunned by the harsh accusation, and an immediate denial rose within her. Before she could voice it and without warning or effort on her part, she suddenly stood in a clearing with trees blocking the view to either side. She crouched instinctively and turned in a slow circle with her hands raised in a defensive fighting stance while her brain scrambled to catch up to the moment. "Nylotte? What are you doing?"

The forest noises she'd barely noticed vanished, and crashing sounds began to emanate from all directions. She reached for her daggers but they weren't there. Cara still wore her normal training clothes and immediately missed the protection of the tunic she'd traded for a concert t-shirt. She'd worn heavy metal shirts exclusively with demonic references on them when working with the Drow simply to tease her, and today's Motley Crue shirt was one of the most effective. *Maybe that's why she's being so witchy.*

When the figures burst out of the foliage, she was both shocked and repulsed. They looked like a drawing figure for a full-sized troll, with long limbs and giant bodies. Worse, they were flat and featureless, hairless, muscleless, and—the worst, as far as she was concerned—faceless. She knew that if she waited, she'd be surrounded in moments so she attacked.

The first waved its arms at her as she dove beyond it, exploiting a gap in the slowly shrinking circle. She bounded up and kicked the creature in the back to propel it along the line it was already taking. The enemies reacted slowly and although they advanced and launched attacks, she found it fairly easy to avoid them and connect with counterstrikes.

The problem was that there were so many of them, and her punches and kicks entirely failed to damage them. *Fine, so it has to be magic, then. Screw you, Drow witch.* She assumed that the woman wanted her to push herself to use different kinds of power, so she tried as hard as she could to fight with force and ice, the ones she'd had middling success with thus far. After several moments of that nonsense, though, she went back to what she was good at.

Cara summoned long whips of flame in each hand and used one to keep extra enemies from closing while she shredded single opponents with the other. She didn't realize how much she was enjoying herself until half her foes had been eliminated and the rest suddenly froze in place. She resisted the urge to destroy them while they were immobile and concentrated on breathing deeply to prepare for whatever her teacher threw at her next.

When it came, it was unexpected.

Demon sauntered out of one side of the forest and clapped slowly. "Well done. A very effective use of fire, Bearer."

Angel's melodic voice sounded from the opposite side of the clearing as she broke the tree line. "You are powerful indeed. We made the correct choice in allowing you the opportunity to win us."

The two beings stopped in front of her, Angel at Demon's right hand as always. The latter asked, "So, did you enjoy yourself?"

She frowned. "You did this?"

He turned his head to his sister—she wasn't sure they were actually related in any way, but since they were essentially identical twins, she'd decided that they would be brother and sister in her thoughts, whether they liked it or not—and laughed. "She's quick on the uptake, no?"

Angel grinned. "Indeed so. But she's still getting used to us."

Cara interrupted before he could make fun of her again. "So this is a mental projection again, right?" They nodded in unison. "What's going on out there?" She waved in the general direction of the sky.

He scratched his nose and looked bored. "Less than a second has passed outside. You are still planning to offer petty excuses for why you fail with other magics in order to appease your teacher."

She blinked, unsure of what to say. Angel filled the silence. "We brought you here because you are suffering a disconnection."

Her mind grasped the last word, and she pictured the paths that Diana and Nylotte had shown her and imagined gaps that kept her from accessing the other magics. "Can you help me with that?"

The dark figure turned to his mirror image. "She still doesn't understand. Are you sure she was our best option?"

Angel laughed and smacked him in the chest with the back of her hand. "What he means is that the disconnect is not in your magic. It's between your heart and your mind."

Now, she was well and truly confused. She ran the conversation through her mind again and still couldn't come up with a clear answer. "So…you're telling me that my brain wants one thing, but my heart wants another?" Angel nodded and she laughed. "You've just described every romantic relationship I've ever been in."

The other figures joined in the mirth, and Cara shook her head. "I don't see what you're trying to say. I'm sorry."

Angel and Demon both smiled. He stepped forward and

touched her face with his hand, and security and surety flowed from it to curl deep into her core and banish her worries. "Fortunately for you, Bearer, we are here to look out for your best interests. She will explain. Again, you succeed, knowing what you do not know and being willing to admit it. Well done." He vanished from sight, and she turned to the woman in white with a smile.

Angel's words caused that smile to grow large enough to hurt. "Your brain is telling you that your teacher is right —that all users of magic should have access to all the forms of magic. But your heart is made of flame, Bearer, and fire is a jealous power. Sometimes, like Demon and I, a being is meant to be a master of one thing instead of a student of many."

A brilliant white light covered her vision, occluding her dagger's avatar. Back in the basement, Cara's voice trailed off as she considered what had happened, then she smiled as happily as she ever had in the training space. She straightened into a respectful pose, her head slightly bowed. "With a great deal of respect for your perspectives and your instruction, my teacher, while I have not tried to fail with the other forms, I no longer wish to pursue them. Can we work instead to make my skills with fire more formidable?"

The room was silent as Nylotte processed her words. Diana hopped down from her crates to stand beside her friend, one hand on her shoulder. She looked at her and asked, "Are you sure?"

Cara nodded. "Never more."

The Drow, who had watched the exchange, huffed out a breath. "You are aware that focusing exclusively on fire will make you vulnerable to those creatures that are resistant to it, correct?"

She nodded again. "I accept that limitation. I'll use bullets for those." Diana laughed and sounded unexpectedly happy and light. *This place is good for her, like a fortress of solitude or something. But one with a wicked-tongued Drow instead of recordings of her parents.*

Nylotte raised an eyebrow and her stern look vanished under a broad smile. "I respect the certainty you have received, my student, and am more than willing to focus your training toward the goal you have set." She looked at the third person in the room and her grin turned into a frown. "If only all my students could possess such mental clarity."

Diana laughed. "Whatever. It gives you a chance to be all superior. You know you love it."

Cara reached around to where her blades were sheathed on either side of the small of her back and touched the hilts. *Thank you.*

The daggers' laughter, perfectly synchronized and complementary as always, echoed in her mind. Their voices blended together as they said, "You are worthy, Bearer. Embrace your power."

She turned to her teacher. "I'm ready whenever you are."

CHAPTER TWENTY-ONE

Diana had brought her paperwork—all electronic and accessed through one of the secure tablets that were scattered around the office—to the fifth-floor conference room. The sun hid behind clouds and gave the space a kind of melancholy atmosphere that fit her current mood. *Paperwork sucks. Too many losses and draws in a row sucks.* Her mental voice added, *"The fact that shadow magic keeps kicking your ass sucks."*

She didn't reply to the taunt. There had been further conversation about how to manage the various "selves" within as part of her training with Nylotte, but the Drow had offered the opinion that anything that helped to ground her student was undoubtedly a good thing. So, she endured and tried to draw useful information from her brain's attempts to make her unhappy. Sometimes, she succeeded. This wasn't one of those times, however, as her lack of success with shadow was already clear to everyone involved.

Maybe I should be like Cara. Specialize. Even as she

thought it, she knew it wasn't a viable path for her. Personally, because she craved the possibilities that came with expanded power options. Professionally, because she needed to be the front-line defense against magic, which required as much flexibility as possible.

She sighed and returned her attention to the tablet to signing documents and verify purchases. *Why the hell does Kayleigh need another 3-D printer?* She shook her head and authorized the request. *Hire good people and stay out of their way. Especially when their AI has control of your house's defense systems.*

She was a half-hour into the mind-numbing task when Tony appeared unexpectedly. He snagged her coffee mug and refilled it from the machine on the counter, then filled a cup of his own and sat across from her. She took a long sip of the bitter brew and sighed. "I think you saved my life."

The former detective chuckled. "Well then, I've accomplished one good thing today, so that's something."

She tilted her head. "Problems?"

"Nah. Only too many options and a decision-making disorder." He set the mug down and leaned toward her with his elbows on the table. "I think it's time to take Starsky and Hutch through a few training sessions. They have potential and have more than shown their willingness to leave the PD behind and go private company. We could use the bodies."

She frowned. "Not for ARES stuff, right?"

He leaned back and shrugged. "Now? No. In a few years, once those two have really learned the ropes? Maybe."

"But you'll keep church and state separate until then, right?"

He laughed and nodded. "Is the Pope Catholic?"

"Okay, then, you have my approval. And my envy. I'd like to get over there more." While her agents still managed the occasional training session in the impressive facility behind the facade of Two Worlds Security Consulting, her free moments were taken up studying with Nylotte or hanging out with Rath. While the troll would be fine with spending time together in the space, the blocks of freedom she had weren't large enough to make it work. "Hey, consider taking Hank and Anik along. And think about running some with Rath, too."

Tony rapped his knuckles on the table twice. "Of course. Everyone must train." He rose and studied her for a moment. "You're looking tired, boss, if you don't mind my saying so."

She looked up from the tablet to spear him with a glare. "I do mind you saying so. Didn't your mother ever teach you to be polite?"

Tony laughed. "She taught me to be honest. That's why I became a detective—because so many people failed to learn that lesson. And you still look tired."

Diana shook her head. "Noted. Get out."

He waved as he departed, and she let out the laugh she'd held back. *Yeah, I look tired. But I'm getting stronger every day, physically and magically. So it's worth burning the candle at both ends a little.*

Her phone buzzed, and she looked down to find a text from an unknown number. She frowned as she read it. **Agent Sheen, your presence is requested by the Lady.**

However, you are no longer permitted to portal into Stonesreach. Please present yourself to her in three hours.

Her frown deepened. If the Lady of the Kemana was upset with her, that was one thing, but revoking her permission to portal in meant that she would have to walk all those steps again. *And climb them again if we don't fix whatever's broken.* She put her palms on the table and used them to push herself to her feet, already feeling the future pain in her legs from the steep staircases that led into the underground city.

She headed to the elevator that would take her to the lowest level of the facility. "Friday, let Cara know that she's in charge for the next twelve hours or so and that I'll be in the kemana." It was standard protocol to hand leadership off when she would be out of contact, and they did it regularly during her training sessions and journeys to Oriceran on sword-searching missions with Nylotte. The AI chimed to acknowledge her request.

The floor was empty when she exited the lift, which was a bonus. She strode quickly to the equipping area and opened her locker. Technology was forbidden, nonfunctional, or both in the kemana, so her guns and grenades would stay at home. Diana withdrew an extra pair of potions, doubling up on her healing and energy flasks as she slid them into her belt. She retrieved the black uniform shirt and donned it but didn't tuck it in to hide the gear she carried. Kayleigh had made her an alternate version of the stylish spy boots a few weeks before without the holster for the Ruger. Instead, each held a stiletto down the back and a brace of throwing knives. She pushed her feet into them and stomped to set her heels, enjoying the echoes that followed.

She was ready to go, but something still didn't feel right. *Okay. If I insult the Lady, so be it. She can cut me some slack in return for making me walk.* Diana pulled the shirt off and located her special vest—the only one on this planet to feature a layer of titanium chain on the inside—and strapped it on. She slipped a bowie knife into the back sheath and put the dark uniform top over it. When she looked in the full-length mirror on the wall next to the exit door, it seemed obvious that she wouldn't really fool anyone, but she hoped to earn a point or two for at least attempting not to offend.

With a sigh over the extra pain the additional weight of the chain would add to her legs, she summoned a portal to the parking area near the kemana's outer entrance. *Maybe I should use my force power and fly through the tunnel instead.* She snorted. *That'd be sure to tick them off.*

CHAPTER TWENTY-TWO

Diana stepped from the portal into a darkened corner of the parking lot. The highway overhead cast shadows in the diffuse light from the clouds, and she materialized unseen. She crossed to the unremarkable gate and freed it with a spell, lacking patience for the icon-search she'd had to do before. With each step along the earthen tunnel, her ire at the situation grew.

She was scowling when she reached the inner door. It was guarded, as always, by a bored-looking Kilomea. "Diana Sheen." He nodded and opened for her as she presumed he would do for anyone magical. Lady Alayne had explained long before that the checkpoint was primarily to keep humans from wandering where they shouldn't be for their own safety as well as for the security of the kemana.

The tunnel transformed from hewn rock to carved stone in the same ivory color that dominated the city beyond it. As she neared the threshold, purple light seeped in from above and tinted the floor with the same shade.

She paused before entering to admire the layout of Stonesreach, particularly the way the streets appeared to be rays of a sun from a child's drawing that emanated from the glittering white castle in the distance that was home to the leader of the community.

And she is not on my list of favorite people, at the moment. Lady Alayne had always been prickly and was clearly much more concerned with the goings-on of the city below the surface than the one above. *Which is appropriate,* she acknowledged with an inward sigh. *I miss the days where things were less muddy. What I wouldn't give for the purity of a fight with Cresnan right about now.* She chuckled at the thought of the first Kilomea she'd encountered, then sobered as she remembered his ultimate fate.

Diana took a deep breath like a swimmer about to dive into a pool and crossed the threshold into the kemana proper. She stood at the top of the long staircase that cut through the rings of modest homes arranged in tiers on the way down. The activation of her danger sense came as a complete shock and her mind reeled as the world slowed around her. Despite her preparations, she'd not really believed there was any peril to be faced on this journey. Her mental voice chided her, *"Always the optimist. Look out!"*

She caught the glow of the fireball from the corner of her eye and leaned back to let it pass through the space her head had just occupied. *Idiots. You should have used shadow. I might not have seen it.* She turned to find the culprit but there was no one in sight. She breathed a charm to dispel illusion but nothing was revealed. Time accelerated again, and she looked down to see a pair of angry-looking Kilomea racing up the stairs from the tier below. Her first inclination was to engage them directly, but that would leave her vulnerable to attacks from the other sides, including from the mysterious fire-thrower.

Acting on instinct, she darted to her left and surged into a full run toward the nearest houses. This level was all dark, as it had been every time she'd visited the kemana. *Damn it. No help to be had here.* That triggered an idea, and she opened her mental defenses a smidgen to try to send her mentor a telepathic message. She stumbled and fell forward as pain lanced through her skull and obliterated the very possibility of thought, and she reflexively snapped the barriers around her mind back into place.

Her hands were bleeding from where they'd scraped the ground but she pushed awkwardly to her feet. The first house flashed past as she ran through what would be its backyard and suddenly, her instincts screamed a warning. An immediate slide allowed her to narrowly avoid the blade that whipped menacingly over her head, and she darted up in a fury. *Enough of this.* She extended her arms and touched her thumbs together to summon a wide cone of fire aimed at her barely seen opponent.

There was a scream as the flame washed over a giant Kilomea, the largest she'd ever encountered, and set him ablaze. In the flickering glow, she saw the two in pursuit had closed the distance and that another she hadn't noticed before emerged from the space between the houses. That one ignored his burning partner and stalked past him as he approached. He swung something that looked like a motherloving halberd, with a curved blade on the left of the long staff, and spikes on the top and right. She thought about drawing one of her various knives, the Bowie in particular, and grinned. *There is enough magic around, and I have extra potions. Let's mess this bastard up.* She put her fists together, one atop the other, and a blade of force extended from them to stop at about the length of a samurai sword. Another trickle of power added fire to the edges. She smiled at her enemy. "I'm ready to dance when you are, scumbag."

Her skills with the sword were rusty as the martial art that had used it was many years in her past. However, some of the basics were still deep in her muscle memory, waiting to be called upon. His downward stroke seemed intended to end the fight in one blow. Diana avoided it by scurrying to the side and watched it pass. She made a horizontal chop with her own blade with the same intent, but he dodged and managed to keep his skull attached to his body. The next attacks with the halberd were stabs with the point, using it as a poorly balanced spear. They were fast enough that she was forced to focus exclusively on defense. She deflected the spear to the left, right, then left again with brisk swings of her blade. Her opponent made his mistake when he whipped the weapon around his head and brought it across, blade-first, in a sideways strike at her midsection.

She had been waiting for an attack exactly like that and closed the distance between them in a fast shuffle to position herself too close to him for the blade to connect. She slashed down, not at him but at the shaft of the halberd, and her flaming force sword sliced through it without slowing. Before he could retaliate, she turned the weapon at the bottom of the strike and chopped it upward, driving forward with her back foot to cleave him from leg to shoulder. He fell soundlessly, the wound so severe it stole his consciousness immediately.

The move finished with a downward flourish and she was surprised when it was deflected by another weapon. She sprawled from the impact and a blade whistled as it cut through the space she'd just vacated. *Oh, right, the first two. Of* course *they have swords too. Why wouldn't they?* She growled at the surrounding darkness, cursed the fact that her tech didn't work, and thought unkind things about the crystals above for being so dim at the moment. Then she grinned, released the sword with one hand, and summoned a fireball in the other.

The glow from the flaming sphere revealed vague shapes at least a dozen feet away around her, which was enough to identify her foes as they materialized from the darkness. The original two were present, at a minimum, although there could have been more given the way all the attacks used the same wicked-looking curved sword and the enemies faded back into the shadows after the attack. She was on the defensive, able to divert their stabs and slashes with one hand but unwilling to commit to more while she didn't know the true number of the opposition.

The solution slid into her mind at the same moment that her body acted on it. When the next adversary darted in to stab at her, she sidestepped to avoid the blow instead of meeting it straight on and whipped the flaming orb the short distance from her hand to his head. He fell back with a snarl and clawed at the burning hair on his face, and the light revealed his friend a few feet away. She generated and threw another fireball and pushed forward while they were distracted.

Diana targeted the second as the first seemed on his way to recovering his balance. Her off hand returned to the sword, and she raised it high, the blade parallel to the ground. She stabbed it forward to pierce his shoulder, repeated the move on the other shoulder as he shifted position to protect the first wound, then finished with a brutal forehand slash to his leg that severed vital muscles. He fell and howled in pain.

The other had recovered and attacked with an outraged shout, slashing his weapon down from her left. She hopped to her right and swept her blade across her body to block the attack but discovered it was only a feint as he suddenly changed trajectory and collided into her. The magical sword vanished when she lost her grip on it, and she stumbled for several steps before she impacted with the wall of the house behind her. The Kilomea was on her immediately, a superior sneer on his ugly face. The range was too close for his blade, so it was hand to hand, the opponents so focused on the battle that there was no room for conversation or even for thought.

His fist came in from high left, and she blocked it with her forearm. He grasped her throat with the other hand and she latched onto his thumb and bent it against the movement of his wrist joint to free herself to breathe. She maintained control of his arm for only a moment as his knee jerked up. Only a hasty downward punch with the hand she'd used stopped it from connecting with her solar plexus. She flicked a back fist at his nose with that hand, and when he intercepted it easily, she pounded the contemptuous look on his face away with an uppercut from her other that had the strength of her force magic behind it. He was lifted from his feet and dropped onto his back. Before he could recover, she leapt into the attack with a shout and pulled her legs up, then straightened them as she descended. Her heels hammered into both sides of his collarbone and shattered it. He growled at her in either rage or defiance, and she finished the fight with a powerful kick to his temple.

She spun, suddenly aware that she'd lost focus on anything other than that single opponent, but no more were visible. She'd won. Adrenaline faded as she leaned over and put her hands on her knees, breathing heavily to draw sorely needed oxygen back into her body. Her brain's return to function heralded the return of her inner voice. *"Hey, Diana, have you considered the fact that the summons to the kemana was a ruse intended to draw you into an ambush?"* Yes, yes, I have. *"Okay, well, here's a reminder. Something attacked you mentally when you tried to call for help, and Kilomea don't have that ability as far as we know."*

Oh, bloody hell. She heard a chittering around her, summoned two more fireballs, and turned in a circle as the new arrivals manifested to try to pinpoint the sound. The light illuminated four portals hovering in the air at each of the cardinal points, presumably with smirking witches and wizards behind them. But that wasn't what struck fear into her. Her eyes widened as she tried to make sense of what she saw.

Are those...Mirennas? With metal claws attached to their hands and feet? Oh, sweet mother of Megalon.

CHAPTER TWENTY-THREE

The alien monkeys had been slightly dangerous and mostly annoying the last time she'd faced them in the basement of the Museum. Now, though, in greater numbers and with the blades to supplement their attacks, they were downright frightening.

Diana flung the fireballs into the oncoming ranks, then used a blast of energy to elevate herself. She arced out of the center of the circle and looked for a place to land when a sudden and unexpected force hurtled her toward the ground. She barely managed to increase her own power to avoid breaking bones as she landed and still had to roll to the side to absorb the momentum of her fall.

A red haze colored her vision as she found her feet. The little monkeys had arranged themselves in a chaotic wave and attacked her the instant they exited the rifts. She turned to fire again and delivered it in large sheets at the creatures' chest height. Some slid under the attack and vanished from her sight. Others tried to jump over it, but she sustained the flames and they fell into them as they descended. The most clueless continued to run forward until they were immolated. She washed the fire down and then up again to ensure that she obliterated the ones that went low.

This is all well and good, but it's draining. Plus, they won't be stupid enough to keep attacking in a straight line. I need to deal with the jerks holding the portals open. She located the nearest, a heavyset wizard with opulent robes and scars on his face. Where Anik's imperfections only served to make him more handsome, this man was repellant in every sense of the word. She felt icky by merely being in sight of him.

Diana sprinted forward on a line toward him, scything flame before her to clear the path. She sensed the little murder monkeys following her, their chittering now a constant hum she feared she'd hear in her nightmares forever. He reacted to her charge by dispelling the portal —*good*—and lashed out at her with a coursing cone of shadow. *Not good.* The anti-magic deflectors under her shirt crackled and popped as they protected her from the attack, and in the next moment she was close enough to act, the Mirennas between them already burned away.

The ongoing power expenditure was draining her, and she feared she wouldn't have time to use her potions if it ran out. To preserve what she could, she let the fire fall and turned to the skills Nylotte so often berated. She leapt high and pistoned a foot into his chest to force him back. The shocked look on his face made their shared moment extra special, and she smiled as she landed and charged his retreating form again. She kicked his legs out from under him, and when he fell, dropped to the ground with an elbow aimed at his sternum. His scream covered the sound of it breaking, but both confirmed he was out of the battle.

The agent surged to her feet but a blast of lightning wreathed her and consumed more of her deflectors, and a quartet of monkeys arrived. She yanked the Bowie knife from under her shirt and used it to slice at the nearest, which careened toward her head with its blades extended. Her lean to the side saved her from its weapons, and her strike drove him past her. The next two attacked together, and she sustained slashes down her left arm from one as she pinioned the other with the blade and thrust it all the way through his chest. The falling primate stole the weapon from her hand, and she threw herself sideways to avoid the fourth, who had leapt at her face while she dealt with the others.

She landed badly and her shin jarred painfully against a rock. Diana cursed herself for not coming fully armored as she forced herself to her feet. She drew a throwing knife from each boot and hurled them at the closest targets. They each struck one of the creatures but only one resulted in a kill. *Dammit. Maybe I need lessons from Rath's teacher.* She summoned another jet of flame and swept it across the nearest monkeys and the witch who doubtless hoped not to be noticed as she held the portal open. *No such luck, wench.*

The rift vanished when the woman shielded and called up fire to absorb hers. The agent switched powers and released a volley of sharp icicles in an arc to rain down onto the woman's head. When she lifted her shield reflexively, she created a sheet of ice under her feet, and the witch slipped. Her defenses failed when she fell, and there was only a shrill shriek, quickly cut off, in reaction to the sharpened missiles that punctured her prone form much like a pincushion.

Her deflectors crackled again and a blast of force lifted her and slammed her back against the rock wall that supported the next tier up. She avoided smacking her head thanks to an instinctive curl as the attack struck, but the impact with the stone cracked a rib—or several. She couldn't tell. *Again. Damn them.* The fact that it had done so despite the Kevlar plates protecting her was a testament to her foe's power. She located the culprit and snarled at the Remembrance's lead witch.

Sarah responded with a smile, summoned a large wave of shadow, and threw it at her. Diana had no idea if the magic might contain another portal to send her somewhere nasty—or even if such a thing was possible—so she took a step and used her own force magic to launch in a low arc onto the higher tier. She ducked behind a building and activated one of the charms in her bracelet to fade into the shadows and become less noticeable to all senses, mundane and magical. *Chew on that, witch.* She retrieved the healing potion from her belt and downed half, then grimaced when she felt the bones move and shift into alignment to meld the broken shards together. It required a monumental effort to keep from screaming during the process, but she managed it.

Okay, time to turn the tables. One of the things that this part of the kemana—also seemingly vacant—had in abundance was fist-sized rocks. She gathered them and scuttled away from her hiding place, gaining distance from the sounds of the monkeys climbing up to her level. She placed them in open locations on any support that was at least as high as the little creatures' heads. As they approached, whenever a stray reflection on their metal appendages revealed one of them, she used her telekinesis to transform the stones into missiles and fired them into and through the skulls of her pursuers.

Diana had hoped the remaining witches and wizards would abandon the portal and search for her, and quiet hisses suggested her wish had been granted. By the time the monkeys were eliminated, she'd run out of rocks and cover as the houses ended at a large clearing that ran for at least a hundred feet, maybe more. It was highly unlikely she'd be able to make the crossing undetected, even with the concealment charm.

She drew the remaining throwing daggers from her boots. Any attempt to strike Sarah with them was a non-starter as the defensive barrier that had thwarted their attempts to tag her would no doubt be in play here as well. The invisible shield might have been why none of her previous efforts to kill her had worked out. She could only hope that her sidekicks weren't quite as prepared.

Her hiding place lay two houses away from the open area. She'd circled to the rear of the domiciles and positioned herself in the alley between the second and third building. From the sounds of the oncoming enemies, they were wisely checking the alleys as they passed. She resigned herself to discovery and stood with her back against the wall of the third house, as far into the shadows as possible.

When the enemy witch stuck her head around the corner, Diana held her breath. The way the woman snatched it back almost immediately made it likely she hadn't been seen. She raised her arms into a throwing position and waited for her to reappear. When she did—and actually stepped fully into the alley—the agent surged forward and hurled both blades at once in an overhand throw. They streaked forward on diagonal trajectories to strike the witch side by side in her chest. *Down and hopefully, out.* She couldn't be sure as the knives weren't that long and she'd had to aim for the biggest target. A better thrower would have found the throat, but that wasn't her. She chuckled inwardly as she ran to reposition in the alley between the houses closer to the clearing. *Maybe Rath could, though.*

She used the moment of chaos sown by her attack to drink an energy potion, confident that the battle would either be won or lost before the draught's impact on her systems caused her to crash into unconsciousness. Power flooded through her and filled her to the point where she could barely contain it. She summoned a force shield as tall as she was in her left hand and stalked into the backyard of the building. *Enough fooling around.*

She didn't expect the ambush, but in her heightened state of being, she didn't not expect it, either. The attack from in front of her was an impressive combination of intertwined fire and shadow as one of Sarah's witches circled her palms in the air. Diana caught it on her shield and had to concentrate momentarily to be sure it properly repelled each assault. The attack from the side, where the main witch had somehow climbed to the roof of the house, proved to be more of a challenge. When her magic sense kicked in and slowed the action around her, she couldn't identify the source. The shadow orbs struck her back shoulder and spun her, drove their daggers of pain and despair into her body and mind, and she almost faltered.

But the energy surged through her, and all she had to do was release it. She set her feet to stop herself from stumbling, and the force shield in her fist thrust forward and continued to block the inferior witch's attacks until it pounded into her at full speed and catapulted her at least a dozen feet. *Heh. She'll be too busy trying to find all her teeth to bother me again.* The agent shoved the pain aside and banished the mental portion of the attack by focusing on how good the magic coursing through her felt before she launched herself upward. She aimed for Sarah, but the witch stepped adroitly aside before she landed and bestowed an arrogant grin on her.

The woman's voice was far more smug than it should have been, given the situation. "Diana Sheen. Yet again, we meet. Today, the outcome will be different, though. I wonder how your team will manage without you?"

As a tactic to make her worry, it failed utterly. She had full confidence that Cara could take her place if she fell and knew that Kayleigh would watch over Rath. Her laugh at the boast was heartfelt and gleeful, thanks to the power flowing within. "Sure, sure. Let's see. I've taken out Kilomea, murder monkeys, and your right-hand people. You've…done nothing useful."

Sarah shook her head. "I've done enough. You're here alone and lack any support." She realized the banter was a play for time and feared that reinforcements might be on the way. *Lady Alayne did tell Nylotte she was concerned about the penetration of the kemana by the Remembrance. Maybe she has more allies here than anyone knows.*

Without replying, Diana moved to attack. She reached for ice and fired it at the witch's feet, hoping to freeze her in place with the unexpected tactic. The other woman deflected it with an unconcerned wave of her wand, then gestured casually to direct another shadow assault. This time, they manifested as tiny darts that swirled and flickered as they crossed the short distance, which made them hard to deflect.

So screw deflecting. She cartwheeled to the side and evaded them as they passed through the space she'd abandoned. When her boots returned to the stone roof, she launched herself forward with a fist extended, moving parallel to the surface. Sarah reacted barely in time, spun away, and shoved her away with a blast of power. Diana rode the new trajectory and landed on the hard-packed soil a dozen feet from the edge of the building. She reached deep for her magic, gathered as much as she could hold, and threw it with both hands to eject a person-sized force sphere.

It covered the distance to the house in a second, crashed into the wall where it met the top, and exploded the two sections apart. The side of the structure caved in, and the shattered roof became airborne. She located the witch among the swirling rubble, waving her wand to try to control her unexpected flight, and put her thumbs together to summon a cone of flame. The blazing line tracked Sarah's path and engulfed her as she landed. The power drained from Diana, moving toward empty, but she gritted her teeth and maintained the attack. She slipped her mind into the magic, sensed the moment when her foe tried to scurry to evade the beam, and moved it with her. It became a battle of magical strength, one she was determined to win.

Her vision grew hazy as her power reservoir evaporated, but she held on and pushed with everything she had to end her opponent once and for all. A scream emanated from within the conflagration as the flames overcame the other woman's defenses and she fled toward the kemana's tunnel, her clothes and hair burning brightly in the darkness. Diana took a step forward to pursue and fell face-down. She fumbled for the other energy potion, but by the time she'd retrieved it, the enemy witch was gone.

She had only enough strength left for two actions. First, she sent a mental message to Nylotte and received assurance that her teacher was on her way. Then, as her vision spiraled into a small dot, she cursed Sarah with every combination of creative profanity she could think of until she ran out and lost consciousness.

CHAPTER TWENTY-FOUR

Deacon ran—literally—into Kayleigh's side of the lab floor, waving a piece of paper. She looked at him, half in surprise and half in mockery. He didn't seem to notice and thrust the page at her. "We've got them."

Both her eyebrows raised as she reviewed the data it listed. "Okay, I get that both Clarke and Tomassi are leaking. But Somers? Really?"

He nodded vigorously. "I know, right? But look closer."

She stared at the information but definitely didn't see whatever he was referring to. She looked up with a scowl. "You're doing this on purpose, aren't you? Trying to make me feel stupid? Well, I'll have you know that it's working splendidly."

"Yes, on purpose. He laughed. "No, not trying to make you feel stupid. I merely want you to appreciate my brilliance."

Kayleigh rolled her eyes. "As if you don't go out of your way to remind me of it, like, daily."

"If you've got it, flaunt it, that's what RuPaul always says." He shrugged and pointed toward his computer setup at the other end of the floor. "Come take a closer look."

She followed him and smacked him gently on the head as he sat in front of her. He chuckled, called up information on each of his many displays, and gestured at the one on the far left. "Okay, that's Clarke, who's the most compromised. You can see that he's deliberately sharing information with...well, all kinds of people. Whatsapp to connect with the Chinese, and Shredder to speak with his Oriceran contact, who appears to be someone not directly connected to Nehlan."

Kayleigh frowned. "How do you know that?"

Deacon pointed at the next monitor. "That's Tomassi right there. He does have the direct connection to Nehlan, as you might recall assuming your memory works better than the rest of your brain." He yelped when she kicked him in the Achilles, then continued with a hint of laughter in his voice. "There's clear evidence that someone has taken over for the dead elf with our dear Winston T, but he doesn't use the same contact route as Clarke's person does. So they must be talking to different people."

She shook her head. "I wouldn't take that one to court."

He shrugged. "I'm eighty percent confident, but it really doesn't matter, anyway. We don't need to know exactly who's on the other end in order to confirm that they're leaking like sieves."

"Fair enough. Kayleigh sighed and chose not to argue the point. "So, Clarke is doing it on purpose with both Chinese Intelligence and the Oricerans. Is that true for Tomassi as well?"

Her partner shook his head. "Nope. He seems to be a willing partner with someone on the other planet and completely unwitting as to the degree he's been compromised by the Chinese. They're running a virus on his devices."

"Shouldn't that be detected somehow? One would hope that Congress in general—and the oversight committee specifically—would have some state-of-the-art anti-malware installed."

"Well, if the chucklehead hadn't downloaded a gaming app for the website he uses, whatever defenses he has would probably have been sufficient. The best part is that in order to get it onto his phone, he would need someone in government IT to help, which means that person is either on the Chinese payroll, or an idiot, or both."

She groaned. "Seriously. These morons are full of surprises."

He turned in his chair and looked at her. "I have another one for you. The virus is magic."

"Meaning the Chinese Intelligence folks are also using magic in their software?"

"You got it in one."

"Damn."

Deacon laughed. "My reaction involved far more colorful language, but yeah, that about sums it up. The game has become real complex, real fast."

"Well, I guess it makes sense. They have a huge population, so the chances of turning up a hybrid tech and magic expert is probably greater than average."

"Exactly."

"So what's the deal with Somers? If you tell me he's

deliberately sharing information with our enemies, I'll have to stop believing in anything."

Her partner sobered and pointed to the pair of monitors on the far right. "I didn't find any indication of willful spilling on his part but his devices are compromised by several different varieties of malware. One is definitely the Chinese, and I haven't traced the others. So far, they resist my own virus's attempts to penetrate their defenses." He shook his head. "There's no way these got on there by random chance. Someone on his staff, or someone he's in contact with, is involved."

She sighed. "Damn. Can we find out who it is?"

"Not with the data we have so far."

"So, what's your recommendation?"

He turned to face her and looked extremely uncomfortable. *Deacon likes the pursuit but isn't fond of the results. I can relate. Unfortunately, that's a luxury we don't have.* "I think that Tomassi and Clarke need to be…dealt with. Removed from the committee. Whatever." He swiveled to stare at the details on the right-hand monitors again as if there were secrets to be discovered. "And everyone who works with Somers—or is friends with him, or related, or any sort of contact, really—needs to be investigated further. Deeply investigated."

She patted him on the shoulder. "I'll let Bryant know about all three of them but tell him we need Somers kept in place until we can dig deeper. Does that sound good?"

He nodded, already back at work to try to track the traitors in their midst. She returned to her lab and sat at her worktable, staring at the pieces of magical drone bug carefully arranged on it. With a sigh, she activated her comms and connected to Diana. "Boss, I have something to tell you that you won't want to hear."

CHAPTER TWENTY-FIVE

When Bryant received the news, he dropped everything he was doing and sprinted to the exit, cursing himself for not having a portal destination prepared. He called for a driver on his race toward the staircase and stood impatiently, tapping his foot at the curb as he waited for the car to arrive. When the black SUV stopped in front of him, he yanked the door open. "Lights and Siren. Go."

The agent was one of DC's best and navigated all the lanes—and occasionally, the sidewalk—with effective madness. They pulled up outside the hospital in as good a time as he had any right to expect, and Bryant punched the woman's arm lightly in thanks as he scrambled out and ran to the entrance.

He broke into the room at full speed and skidded to a stop at the sight of his boss, Carson Taggart, awake and sitting in his bed. The electrical current devices they'd used to keep his muscles active while he was in the coma had apparently worked, as he seemed capable of relatively easy movement. He grinned at his subordinate's enthusiastic entrance.

"You really ought to be a little more dignified, Bates. What will the rank and file think?"

Bryant couldn't restrain his grin. "Well, now that you're awake, I am the rank and file—and happy to be, I should add. I'll go back, retrieve your secure tablet, and it'll be like you never left."

Taggart shook his head with a half-smile. "That won't happen, I'm afraid. The doctors tell me I'm stuck in here for at least another month in recovery and should avoid undue stress."

He shrugged. "Okay, I can handle it for one more month if I need to."

The other man shifted in his bed and a grimace flickered across his neutral expression. A little weight entered his tone. "When I say won't happen, I mean ever, Bryant. I'm done with ARES, other than wishing you all the best. It's time for me to focus on enjoying whatever time remains of my duration on this planet."

He sat heavily in the chair beside the bed and blew a few errant strands of hair out of his face. *Damn, I need to get it cut again already? Where did the time go?* He shook his head morosely at Taggart. "Why would you do this? What did I do to make you hate me?"

His boss—former boss—laughed. "Don't be a nitwit. You did it to yourself, exactly like I did. Nothing comes from success but enduring punishment, my boy."

"Damn." He exhaled forcefully. "Are you seriously going to stick me with this? No training or anything? Maybe you could come back for a few months."

Taggart shook his head. "No chance. I'm done. But you can always come to me for an old-timer's perspective on things."

He grinned. "In that case, I have something to run by you."

Bryant did have a portal destination for his next stop, so he called to dismiss the car and found an empty room nearby to cast it in. He stepped through to the secluded corner in the Congress workspace and stopped in a restroom to make sure he was ready. The trepidation he felt didn't show on his face, and his suit was still well-creased. *It's all good. Let's go cause trouble.*

A moment later, he tapped his watch to alert Finley he was on his way, confident that the other man had arranged the matters under his control properly. He entered the conference room to find the same arrangement as the previous meeting, with Finley on one end, Cyphret, Tomassi, and Clarke to his right, and Somers and Hughes to his left. Once again, he took his time as he retrieved a cup of coffee and enjoyed the irritation that emanated from the trio he'd started to call the "anti-party." *Because they're against ARES and because they'd be no fun at all at a party.* He snickered quietly as he filled his mug and turned to the table.

Bryant lowered himself into the chair and flashed a wide grin at the senator on the opposite end. Finley shook his head and raised his chin in a signal for him to begin. He didn't get a chance to start before Clarke, again theatrically irate, demanded, "Why have you called us here yet again? Is it to resign? Because I can't think of another reason that would make this annoying repeat worthwhile." Beside him, Tomassi nodded. Cyphret sat with her arms folded and hadn't reacted to the man's provocation. *One point for Janet.*

He took a slow sip of his beverage for no purpose other than to irritate Clarke, then set it on the table. "In fact, I have a very good reason for asking you all to come together again. You'll recall that at our last meeting, I informed you there were secrets leaking from this group. Additional evidence on that matter has come to light, and I thought you would want to hear it right away. Senator Finley agreed. So, here we are."

Ellyn Hughes, no-nonsense as always, rapped a knuckle on the table. "Don't keep us in suspense, Special Agent in Charge. Which staff is the culprit on?" Bryant felt a surge of warmth for the woman, in part because she was hopeful enough to think it wasn't one of the people in the room and in part because she was one of those unstained by even a hint of corruption.

He nodded. "Senator, I regret to say that the leaks are not coming from staff members. Instead, someone on the oversight committee is directly responsible for them." He kept his gaze locked on hers but saw Tomassi blanch and Clarke get a nasty look on his face in his peripheral vision. He waited in silence until, after several seconds, Cyphret demanded, "Well? Who?"

His expression deadpan, he turned to the man on his left as he and Finley had agreed in advance. "Senator Zachariah Clarke, it is my distinct pleasure to tell you that your presence on this committee is no longer needed. You have been a very naughty boy." He couldn't resist taking a shot at the man's immense pride, and the jab had its intended result. His target bolted from his seat, red-faced and sputtering.

"Preposterous. Lies. I will see you broken for this, Bates."

Finley shook his head and looked sad. "No threats, Zachariah. I've seen the evidence. They know about your messages. It's frankly embarrassing that you weren't better at hiding them since you're a member of an actual secret group." Clarke gaped and the door to the far hallway opened to reveal a pair of burly men in dark black jackets, clearly FBI agents given the circumstance. The senator continued to protest his innocence as they locked the cuffs around his wrists and escorted him from the room.

The others—save Tomassi, who still looked like he was about to throw up or pass out or both—turned toward Bryant. Hughes spoke for them. "Explain." Her voice was cold and dangerous, appropriate to the moment. He pulled his phone out and pressed some controls to access the display at the end of the room. Another few strokes brought up the evidence against Clarke, now available for them all to see, including logs that showed how often he had shared information.

The senators gazed at it and made sounds of disbelief before they settled back in their chairs and looked shaken. Somers gave a low chuckle. "Well, that's something. Do you have any more surprises for us, Bates?"

He turned to Tomassi. "How about it, Winston? Any more surprises for this meeting?" It was cruel, but dammit the hypocrite deserved it. *In spades.* The man gaped for a moment, then tears seeped from the corners of his eyes and he lowered his gaze to the table. "I didn't... I didn't mean to...it simply got out of hand. I wasn't sure they were watching, but I guess I should have known. I—" He put his face on his folded arms and sobbed into them.

Bryant stared at him momentarily, his expression twisted in distaste, then turned to the others. "Senator Tomassi is a fraud. He gambles and is in way over his head and failed to realize that the site he used was a trap by Chinese Intelligence. He's been a source for them for ages. However, what he fails to mention is that his addiction has been funded in part by selling secrets to enemies on Oriceran, specifically to Nehlan."

The others stared at him, but no one spoke. Finley broke the silence several moments later as a woman in a dark suit entered. "Winston, Agent Carlisle will take you for debriefing. We'll need you to work with the FBI to fix some of the things you've broken." She pulled him to his feet, not entirely gently, propelled him out of the room in front of her and closed the door when she exited.

Somers looked at Bryant. "Son, please tell me you're finished. I don't think my heart can handle any more shocks today."

He grinned. "All done, Senator Somers. We believe the leaks are filled now." *Minus yours, which we'll keep open deliberately.* "We should be able to use Tomassi to feed disinformation for a while, but he's not the type to hide something this big well. He'll screw it up before long, and he'll be headed to prison. Maybe we can get him a cell next to Clarke."

Finley addressed the group in an emotionless, businesslike tone. "The oversight committee is operating outside designated parameters. As such, no non-critical actions shall be taken until we have acquired two new members. I will oversee the search and decide on the additions in consultation with the vice president, as specified in our orders of operation. Barring an emergency, we are officially on hiatus until further notice."

The other senators filed from the room, displaying various degrees of stunned surprise and unhappiness at the turn the day had taken. Finally, only Finley remained, and Bryant crossed the empty space between them to shake his hand. "Well done, Aaron."

The man shook his head. "Well done you, Bryant. I hear Taggart is awake. Will this be your last meeting, too?"

He sighed. "No, the old man is turning his papers in and heading off into the sunset. It looks like I'm stuck with the job."

The senator slapped him on the arm. "You're great at it, and you'll continue to be great at it. The work suits you."

"On the whole, I'd rather be on a beach drinking a margarita."

Finley smiled. "There's time for that, eventually. Look at Taggart." He laughed as Bryant groaned at the thought of the potential decades of this nonsense ahead of him.

CHAPTER TWENTY-SIX

E ven though Hank had begged off at the last moment, Cara wasn't willing to give up one of her favorite nights of the week. She entered the warehouse to the now-familiar sounds of fights in progress, with crowd members cheering or booing the combatants in the ring.

Her path to the front was blocked several times by large bodies in motion and a couple of others by people she knew who greeted her and offered her high fives. She wasn't short by any means, but those who embraced recreational underground fighting tended to be on the large side, more Hank's size than hers.

It was a situation that worked to her advantage, as most folks didn't give the proper level of fear and respect to those smaller than them, which guaranteed her an opponent on any given night. There had been a couple of occasions where Hank wasn't able to play because he was the biggest person in the room and no one was willing to take him on. She'd offered, but he had only smiled and demurred, clearly uncomfortable with the idea of battling a comrade in the mostly rules-free environment.

Unusually, there were several other women present. One of them was warming up in the corner using MMA-style kickboxing moves. Cara leaned against a pole and watched as she unleashed a tricky combo of back hook and jumping crescent kicks that looked strong enough to defeat anyone. She had good balance and muscles rippled on her bare arms and legs.

A man came up to talk to her, but she shook her head and he retreated with a wave. That was another thing Cara liked about the place. Despite the fact that they'd all gathered to pummel each other into unconsciousness, there was an appealing lack of pretense. Declining to fight wasn't treated as a rejection but simply a moment of conversation between two people with similar goals. It reminded her of the best moments in the Army and of many moments with her BAM team since.

She wove through the rowdy crowd to stand slightly outside the woman's line of sight. When she turned and noticed her, Cara smiled, and the other woman returned it before she approached her to chat. Her face suggested that there was Italian or Spanish somewhere in her bloodline, but it was otherwise unremarkable—pretty but not gorgeous, encouraging but not begging. Her hair was short, spiky, and bright purple, bringing Rath to mind.

Cara stepped forward to greet her halfway. "Hey."

"Hey." The woman ran a towel over her neck to wipe away the sweat from her warmup. "I'm Brin."

She nodded. "Cara. Nice to meet you, Brin."

Her new acquaintance wagged a finger. "Ah, I've heard

about you. All good stuff. You command respect around this place."

"There have been a few decent fights, yeah." She shrugged. Are you interested in a bout?"

Brin smiled widely. "Oh, definitely."

It took about twenty minutes before the backlog cleared and they had their turn. In the interim, they chatted about neutral things, neither sharing any personal information. By the end of the interval, they were fairly well caught up on one another's guilty television pleasures, favorite movie stars, and bands they thought were terribly overrated.

The two strode into the ring to cheers from the surrounding crowd. There was a catcall at Brin, who spun in annoyance before she smiled and flipped off the man, who was apparently a friend. She shook her head as she turned back to Cara. "He's an idiot. Sorry."

She laughed. "We all have them. Remind me to tell you about Tony sometime."

The referee, a giant with a hairless scalp and face, very dark skin, and an attitude of unbridled authority, stepped in. He confirmed that they both knew they weren't supposed to kill or maim one another, then retreated from the combat ring and blew the silver coach's whistle fastened around his neck.

Cara ran forward, light on her feet, and wasn't surprised when the other woman chose to circle. Since she'd seen at least a little of Brin's fighting style but hadn't revealed her own, she had an initial advantage her opponent would want to eliminate. Stretching out the opening of the fight was a good way to accomplish that.

She moved in and cut directly across at her purple-haired foe, and Brin surprised her by stepping forward as well, her hands raised like a boxer. The woman jabbed with her left, and as Cara moved to the right to avoid it, the other fighter executed a half-spin and drilled a punch into her stomach.

Wincing from the aftershocks of the blow, she skipped back. *Damn, she hits hard.* She advanced again, leading with a jab, and followed with a hook and jab combo when the other woman dodged. The second thrust caught Brin in the chest a couple of inches below her throat, and she nodded with a grin to acknowledge the touch. Then, she spun so fast that Cara was momentarily frozen in surprise.

She managed to raise a hand to protect her head an instant before the woman's heel reached it. The fingerless glove cushioned the blow but it still exploded stars into her vision and made her ears ring as she staggered to the side. She swung a wide hook with her left but missed as her opponent drove in and rammed her shoulder into her midsection, levered her up, and thumped her hard onto the mat. Before she could recover her wits, the woman had her leg and arm locked. Cara tapped out and let her limbs fall where they would while the world spun above her.

The purple hair appeared in her vision first, followed shortly by Brin's smiling face. She reached a hand down to help her up, and she accepted the gesture. They hugged it out to end the match, and she headed for her bag and the ibuprofen that lay within. She also had a healing potion, an extra hedge against someone taking major damage at the fight, especially if that someone happened to be her. But she dismissed the need for it and decided an aching head would be a good reminder not to underestimate her opponent.

As she staggered out the door onto the street, still wobbly, Brin followed and stepped beside her. "Hey, are you okay?"

Cara nodded and regretted it immediately. "Ow. Yes, okay. A little hazy, is all."

The other woman pointed ahead. "My car is two blocks up."

"My bike, too."

The women walked together to their respective vehicles and said their goodbyes. Cara asked for a rematch and promised a better effort, and Brin laughed and accepted the challenge. She was grinning when she kicked the motorcycle to life and pulled out of the parking lot, headed for her apartment.

The good feelings lasted only five blocks before the AI in her helmet informed her she was being followed. She said, "Show me," and Quinn outlined three different cars in the rear-view angle provided by the camera on the back of the headgear. "Magnify." Her virtual assistant complied, and the closer look revealed there were four people in each car. "Damn. They're loaded for bear."

She revved the accelerator and the bike increased speed, but the chase vehicles matched it. "Connect to Kayleigh." There was a brief pause before the ping sounded in her ears. "Glam, Croft. I'm on my bike and being followed by three groups of thugs, according to Quinn." There was a rustling sound, and she heard the tech sign off from her online video game.

Kayleigh began to strike keys loudly. "Okay, I've

dispatched two watcher drones from nearby. The first should be on station in about fifteen seconds. Take your next left." The ARES watch they all wore provided GPS tracking down to within a foot.

She obeyed the command and slewed the bike through oncoming traffic to extend her lead over the others. The motorcycle bounced as she hurtled onto the bridge at high speed and crossed the river toward downtown.

"Okay, I have eyes on you. Take the tunnel, then make a right on the other side." The small channel cut through a hill that supported a University and hospital above. She wove through the traffic inside and rocketed out the far end, leaning the bike sideways to execute the turn without losing too much velocity. "My second watcher is now with you. The defense model will intersect your path in about a minute if you keep going in that direction."

Her mind worked furiously. "It would be useful to see who these assholes are. Is there a good place for an ambush nearby?"

"Wait one." Again, the sound of clicking keys and of a side conversation she couldn't make out—presumably with Alfred, the house's AI—commenced. "Yes. Are you sure that's what you want to do? I only have one drone for support."

Cara thought about it and an idea emerged. "What if you blast one of the cars with it and bring it back after? That should improve the odds right off the bat, and I'm sure I can hold my own until it returns."

There was a delay before Kayleigh replied and sounded tenser than she had previously. *Probably because I asked her to stun a group of fools driving at high speed.* "Yes, but only if we do this at the railyard."

She grinned as she pushed the accelerator to the maximum. "That's a perfect place. Let's turn the tables on these bastards."

CHAPTER TWENTY-SEVEN

The sight and sound of the trailing car crashing into the barrier at the side of the road behind her signaled the arrival of Kayleigh's drone on the scene. Cara swung her motorcycle over the first two sets of train tracks, momentarily airborne both times. She turned right to take a path between the stationary trains and cut across another set of tracks when there was a small opening between two disconnected cars. She braked and walked the bike back between the sections of the train to protect it, then hooked her helmet over the handlebars.

"Status, Glam?"

The tech seemed distracted, which was likely because she was flying three drones, one of which had stunned the driver and passengers of a moving vehicle. Knowing her, she'd already put in a call for an ambulance as well. The police would be the next logical connection, but BAM Pittsburgh had a standing policy not to involve them in anything directed exclusively at agents. "You have about thirty seconds. Alfred says there's a low probability that they'll try to use the vehicles against you."

"Okay, that makes sense. We've defeated them often enough that they need to make it personal. Besides, why bring so many people if you only plan to ram me with a car? Nah, they want to deliver a message." She unlocked the hidden compartment under the motorcycle's seat with a finger scan and withdrew her lightweight utility belt, Ruger, and Glock. Outside weapons were appropriately forbidden in the fight club space. She strapped it on, slid the pistol into its holster at her hip, and reached behind her to tap the hilts of her daggers. The revolver went into the hideaway holder in Kayleigh's spy boots, which weren't really necessary anymore since she had her own blades but which were stylish and comfortable and worth wearing anyway.

"Ten seconds."

Cara stepped into the open and faced squarely down the empty space between the two trains. About seventy-five feet away, two cars bounced over the tracks and slid on the ubiquitous gravel as they made the turn. They braked abruptly as expected, and eight people piled out of them. They were dressed in street chic and obviously wore their own version of what they thought of as cool. Each carried a pistol in one hand and a weapon of some kind in the other, and they held them out like the threats they were.

She smiled. Under her breath, she asked, "Time until the drone is back?"

Kayleigh cursed. "Our friends are smarter than expected and way more well-equipped. They disabled it as it was returning. It seems to be a localized disruption to the software. It's grounded and maybe destroyed. I can't access it."

She rolled her neck. "Okay, the degree of difficulty has increased but is still acceptable. Make a note to find out where they got the tech. That's military-grade, and I thought only the authorities were supposed to have it. Well, and Brownstone." The stories of the legendary bounty hunter making the local PD's drones fall from the sky were absolutely secret, which of course meant they traveled the underground chat rooms catering to the military and police as fast as fingers could type. She still had access as a former member and spent many an evening relaxing and chatting with other Army folks online.

"On it. Hank is rolling but won't be at your location for at least fifteen minutes."

"Well, he'll miss all the fun then." She raised her voice and tilted her chin. "Hey, friends, what's going on?" Her hands were warm with barely contained fire magic, and she held them loosely at her sides, ready to attack or shield as events dictated. She had noted no wands among those who confronted her, which gave her confidence even though she was outnumbered.

The man in the lead twitched his pistol at her. "You've caused trouble for us. We decided it's time to end that."

"Okay, this would be the part where you climb in your cars and drive away before you have your asses kicked. I'll give you ten seconds to get moving in the opposite direction." She glared at the man in front and tried to break his nerve. *Cow the leader and the pack will follow.* Instead, he raised his pistol and fired, which was the signal for his crew to do the same. Cara was in motion as soon as the gun began to raise, summoned a wall of flame to block the shots and their view of her, and darted to the side in case they carried anti-magic rounds. The barrier deflected the bullets, and she grinned. *Amateurs. They obviously assumed that since they weren't after Diana, they didn't need to come loaded for bear.*

She maintained the fire for a few seconds while she crept ahead on the top of the train cars nearest her, then let it fall to reveal that she'd vanished. The reactions from half the goons were comical as they searched frantically for her. The other half—the more professional members—ejected and replaced magazines in their pistols before they continued to move slowly forward. She judged that five of them might have vests under the hoodies she thought were too hot for the summer weather. The others wore shirts that were either too thin—or too skimpy in one case—to hide them. She shook her head at the latter. *Lady, it's not a fashion show. Crop tops aren't appropriate for armed combat. They're strictly for hand to hand.* She snorted and drew the pistol from her hip.

Cara fired the first six bullets quickly, two each for the unvested enemy, and aimed for their arms even though it was against protocol. She didn't feel particularly threatened and wounding these warrior wannabes would probably take them out of the fight completely. They didn't seem like the grit-your-teeth-and-keep-fighting kind. *More like the run away bleeding kind.* Three of the bullets struck home, two into one of the women and one into a man in a muscle shirt. The rounds she directed at crop-top missed. She ducked out of the line of sight of the others when they fired in her general direction. *Nine shots left.*

The whir of the drone intruded an instant before Kayleigh spoke. "Okay, two have jumped into the rearmost car, and the other six are looking at you. Also, ally incoming." The agent frowned and in the next moment, Rath's gleeful voice sang over the comms.

"Here I come to save the dayyyyyyy." He flashed into view, folded his wings, and arced to land feet-first on the woman in the half-shirt. The impact shoved her into the side of the nearest vehicle and she fell face-first. Two canisters careened toward the remaining five hostiles, and they detonated in a conflagration of bright light, deafening noise, and solid concussion.

Cara jumped over the lip of the roof, twisted to grab the ladder that led down, and slid to the ground with her hands and insteps locked on the outside. "Rath, you make it too easy." His laughter was followed by the sound of his stun batons firing.

Kayleigh was clearly amused by the troll's antics. "Four left."

Cara found the nearest adversary—a woman who was bleeding from her ears—and swept her feet out from under her. The assassin landed on her side with a thud and the crack of a breaking bone. She shook her head. "Rath, I'll bring them down and you stun them so I don't risk hurting them any more than necessary." *Amateurs may have been too generous a description of these fools.*

In response, he began to sing again. "When criminals in this world appear..." His baton snapped loudly. "And break the laws that they should fear..." She shook her head and tuned him out as she stalked forward toward the next target. This one managed to recover his wits enough to brandish the tire iron he carried at her, but she stepped in and delivered a punch to his chest as a distraction before she kicked him in the crotch. He crumpled and she moved on as the shock batons discharged again. "The cry goes out both far and near…."

Kayleigh was laughing now, doubtless at the troll's ongoing song. "Two remaining. Careful, they're moving to surround you."

Cara stopped, and the dust cleared to reveal the promised opponents, one to her left and one to her right. "Howdy, boys. Are you really sure you wouldn't rather sit down and let us knock you out until the authorities get here?"

"Eight minutes for the police," the tech interjected. "You'll want to be out of there by then." There was always the chance that an overzealous patrol officer might decide to waste their time by demanding they come to the station. Standard procedure was to avoid that possibility by not being there when they arrived.

Her opponents looked at each other while the tech was speaking and raised their pistols together. With a sigh, Cara launched darts of flame from each hand to jolt the guns from their hands. "Last chance, fellas." They lurched forward with their backup weapons—a tire iron for the man on her left and a military surplus KA-BAR knife for the one on the right. She drew her daggers and swept them out to intercept the attacks, guiding both in front of her and down. The man with the longer weapon was more exposed, and she skipped forward to deliver a side kick to his thigh that brought him to one knee.

"He's yours, Rath." She turned to the other, who held the knife before him as if it would stop her approach. "Have you ever used that before?" She tossed her right-hand dagger, Angel, in the air and caught it reversed, the blade laying along her forearm. With a broad grin, she gestured with Demon. "See, this way, you can slash." She shuffled in and whipped the edge at his face and he stumbled back, his hands raised in a panicked defense. "Or stab." She drew her arm back from the far end of the first strike and drove the point at him.

He tripped over his own feet as he tried to retreat. She looked at him and shook her head. "You know, if y'all were going to interrupt my pleasant evening out, the least you could have done was be competent." Her diminutive partner thrust his batons forward from behind and the man fell without having ever known the troll was there. "Idiots."

"Idiots," Rath echoed,

"Four minutes on the women and men in blue," Kayleigh warned. "Get moving." Cara made a circuit of the fallen and collected their phones and whatever other personal items they carried for investigative purposes. She accelerated out of the main entrance of the railyard as the sirens came into audible range. Quinn gave her a feed from one of the overhead drones, and she saw the police cars racing into the yard as Rath glided above them, headed for safety.

She grinned with the satisfaction of a job well done, then sobered. "Glam, we have to find out how these bozos knew where I was. Plus, I need a drop-off point for these phones." ARES quarantined enemy gear off-site until it had been checked for trackers. "First, they target Diana and now, they attack me. For an allegedly secret organization, we don't seem particularly secret these days."

CHAPTER TWENTY-EIGHT

Sloan was reviewing his ideas to tag Sarah with the bug Kayleigh had provided when his phone buzzed. He cursed in annoyance at the interruption, and again in annoyance at the world in general, and picked the device up. It unlocked to reveal a text message from Mur. **Pickup in ten minutes.**

What the hell? There were no plans for the gang to meet today, and he'd had no other invitations or summons from anyone on the human side of the Remembrance. It was rare that something took him completely by surprise, but this request had accomplished it. He bundled his thoughts about action against Sarah and shoved them into the corner of his mind, letting the memories and attitudes of Tommy Ketchum flow back into place. He'd seen recordings of himself as he shifted into his cover roles and knew his expressions and body language would change to represent the persona he adopted.

The agent rose from the couch with a groan and strolled into the bedroom to get dressed. Tommy had decided to take a hint from his bosses and had purchased nicer clothes with the profit-sharing from some of their side operations. He donned a suit and a dress shirt and slid his feet into his shiny shoes, the entire ensemble a matching shade of black. A minute remained, barely enough time to mess his hair up in a manner appropriate to the character. He headed out his apartment door as Mur pulled up in his big black pickup.

He jumped in, and the man gave him a quick smile. "Nice outfit, copycat." He swung the wheel and merged into traffic without delay.

"Only learning from my betters, you know how it is. What's going on?"

The big man shook his head. "I'm in the dark on this one. All I know is that the boss said to pick you up and get to our own base." He meant the humans' hideout, not the main Remembrance facility. "He sounded angry. Really angry."

Sloan considered his next words carefully, then decided to go for it. "You'd warn me if he was mad at me, right? Like, give me three steps toward the door?"

Mur nodded without meeting his eyes. "I can't think of a circumstance where I wouldn't." *That's reassuring. Kind of. It doesn't put me in the clear, though, if he finds out my secret.* The man's voice lowered as if he was saying something that scared him. "Between you and me, I'm not sure that he's completely keeping it together these days. I don't know if it's the surgeries, or the pressure, or what the hell else. But he's not...balanced."

"Yeah, I kind of got that idea at the restaurant."

The other man shook his head. "That wasn't nearly as

extreme as some of the stuff he's said. He's ready to kill Sarah and is waiting for an excuse or an opportunity that'll keep the rest of the magicals from attacking him. Plus, he talks bad about the guy above them—the one from the other planet—like he wants him dead too."

"So he wants to be king?"

Mur sighed. "That's the thing. I'm not sure there is an end goal. It's more like he's ready to start killing and not stop until he's gone through everyone on his list."

Sloan grimaced. "Like the movie says, some men simply want to watch the world burn. Maybe Marcus has become one of those guys." He chuckled. "I guess I better work twice as hard to stay on his good side."

A couple of dark laughs escaped Mur. "You and me both, brother."

They walked through the doors to the humans' bolt hole to find about half the group there and Marcus nowhere to be seen. The space was a converted mechanic's garage with five bays that had formerly accommodated cars and now provided room for people, weapons, and stolen goods. A small cluster of four men stood alone in the corner and looked nervous, and Sloan instinctively tried to peer into their feelings. Once again, he failed to convince his magic to appear. *Dammit, everyone else is getting training. Maybe I need it too.*

Another three cars screeched to a halt outside and their occupants strolled into the room as if nothing was wrong. He exchanged glances with Mur, who shrugged. *It seems like only he and I are worried. I'm not sure if that's overreaction on our part or stupidity on everyone else's. After the scene at the restaurant, anyone with an ounce of sense and something to hide should be damn concerned.* His thoughts were interrupted by the arrival of their leader, who barged out of the former customer lobby into the open portion of the workshop.

He strode to the center of the space, not speaking, an angry glare on his face that he swept across each person as he walked. Individual conversations fell silent under the look. When he stopped moving, he looked around with his hands on his hips. He spoke in a snarl. "I thought I had been clear. Then, when I discovered that people were confused, I made an example of two of you to ensure that I was clear." He suddenly yelled, startling everyone in the room. "But apparently, some of you are too stupid to get the damned message."

There was a visible unanimous recoil as most of those present took a step away from the wild-eyed man in the middle. He raised a hand and pointed at the foursome that sneaked toward the exit. "These people, for example." He lurched into motion and almost ran across the space to stop them from advancing further when he positioned himself between them and the doorway. "Would you like to explain to everyone what you and your idiot friends did last night?"

None of them spoke. Sloan wasn't sure if they were frozen in fear or simply unwilling to play the man's game, but it was a bad look either way. Marcus laughed. "Really? No words? Well, let me share with the group." He turned to face the rest of the gathering. "Twelve people," he paused, then yelled "Twelve idiots," before he lowered his voice again. "Twelve idiots decided to take it upon themselves to attack one of our enemies."

Looks of disbelief flickered across the faces of those closest to Sloan, but he couldn't pull his gaze away from Marcus to check the rest. *Holy hell, he's either lost it or is almost ready to.* "These four were the lucky ones. They managed to crash their car on the way and missed the actual battle." One of them looked about to speak, but the man near him grabbed his arm to prevent it. "The other eight are currently locked up."

He spun to face the offenders. "I don't even want to know what you were thinking. Or if you were thinking, which seems damn unlikely. But let me tell you what you've accomplished." He paused, and every person in the room held their breath as they waited for his next words. They were low and threatening. "You didn't kill the woman. You didn't kill her helper. You didn't manage even to wound either one of them, as near as we can tell." His fists clenched and unclenched as he spoke. "But you did reveal our knowledge of the woman's whereabouts. And you reduced our numbers. For. No. Bloody. Gain."

He followed the finishing shout by raising his arms, which were once again clear of obstruction due to his rolled sleeves. Lightning discharged at the quartet from the left. The wide cone caught all of them and they jittered and danced involuntarily. The right arm fired a fan of tiny projectiles that looked like long needles at head height. The flechettes penetrated the soft tissue of their faces, and they howled as they fell with their hands over their torn flesh.

Marcus didn't speak or move other than to maintain the electrical assault until all four were dead. When it was over, he turned to the larger group and glared at each of them in turn. Sloan felt the implied promise that he, too, would face the leader's wrath if he stepped out of line. Their leader stormed from the room, pausing briefly to mutter to Mur, "Clean that up," before he continued and vanished from sight.

Sloan's companion looked at him and shook his head. He responded with a slight nod and accompanied him as he gathered trusted people to dispose of the remains of the four transgressors. *Okay, the verdict is in. The Remembrance now has* two *certifiably insane leaders.*

CHAPTER TWENTY-NINE

The message from Lechnas had invaded his dreams, one of Dreven's least favorite methods of receiving missives from his master. The communication had been unequivocal, demanding that he take matters on the other planet in hand personally. *Clearly, my underlings have failed again and failed to report their failure.* He shook his head in frustration. *Well, at least he didn't kill me out of hand as he threatened to do. Where there's life, there's hope for an improved outcome.*

He gathered his most important implements and weapons. *If the goal is to sow chaos, it's better to bring more than less.* Despite the tension involved in the assignment, part of him looked forward to personal involvement. After a year of managing others and coddling his colleagues in the circle, to have the chance to act directly would be a pleasure.

The small smile turned into a frown as he remembered his last personal encounter with a human. *Stupid woman. I had her, dead to rights.* He shook his head. *Sometimes, it is better to be lucky than skilled, I suppose. Next time, her luck won't save her.* When he judged he had gathered all the items he could reasonably take, he created a portal to the office the annoying witch used. Through the rift, he saw that the door was open and the room was empty. He stepped through and dropped his bags as he heard shouting through the opening.

At the foot of the stairs, the human and magical leaders of the group confronted one another, their respective followers arrayed behind them. The man had his metal arms folded, which was surprising since he'd expected to see only one. The witch had a hood over her head and her back to him but pointed a finger into the man's face. It was clear that the potential for an all-out escalation had increased and would become inevitable if the two didn't rein it in. He watched for a moment, considered whether to let the scene play out unhindered, and decided he couldn't afford the number of soldiers that might be lost.

He strode down the stairs and the loud noise startled everyone on the floor. Their heads turned, and he saw that the witch's hair had vanished, which explained the covering. She bowed slightly. "Welcome, Dreven. We did not expect you."

He waved dismissively. "I didn't wish you to." He reached the bottom of the stairs and looked at both groups. "What transpires here?"

Sarah gestured at her counterpart. "His people carried out an unapproved attack on one of our enemies. They failed due to their arrogance and now, our position is weakened. He suggests we should try the same tactic again on more junior members of the woman's team. It's idiocy."

She shook her head. "Remove the head and the body dies. Remove an arm, and well…" She glanced askance at the man. "The head continues." The unspoken "unfortunately" hung in the room.

Dreven faced Marcus, whom he'd judged to be reasonably useful for a human. He saw fury in the man's eyes, although it didn't reach his body language, which was soft, quiet, and all the more threatening because of it. "True?"

He shrugged. "Not the whole story, but true. The ones who acted did so without permission. Those who were not arrested paid for the mistake with their lives."

"At the hands of our enemies?"

"No."

Dreven nodded. "Acceptable. However, it has become clear that neither of you can be trusted to handle the tasks I have given you. Again and again, you have failed. That ends today." He turned to the stairs and climbed them halfway to ensure that every eye could see him. "For too long, this group has targeted the wrong opponents. It's time to start at the top and work our way down."

There were several nods, no doubt from people thinking of the woman who had eluded him. "To do this, amusingly, we will start at the bottom." The nods stopped and turned to confusion that spread through both groups. He watched it flow with amusement. "Underground, in fact. We will invade the Stonesreach kemana during their night."

The shock that circled the room was a wonderful thing to behold. *I've been among alleged equals for too long. It's kind of nice to actually be in charge of those who are clearly inferior and know it, rather than merely acting as designated leader.* He smiled. "When we do, a group will cause trouble at the palace to draw attention there, but that is not our main objective. Instead, our goal is threefold. First, we will show those in the kemana who have been too afraid to join our cause that they have support and should emerge from the shadows. Second, we will upset the delicate throne Lady Alayne rests upon. When her citizens are in crisis, she will have little energy to spare to assist our enemies on the surface. Finally, we will strike at the one person who is most pivotal in the equation governing the balance of power in this city."

He gestured at the two groups below. "Prepare. We will move in several hours. Summon those who are not present and collect all the simple weapons you are able to acquire. Technology can't be relied upon below, so we will use what we have and trust in our magic to make the difference." He pointed at the two who led the rabble. "You two, upstairs. Now."

He reclined in the chair behind the desk when they arrived after a short delay to give an initial set of orders to their followers. Sarah took the single remaining seat, which forced Marcus to stand. The man leaned against the closed door with his arms folded and tapped his fingers in an irritating fashion. Dreven decided to let the petty insult slide. *There are bigger concerns.*

"The first thing you should both know is that my superior has demanded results and informed me that lives will be forfeit if there is any failure. Rest assured, yours will be spent before mine. I suggest you consider that when you lead your people in the battle to come." Both nodded in response but neither seemed to truly grasp their subordinate positions. Again, he decided to delay disciplining them. If he was not forced to sacrifice them in the fight under the city, he would deal with them thereafter.

"The second thing to know is that we will burn this city to the ground, if required, to accomplish my master's objectives. I care not for what priorities you've had before. You now serve his will by serving mine. Have no doubts about the relative importance of our goals. Mine are paramount and yours are secondary at best." Again, they nodded without speaking.

"The last thing is that we have multiple targets to take care of tonight. We can hope the move on the palace accomplishes something useful, but I doubt that it will. There's a reason they built the city center like a castle, after all. But there are several places that require our attention." He flicked his wand, and all the objects on the desk swept aside and shattered on the floor. A wave summoned an illusion that displayed an overhead view of the kemana. Four locations plus the palace were aglow, surrounded by featureless blocks representing the other structures. "Three of these buildings are important simply for what they hold. We will break in and steal the weapons and items within to use to our advantage."

He tapped the wand on one of them, and it grew to show a two-story shop with windows on all sides and an entry on street level. "This one, however, is the real prize. We want what's stored within here most of all, as they are some of the rarest items to be found in the kemana. But more, we want the woman who lives and works there." He dismissed the image and looked at his underlings. "You failed to look behind the curtain. Diana Sheen and her team would not be nearly as successful as they are without the guidance and assistance they receive from the Drow, Nylotte. She has been seen traveling with Sheen several times and is thus our enemy as well."

Dreven rose to his feet and stared at the two people in his office. Each wore a bloodthirsty grin appropriate to the upcoming event, and he couldn't bring himself to care about what personal desires or characteristics drove them. It was enough that they anticipated the chance to wreak havoc in Stonesreach. "Go and prepare. There's no time to waste."

CHAPTER THIRTY

The telepathic message from her teacher was an absolute shock and she actually dropped the bottle of beer she'd carried into the living room.

"Diana, Stonesreach is under attack. Get here as soon as you can."

She looked down with an open mouth at the shorts and t-shirt she wore, then yelled, "Rath, come to me." She activated her comms and sent out a general alert to the team, calling for them to gather at headquarters as fast as they could get there. Rath arrived at her side as she reached the bedroom, and they portaled to a disused corner of the bottom floor of the base.

They headed to the lockers as the others reported in. To the non-magicals, she instructed that they should gear up and hold awaiting further developments. She told Cara and Hank to get there as quickly as possible. Each gave an ETA of less than ten minutes, which was reasonable. She donned her equipment and shoved extra potions into her belt, then holstered the Glock and her Ruger and retrieved spare magazines in case the battle ranged beyond the magical city. She snagged the Bowie knife from Tony's kit and set it on the bench, making a mental note that they should have some additional ones around in belt sheaths for moments such as this.

Rath hopped up beside her, already geared up and carrying his batons. Even without the shock function, he was impressively skilled with the weapons. A trio of throwing knives was strapped at his left and right ribs, angled for easy draws. She grinned at him. "You're like a walking arsenal, these days."

He laughed. "Say hello to my little friends."

She rolled her eyes. "Can't you stick to the bubble-gum action movies?" He shook his head, and she sighed. "Fine, be that way. Make sure they're sharp because this one will be tough." Hank and Cara burst through the door from the parking garage and rushed to their lockers.

Kayleigh followed them in. "Any word from Sloan?"

"I assume this either happened so fast he couldn't alert us or he's been under the eyes of the boss guy the whole time. He might have been too successful at infiltrating the group."

The tech grimaced. "What do you need from me?"

Diana thought about that for a second. "Let's position drones near the tunnel exit. You know where that is, right?" She nodded. "Also, keep an eye open around the city. It's always possible that they're making a move down below as cover for an attack on the surface. God knows, they love their distractions."

"Gotcha, Boss." She jogged over to the core and began

to punch the buttons to bring it to life, already deep in conversation with her AI, Alfred.

The slamming of a locker caught her attention, and she turned to find that the others had dressed in record time and were almost ready to move. "Remember, tech's not a thing. You'll have to rely on magic, magic weapons, and things that cut or strike."

Hank grinned. "I've wanted to say this since I got here. Hank Smash!" He imitated the giant green superhero and inspired a gale of laughter from Rath.

Cara rolled her eyes. "Honestly, if the macho in here gets any thicker, I'll find it hard to breathe. Can we go?"

Diana nodded and summoned a portal to Nylotte's basement, and they sprinted through as soon as it materialized.

They raced up the stairs to where the Dark Elf stood with her arms folded and looked out the windows of her shop's first floor. She turned as Diana emerged from the staircase. "These have to be Remembrance people. There's no other explanation."

"No one on Oriceran would be interested in attacking the kemana?"

"There's no reason for it. Plus, there are humans here."

She laughed but it carried little humor. "That'll annoy Lady Alayne to no end."

The Drow nodded, but there was no mirth in demeanor. "What I can't understand is why. I can't see what they could possibly hope to gain."

Diana shrugged. "We don't need to know their objective to stop them. Will you stay here, or will you come to fight?"

Nylotte looked torn, then visibly forced herself to choose. "I'll stay here. There are things in this shop that I wouldn't want others to have."

"Good deal. You'll come if I'm dying, though, right?"

Finally, her teacher's mouth quirked in a hint of a smile. "Maybe."

Cara laughed. "If we're in trouble, I'll call. She likes me better."

Diana yanked the door open and raced into the avenue. There were sounds of explosions and bright lights from the direction of the palace, but she immediately rejected that as a location where they could make a difference. *Lady Alayne has more than enough defenders. The rest of the city doesn't.* She led the others through the nearest cross street to enter the main thoroughfare.

It was absolute chaos. She stared for a few seconds and tried to make sense of it. The impression was that it was civilians, shopkeepers, and residents who happened to be nearby who now engaged the attackers. She wondered why the entire city wasn't up in arms but assumed there was probably a magical veil hiding the action from those not already involved. *Or something. What the hell do I know about large-scale magic? Clearly, anyone with the audacity to attack the kemana would have a plan in place for that.*

An explosion sounded from a couple of blocks distant and smoke billowed into the air. A surge of people screamed and ran from the noise, and Diana began to push her way toward it, her team close behind. When they finally reached the area, they saw that the entire facade of one of the buildings had been blown away and the front rooms on both floors were visible from outside. Humans scurried around inside, carrying duffel bags that resembled army surplus. Diana yelled over her shoulder. "It looks like they're robbing the place, let's get in there and—"

Her words were cut off by another explosion, almost identical to the first, that echoed from the parallel street. Smoke rose over the top of the roofs nearby, and a flickering glow suggested fire. She growled, struck with indecision.

Cara solved it for her. "Hank and I will go and investigate. You deal with these assholes."

Diana watched for a moment as the other two bolted toward a cross-street, then tilted her head to look at Rath. "Ready, partner?" Amongst the chaos, his normally happy personality had been replaced by as serious a demeanor as she'd ever seen him wear. He nodded and stared ahead at the entrance to the broken building. She promised herself that she'd make whoever created the situation that stole the troll's smile pay. "All right. Let's do it."

She ran toward the house and yelled once more. "You go low, I'll go high." She triggered a blast of force and sailed toward the second-floor room and its two suddenly concerned thieves.

Cara led Hank onto the next street, where they immediately found a cluster of people running together and carrying matching machetes. *What the hell? Did they rob an army-navy store to prepare for this adventure?* The weapons would have been enough to indicate that they were on the wrong team, but the way they laughed and swung them at any non-humans in range verified it. She wondered for a moment where the magical component of the attack was but decided that such questions were incidental. You didn't ask about dessert when your steak dinner arrived. She targeted the one at the rear and launched a handful of fire darts at his legs. They struck true, and he fell but his screams alerted his comrades.

They turned, and she made a quick count. *Seven left. Huh. That's hardly fair.* Despite having two each of healing and energy potions, she didn't want to waste her power on the trash mobs. *Heh. Kayleigh and her video game terms. It fits, though.* Hank bolted past her and advanced at a run toward the lead invaders. He'd explained once that his magic was different than most, starting out weak but strengthening as he used it. He shifted direction to the left, and she angled to the right. The enemy had fanned out into four at the front and three at the back and stupidly, remained close enough that they'd be in the way of each other's weapons. That proved to be a problem for them as Hank went all the way left and so positioned the enemy's body closest to him as an obstacle to the one nearer the center.

She'd seen her partner display his skills several times in the fight club, but to watch him go all out was something entirely different. He lashed out with a low kick that hammered his armored shin against his enemy's unprotected one. When the man bent involuntarily, he raised his left fist high and brought it down onto the back of his neck. He crumpled without ever completing the machete attack he'd started. That left two in Hank's range, and she noticed that both looked nervous before her own adversaries claimed her attention.

As she closed the final feet separating her from them, she drew her daggers. A woman was closest and she snarled at her and whipped the machete around in a strong horizontal chop. Cara ducked to let it pass over her head, then darted up and kicked her overbalanced opponent in the ribs. The force of it shoved the woman to the side as she flailed in an effort to regain her balance. The man beside her swung his weapon, aimed at her skull, and she caught it on crossed daggers and delivered a front kick into his groin. He grunted but didn't go down, and she gave him a point for wearing protection. It failed to save him from her next attack, which was to guide his machete past her with one blade while she thrust the other deep into his thigh. He collapsed, dropped the machete instinctively, and clutched the wound as she turned to face the third.

He was already running away down the street, along with another who had chosen not to tangle with Hank. The big man had an enemy at his feet and looked disappointed to see the next one fleeing. Cara grinned at him and tilted her head at the runners, and he nodded, shouting, "Race you." He sprinted in pursuit an instant before she did.

Diana landed cleanly on one side of the large room. The looters had seen her coming, and she was immediately under attack. The one closest swung a baseball bat at her head, and she leaned back to avoid it, pushed forward before he could bring it around, and prevented him from doing so. She punched him in the solar plexus and he folded as she brought her hands down on the back of his head at the same time that she drove her knee upward. His nose shattered and he collapsed, then flopped over and rolled out of the building.

She was already on the move toward her second opponent. He'd brought a sword that looked like something out of *Kill Bill* and held it in a stance that conveyed some mastery of the weapon. She shook her head. "No time. Sorry." She thrust her hands forward and seared him with a cone of force that hurled him through the wooden railing and down the stairs. The sword spun free to clatter on the floor. Diana charged through the other rooms on the second floor but found no marauders. *Dammit, I should have thrown Rath up here and stayed downstairs.* She dashed to the first floor and narrowly avoided a high-speed lamp. *You have to be kidding me. What is this, amateur hour?*

Rath was ahead of her with two bodies at his feet. The troll swiped projectiles out of the air with his batons as he walked toward the last enemy in the room, a woman who had apparently lost her weapon—to judge by the baseball bat lying behind his position—and had resorted to whatever the environment could provide. Seeing that he had the situation in hand, she cleared the first floor quickly as well before she hurried to the basement. It, too, was empty. She returned to find Rath standing over the unconscious woman, shaking his head.

The reason for the mostly vacant building dawned on her as another two explosions resounded from other parts of the city. *Diversions, and enough of them that we can't know what's real and what's not without investigating. And maybe the soldiers don't even know. Damn, this is bigger than I thought. What are they up to?*

The runners were fast, Cara had to give them that. They took an unexpected turn and ran into a shop, and she and Hank followed. They waited inside and put up what was probably the best fight they could but fell quickly. The two exchanged glances, and Hank got as far as saying "What the hell?" before the building exploded around them. The detonation hurled them out into the street, and they landed hard, slid across the stones, and thunked painfully into the structure on the opposite side of the lane. Cara coughed and blood emerged from her mouth. She couldn't move, and the pain in her skull was almost unbearable. She tried to speak, but it only came out in a whisper. "Hank. Help."

An eternity later, he crawled into her visual field and tipped a vial to her lips. It coursed into her throat and she swallowed reflexively, then gulped about half, knowing what was coming next. She screamed as the potion did its work to repair her insides. She handed the flask back to him, and he drank the rest, managing to rise as he healed. He extended a hand, and she used it to climb to her feet. She shook her head. "So, that sucked."

"Yeah, I didn't expect a trap."

"No one expects one. That's why they're called traps."

A familiar, unexpected, unwelcome, and satisfaction-filled voice sounded from the empty street nearby. "Ah, but smart people are always on the lookout for traps." Marcus appeared with a skinny wizard at his side who was lowering the wand he'd used to conceal them. Behind them were a dozen of, presumably, Marcus's best fighters. She saw Sloan standing beside the man in black like he had at the football stadium. His face was a study in neutrality, but there was fear in his eyes. Probably for her.

Cara didn't waste words and leapt into the attack.

More explosions detonated in different places around the kemana, including the one that was the trigger for his group to move. So far, the random detonations had seemed to serve their purpose, providing cover for the actual thefts. The first team had already returned and been portaled away ahead of schedule. *All according to my plan.*

Dreven strode forward from the shadows where they'd concealed themselves, heading toward the prize he most craved. Sarah walked a step behind him to the left and six of her best wizards and witches trailed them. He grinned in anticipation of seeing the look on the Drow's face when her worst nightmare knocked on the door. It had been a long time, but he dearly hoped she'd remember him. If all continued to go according to plan, he'd be the last thing she'd remember. Ever.

CHAPTER THIRTY-ONE

Diana was unable to shake the idea that she was being played. It wasn't a sense like her magical warnings of danger and it wasn't intellect telling her so. But somewhere deep inside, beneath even the ever-taunting mental voice, the certainty that she was doing what the enemy wanted poked at her. *Okay, if the explosions aren't the real thing they're after, what is?* She couldn't get her head around it and turned to Rath. "What do you think is going on here, buddy?"

He frowned. "Idiots. Clever idiots. Distracting. Where aren't they distracting?"

"Good question and I can only think of one way to find out. I'll be right back." She concentrated, then used a continuous blast of force to push herself upward toward the purple stones far above. When she was high enough to see most of the cavern arrayed below her, she swallowed her fear and combined her magics to turn in place, looking at all the sections of the kemana. There were explosions all over the lower part of Stonesreach, save one area. The street that serviced Nylotte's shop was free of fire, as notably quiet as the unaware houses arranged in tiers around the city. *Dammit, is that where they're headed?*

She decreased the power feeding the force magic and descended quickly. A final blast buffered her landing, and she only stumbled a little as she transitioned from air to ground. Rath had moved away from their initial position and swung his batons at someone farther down the main road. She dashed to his side, but he finished the street soldier with a baton to the knee followed by another to the head in the moment before she arrived. As always, she was impressed with his skill and the way he used his size as a benefit rather than a liability.

"I think they're after Nylotte's shop."

She raced toward the cross-street as fast as she could with the troll a few steps behind. With each second that passed, she was more convinced she was right.

Cara's viewpoint had narrowed to one thing—the half-robot-half-man ahead of her. She'd had enough of their seemingly endless courtship and was determined that this would be its culmination. The Daggers' enthusiasm for the prospect suffused her with confidence. Dimly, as if from a distance, she noticed the others behind him but they were shadows and virtually irrelevant. She spread her hands wide and launched a volley of fire darts into the mass while she attacked him, an almost automatic reflex since she'd more or less dismissed them from her mind. Fortunately, she retained sufficient perspective not to shoot toward Sloan, however.

Marcus moved forward to meet her, a poor strategic decision given that he'd brought so many in support but she understood completely. It was one-on-one, regardless of the actual numbers surrounding them. She slipped her daggers from their sheaths and swung them in a curved flourish as she continued. The range was twenty feet when she noticed the wizard's lips move and his wand twitch. Without any conscious intention to do it, she hurled Angel at him in an underhand throw. The blade spiraled rather than tumbled on its path to embed itself in the mage's throat. He fell, and she had only a moment of concern over discarding a weapon before the dagger rocketed back at her. She raised her hand, and it smacked perfectly into her palm.

She skidded to a stop a dozen feet away from Marcus. By some unspoken agreement, they'd both moved toward a relatively empty section of the thoroughfare where their conflict wouldn't be hindered by the rubble created by the plethora of explosions. He shook his head, and there was a little respect mixed with the sneer he wore. "You're such an irrelevant part of all this. Why are you so vexing?"

Cara grinned. "It's the ones who fly under the radar you have to watch out for. Not everyone can be a terminator with training wheels."

It took him a second to process the insult, and he responded with the language they both understood best. He reached into an opening on his left arm, clutched something, and a string of metal spheres suddenly arced toward her. She remembered them from the stadium and knew better than to ignore their threat. An effort of will summoned a curve of fire that redirected the explosives back toward the people he'd brought with him. Her worry sparked for a moment along with the fear that she'd sent them at Sloan or Hank, but it vanished beneath her desire to end her nemesis. They struck and rolled but failed to detonate. *That's handy.*

She grinned. "I surely hope you can do better than that." She tossed Angel in the air and gestured with her empty hand to dispatch darts of fire at his face.

Hank had been enjoying himself an inappropriate amount, right up to the moment that the tiny metal balls clattered on the ground at his feet. When they failed to detonate, his good humor reasserted itself. When Cara had charged the leader, he had crossed behind her and headed for the side of the enemy contingent farthest from their undercover ally. *Hopefully, he'll extract himself before I get there. I'd hate to have to smack him merely to maintain his story.* The criminal on the end was a big bald brute, fat with muscle the way NFL linemen were, and carried a fireman's ax over one shoulder. As Hank arrived in range, the man burst into motion and hacked at him with the weapon without altering the bored-looking expression that covered his face.

He smacked the descending attack aside with a perfectly timed strike of his right palm against the flat side of the head. A quick pivot and sideways shuffle put him safely inside the ax's range. He caught the guy in the mouth with a back fist, then whipped the arm in a semicircle to hammer at his groin. The first blow didn't affect him much, but the second did, driving the breath from him in a whoosh despite the guard he wore. The agent stepped away slightly to clear the path, then crouched and exploded upward in an uppercut. It blasted through the hasty block the man tried to impose and connected with his chin with a crack of breaking bone. He fell limply to the ground.

The punches had built his magic pool, which he could use to increase the intensity of his own strikes or to heal himself. Both abilities were limited solely to him, a fact that had filled him with angst as he watched one of his Air Force buddies bleed out from a shoulder-mounted rocket that struck their chopper during his final tour. None of the experts he found was able to identify a way for him to apply his healing power externally. He also played fair and didn't employ it during practice fights, although it would activate on its own if he was critically injured as it had after the explosion a few minutes before.

He used a portion of it to increase the strength of the skipping sidekick he delivered into the torso of a marauder who thought he was far enough away to be safe. The man careened six feet before he landed and skidded on the stones for a few more. Hank's enjoyment vanished again when he turned in time to meet four of Marcus's followers who targeted him with a coordinated assault.

Rath pounded along at Diana's heels as they cleared the path connecting the streets and rounded the corner toward the Drow's shop. A body shattered the glass windows and the cross-frame that held them and catapulted through to land on the street, groaning. It was a witch, to judge by the wand that hung on a safety cord from her wrist so she wouldn't lose it. *If, you know, she wound up taking an unexpected flight or something.* He felt Gwen's absence when he realized there was no one to hear him if he made a wise-crack and frowned deeper. *Stupid Remembrance.* The fact that the question of who was following the Griffins remained unanswered nudged him as he advanced on the woman, who struggled unsteadily to her feet but hadn't yet noticed him. He'd almost reached baton range when she launched an attack into the building that required her to turn slightly and she saw him. Diana had already vanished into the shop's interior.

The witch's scream as he leapt at her was amusing, but she reacted quickly and raised a barrier of shadows between them. He struck it and was as surprised as she was when he plowed through it without slowing. The deflectors on his vest imploded with a single loud snap. She lurched to the side to avoid him, but the baton he whipped out as he descended caught her in the arm. She yelped, retreated, and raised the wand with a snarl.

Drat. No more magic absorption. He took four steps to the right—enough to look like he was committed to advancing in that direction—then reversed course. The thin cone of shadow struck the building behind him with no effect that he could see in the instant he was facing that way, but his gaze shifted to the witch again, who now tracked the wand toward him. He dove to the side in a shoulder roll, dropped his batons, and found his feet with his throwing knives held lightly in his fingers, exactly as Chan had taught him. He visualized the future trajectory of the witch's arm, which seemed now to be moving in slow motion, and hurled the one in his left hand, then followed it with the one in his right.

Both blades struck but neither flew true. The first transfixed the woman's wrist, several inches away from the wand-holding palm he had actually aimed for. The second, which he had aimed at her upper arm in case he missed with the previous throw, stabbed into her shoulder. The limb fell limply and she looked at him in disbelief for an instant before the pain arrived and she staggered aside. Tears streamed from her eyes as quickly as the curses passed through her lips. Before she could put together the idea of using her unharmed hand to attack, he scooped his up batons and charged, broke her off-hand elbow, and vaulted up to finish her with a spinning blow to the temple. She went down in a heap, and he landed facing the building, which was now aflame.

Nylotte had moved from irritated to annoyed to outraged in moments as the barriers around her shop—which should have easily blocked anyone trying to enter—had fallen one layer after another. She'd delayed the attacking witches and wizards with illusory enemies as they swept inside in an effort to get a picture of the strength she faced. Six entered, and she had blasted the only one with the temerity to try to descend the basement stairs with a fierce ball of force. The sounds that had followed suggested that the witch had broken her windows on the way out.

She'd done a fair amount of renovation after she'd purchased the shop, including using her magic to enlarge the underground portion. Lady Alayne was unaware of that, she was reasonable sure—not that the "ruler" of the kemana would have involved herself in any case. *Still, one likes to keep one's secrets.* She had laid a number of well-concealed traps and charms throughout the space that were inert until she powered them, a step she'd taken when her first external barrier fell. Several went off as she made quick trips away from looking up the stairs for enemies in order to snag things lying around the basement and throw them through the open portal to Diana's bunker on Oriceran.

There had been more than enough time to prepare for battle in the interval between the initial indication that the city was under attack and the direct assaults on her establishment. She had treated the invasion as a dire threat aimed personally at her from the first instant, paranoia having served her well in many similar instances before. *And on this particular occasion, it seems like it might be completely true.* Memories of her flight from her home planet, hounded by enemies seeking her blood, surfaced only to be instantly banished back to the box she kept them in. She'd had decades to master her own mind and was unwilling to let it weaken her.

She wore the black chain top and leather straps that always comprised her base armor. Knowing there wouldn't be much travel involved, she'd chosen a heavy pair of boots with dull metal points on the soles and blades following the lines of the toes and heels. Her gloves ended in talons as well, except for her thumbs and ring fingers, which she might need to open the healing or energy potions she carried in a belt around her waist. The cinch also held a vial filled with sand and another with ball bearings. Finally, she strapped on large bracers to cover her outer forearms, dotted with tiny anti-magic deflectors. The trick to making the deflectors work against enemy magic but not limit one's own had been a secret that took long and arduous research to reveal and required priming the crystals to be used for that purpose in a particular way. Since she'd connected with Diana, there had been further opportunities to test the arrangement as the agents used them and had now devised varieties that could use chips instead of full crystals, but at a far smaller range.

As a backup, she wore a pendant with another deflector in case she missed a block. Finally, she'd strapped on the thigh sheaths that carried her blades. They were strictly for stabbing and blocking, with large curved ornamental guards for catching opponents' weapons. She heard the flames before she saw the telltale flickering, and sighed at the loss of her bedroom, which had held the most explosive trap. Deactivating the basement wards once she retreated down the stairs was unfortunate but necessary, as she didn't want to be caught in them if the invaders activated them.

Her time for contemplation ended as her foes solved the question of how to descend without getting killed by hurling a fireball into the staircase, which reduced it to splinters. She summoned shields to avoid the shrapnel, but when it had finished flying, there were four other figures in the basement. One of them was in an ornate set of armor, a hallmark of ages before in Oriceran's history. It was leather and chain, like hers, but made of interlocking sections that required assistance—or detailed magic power—to don. The pieces were black with golden trim, and the wearer radiated smugness from beneath the helmet that covered half his face. As she lowered her shields for a better look, he spoke and she snarled in fury at the realization of who stood before her.

Dreven's arrogance was fully audible in his tone. "Hello, Nylotte. It's been a long time."

The Drow was balanced on the knife's edge between her desire to rip him and his accomplices to shreds and her need to remain focused so they couldn't distract her and liberate any of the powerful items she stored in the basement. Even one would give the enemies above a significant enhancement in their ability to wreak havoc on the city.

His next words tipped the balance. "I've missed you, wife."

She screamed as she gave in to the rage and committed to ensuring that one of them didn't leave this room alive.

Diana had sprinted up to the second floor of the shop immediately upon entry and discovered an enemy waiting for her. The wizard crouched in a corner as she ran into the bedroom and fired a force bolt at her feet as she entered. She calculated the angles and realized it wouldn't hit her, and she slid to a stop and turned to him at the same moment that the ward he'd triggered with the shot exploded.

The detonation and resulting flames hurled her into the far wall above the bed, and while the anti-magic deflectors on her vest consumed the flames themselves, they did little to mitigate the effects of the explosion. She landed on the soft mattress and rolled toward her adversary, who had already fired bolts of shadow at her. A quickly summoned force shield protected her while she regained her feet within striking distance, and she whipped a kick at his head. He curtailed his attack and tapped her foot with the wand, and she spun away as if he'd struck it with a hammer. She set it down and discovered it would bear her weight, but barely. *Damn. That sucked.*

He looked quizzically at her, then brightened. "It's you."

With a growl, she launched darts of flame from her fingertips at the wizard, but he intercepted them with a swipe of his wand and deflected them in every direction to add to the smoke and fire surrounding them. *I don't have time for a magic battle with this guy.* She snatched the extra Bowie knife from her belt and flung it at him in one continuous motion, and he brought the wand up to deflect it. In the interim, she pushed forward and rammed his midsection with a knee as she carried him into the wall behind him. He folded, and she raised her hand for a punch. She never had the chance to complete it as he grabbed onto her and bowled them both through the room's window into the street below.

Diana landed hard but she'd used her telekinesis as they fell to ensure he would be beneath her, so she avoided damage. She rolled off, a little dazed, and her magic sense kicked into gear. The world slowed as she rolled again and scrambled to her feet, already seeking her enemy.

She found her standing a few yards away with a wizard by her side. Sarah grinned. "Finally, you're here. It's time to die, bitch." Shadow tentacles were already stretching toward her from the witch's arm as both her opponents lifted their wands.

CHAPTER THIRTY-TWO

Whatever dislike Sarah might feel for her, Diana's loathing for the Remembrance witch far exceeded it. She shouted in rage and summoned her force sword as she whirled to slice the tentacles as they reached for her. The wizard broke away to put distance between her two enemies and rendered the fan of fire she planned to send useless. Instead, she snatched his wand with her telekinesis. It spun out of his hand but a shadow bolt sent it off in a different direction before she could catch it.

Diana rolled without looking at her opponent, confident that more of the coherent darkness would be headed her way. She came up next to the shop and summoned two bucklers of fire, then focused on Sarah's attacks. Torn between attacking the defenseless wizard or focusing on her nemesis, she chose the latter when she saw Rath approach the fallen wand at a run. She stalked toward the witch, but while she could easily handle the incoming shadow bolts with the shields, the tentacles proved her strategy flawed. The bucklers failed to block them, and she wound up with the appendages wound around her wrist. She scowled and tried to break free, but they remained tight.

While she was distracted, the witch summoned more of them, this time from her wand, and snaked them around her other wrist. She put all her strength into a pull to yank the wand from the witch's hand but stumbled back as the shadow ropes simply grew longer. *Okay, let's see how long they can grow.* Diana stepped forward to get a little slack and pointed her palms downward. She reached within for force and blasted upward, trailing the tendrils beneath her. At ten feet, they simply moved with her but at about fifteen, they yanked at her hands and dragged her downward. *Sure, let's do that.* She added her own push to the pull and rocketed at the witch with her fists leading. When she was a dozen feet away Sarah realized her plight and stopped, and the agent pulled up and launched ten fire spikes at her, followed by two more identical volleys.

The witch dodged with her own snarl, and Diana landed as Rath vaulted onto the wizard. His double-footed kick felled the man, and the troll applied a prodigious beating from his batons until his opponent lay curled up and immobile. As a final gesture, he snatched the wizard's wand and snapped it in two. Without any indication of what he was about to do, he dropped the batons and spun to hurl two daggers at Sarah. One missed, but the other struck and drew a line of blood along the left side of her scalp. It was only then that her lack of hair registered with Diana. *Hah. So my fire did do some lasting damage.*

The witch's gaze shifted to the troll, and Diana saw death in them. She shouted, "Rath, help Nylotte," and cast a wall of flame between him and Sarah. Almost instantly, she felt the price of the action in her diminishing strength. *I still have enough for you, witch.* He sprinted past her and hurdled through the broken window into the blazing building without a word. She turned to the other woman, her voice dark and fierce. "Targeting my friends is never a good idea. And I'll teach you why."

The quartet of enemies barreled into Hank and rained kicks and punches while they swung their weapons at him. He couldn't make out who had what but focused on blocking the things they held and weathering the other blows. Their greater numbers became a disadvantage as he spun and dodged and put them in one another's way as he retreated. A counterattack opportunity opened, and he hammered his fist into the nearest hostile's face, dropping him instantly.

He'd failed to use his magic, though, and he stumbled awkwardly as the scumbag caught hold of his legs. A baseball bat struck him in the shoulder with enough force to bruise but not enough to break, and he grunted at the pain before he shoved it away. *I have no time for you right now. Come back later.* The one on his left held a machete and circled slowly to try to obtain a window for a clean blow. Hank sidestepped and lashed out with a fist to punch him in the solar plexus. The magic he put behind the blow— about half of what he had remaining—fast-tracked the man into those who hadn't joined the struggle yet and all toppled in one ungainly heap. Sloan pulled his boss out of the way in time to avoid damage to either of them. *I'm not sure how you're staying out of the fight, my friend, but keep it up.*

Now, there were two plus the one on the ground, and a quick stamp broke the arm wrapped around his calf and took the third out of the battle. Hank smiled at the others, who had taken a step back. "If you boys are smart, you'll decide that this is a great time for a walkabout and find your way out of Stonesreach—and out of Pittsburgh." They looked at each other, and for a moment, he thought he had them, but they turned in unison and attacked. *Oh, well. I tried.* He gave them credit for arranging themselves effectively, as their attacks didn't hinder each other. The one on his right was left-handed, apparently, and the one on his left the opposite. Their weapons whipped from the outside, and he backed away from the first swing to see how they'd respond.

Their discipline was good, and they didn't break formation. *Okay, then.* He darted at the one on the right and arced out far enough to avoid the blow from the other. The machete flashed, and he raised his arm in a simple high block and caught the blade on the armor plate that protected his forearm. His adversary realized he was screwed the instant before Hank's forehead smashed into his nose and obliterated his will to continue fighting. The man crumpled, senseless.

He turned to the final opponent with a grin. "Run along, now." The man dropped his weapon and hightailed it down the street. Hank paid him only a second of attention before he turned to check on his partner.

Nylotte didn't like the odds. Four to one was doable, but less so when one of them was as accomplished as Dreven. She spun to obscure her movements and popped the lids on both of the non-healing flasks. She threw the ball bearings into the air with a shout and emptied the sand onto the floor surreptitiously with her other hand. A burst of force propelled the tiny metal spheres at her foes, and if those ranged against were the below-average practitioners the Remembrance had shown in the city so far, she might have hoped they would connect. But Dreven tilted the scales in their favor.

As expected, the balls suddenly veered away pepper the far wall as one or more of the invaders directed their own force blasts at them. She made a show of waving her arms to summon a big spell as she circled to her right, and snuck a small breeze into the magic, only enough to lift the grains of sand from the floor and send them across the room. She scythed a line of flame that stretched to include them all, and each reacted to block it, but while they were distracted, her secret weapon floated toward them.

The nearest advanced, extended a shadow knife from the tip of his wand, and swung it in a vicious arc aimed at her eyes. Nylotte raised the bracer, and its armor halted the force of the blow. The clever wizard transformed the blade to tendrils, but they evaporated as the chips on the vambrace did their work. She noticed her plan was working as the three who weren't Dreven started to blink and expressions of pain dawned on their faces.

She activated one of the charms on her necklace, and

mirror images of her appeared and launched attacks. During the distraction, she used another charm to melt into the shadows and circled behind the wizards and witches. Dreven didn't fall for it, however. He turned and shouted but his warning wasn't quick enough to keep her from hurling force blasts into the back of each of the other three's heads. His cohorts collapsed, face down, and left the two old enemies to face one another alone.

The Drow launched a stream of wickedly pointed icicles at him and dragged the attack from his feet to his head. He stepped aside, and when she adjusted it to follow, applied his magic to flip them and fire them back at her. She summoned a wall of flame and used the steam as a distraction to shift position while she built balls of ice in each of her hands. When she was satisfied with the size, she threw them up and thrust them forward with force magic as soon as he was visible. He batted the one aimed at his face out of the way and took the blow on his armored groin without apparent effect. She laughed. "So, still nothing notable enough to do damage to, ey, Dreven?"

He snarled a curse and stretched his wand arm out. A cage of lightning reared up around her. With another twitch of the wand, it began to collapse inward and the sparks threatened to reach her at any moment. She rolled her eyes. "Please, give me a little credit." A wave of her vambrace in a circle cleared a section momentarily, and she stepped free to drive two force punches at him.

The wizard slashed contemptuously and they veered past him and into the wall where her staircase had been prior to its unfortunate destruction. "Death is all you deserve." He sketched a strange figure in front of him and shadow tendrils appeared from below her to wind around her limbs. With a deft movement, he yanked them tight as others ensnared her body. The first ones fell victim to the deflectors in her bracers and on her necklace, but there were so many that she couldn't destroy them all.

She fought against them to ensure that she'd have room to relax and use the slack to escape in the instant before the tentacles sensed it. An unexpected but welcome sight at the top of the stairs had changed the situation and now, it was about words rather than power. *Although perhaps words are the greatest power of all when it comes down to it.* She summoned a sweet smile. "Aww, are you still heartbroken, Dreven dear?"

He snarled, and the tendrils squeezed, legitimately pressuring her breathing. She wouldn't have too long to taunt him before matters became urgent. She gathered enough air to speak. "Sure would...be lousy if you came all this way...and lost because...you underestimated your foe." He stared at her and broke into laughter as he stepped toward her bound form. *That's it, only a couple more steps.*

Three things happened in rapid succession. First, he put his face next to hers and was livid as he spoke in a growling tone. "It is you who underestimate me, Drow." He made the word sound like the worst name he could possibly have called her. "You always have."

Second, she choked out. "No...you did...exactly...what I thought...you would." At the same time, she saw the flicker in the corner of her vision. That led directly to the third, and she relaxed her muscles to free up enough space to summon force swords in her hands. She yanked them upward and sliced the tendrils on the top half of her body into two parts, then cut down to do the same to the lower half as he began to react. But the troll's blades struck true— an amazing throw from the first floor opening under the circumstances—and dug deep into the space between his shoulder armor and the base of his helmet. His eyes flew wide as both thrown knives penetrated into the back of his neck. His mouth gaped, unable to form useful words.

Nylotte stepped forward and drew her daggers, spinning them once as she raised them to the right level. She stared her opponent in the eye and shook her head. "You always were an idiot. And I was a bigger idiot to believe your lies. But now, the scales are well and truly balanced. You destroyed my former life. For that, it is my privilege to end yours."

She thrust the blades forward with as much righteousness as she had felt toward any action in her existence and stumbled sideways as a rift opened under his feet and sucked him away from her. A scream of defiance tore its way out of her lungs, but there wasn't enough rage in the universe to propel her into the unknown darkness after him. She looked at the head of the stairs, the only place that someone could have seen the goings-on to cast the portal that perfectly, and saw the troll face down on the floor.

She launched herself to his side with a blast of force and cradled his crumpled form in her arms. With a level of concern she would deny to her deathbed if called on it, she brushed the purple hair out of his eyes and felt his head and neck for wounds. None were present, but he still refused to breathe. She put her hand on his chest and sent her own magic into him, a last-ditch healing effort that risked severe damage to the caster. Part of her mind rationalized it while she worked. *If her troll dies, Diana will be inconsolable and be unable to achieve her full potential. Thus, I must save him.* An observer, though, would have seen the caring look on her face and realized that the blustery Drow had a soft spot for this troll, and maybe even—possibly—other small and vulnerable creatures.

Rath coughed as her magic found the blockage and cleared it and he began to breathe again. The Dark Elf kept her magic in him until he was stable, then withdrew it slowly. She set him down carefully and bolted to her feet, anger at Dreven's vanishing act driving her again. *First, I'll find a healing portion for the troll. Then, I'll kill each and every one of Dreven's people until someone tells me where to find him.*

Marcus raised his arm instinctively to block the fire darts she'd launched at him and seemed surprised when they scorched and deformed the metal. The emotion turned to fury, and he drove toward her, swinging his left fist in a wicked hook. She put the information together as she ducked under the punch and dodged aside from the kick that followed. She couldn't help but laugh. "Your arms don't work right down here, do they?"

He growled and drew the daggers from his belt. "Everyone has challenges. You're not good enough to beat me one-on-one."

She realized she'd never have a better chance than this to kill him. Above, his mechanical arms gave him an advantage. He'd obviously internalized the confidence he drew from them, perhaps never realizing that they wouldn't provide such a large advantage in the kemana. *Maybe I can't cut your arms, but that's not the only place you can bleed.* Cara darted in, licked at his face with Angel, then thrust Demon at his stomach when he blocked the first strike. He took the tiniest required step to avoid the thrust and countered with a slash that sliced her cheek from immediately under her eye to her chin. She resisted the urge to touch it and circled to attack again.

He stepped forward to intercept her. The two exchanged a flurry of blows, slashes, and thrusts barely blocked in time or cleverly dodged, and broke apart with neither having scored. Her face was throbbing, but she pushed the feeling away and focused on her enemy. Everything in her wanted to make him bleed and suffer. She started to move again but felt a weight in her stomach she attributed to the Daggers. While their combat suggestions came through in perfect clarity without requiring her to retreat to their shared mental space, their other communications were sensed rather than understood.

Demon and Angel urged caution. Cara sighed and whined in her mind. *But I want to stab him!* The image of a child version of herself stomping her foot made her laugh, and instead of advancing, she retreated, holding her weapons in a guard position. "Marcus. Last chance. Surely prison is better than bleeding out on this street."

He shook his head. "Clearly, you've never been to prison. And I'll never go there again."

She shrugged. "I guess I can't argue with that." She sheathed her blades and summoned her fire to release a cone from each hand that merged on his chest. He thrust his metal limbs in the way and pushed forward against the power of it in an effort to reach her. She dug deep and threw more of herself into the attack, willing it to penetrate his defenses. After a moment, it did and burned through his arms and into the body behind them. He wore a startled look as he fell to his knees and toppled slowly onto his side as the light in his eyes faded.

Cara raised her gaze to his remaining followers, who numbered Sloan plus two. She shook her head. "We've done enough to each other tonight. Get out of here. If I see you again, you're dead. Exactly like him."

They ran. As Cara watched them go, Hank stepped up beside her. He sounded full of all the energy she wasn't. "How does it feel, having beaten him?"

She shrugged. "I thought it would matter more, like a weight would lift or something."

He nodded. "I understand. Maybe it'll come with time."

"Maybe. But for now, there's still work to do. Let's go clean up the streets."

He grinned and slapped his fist into the opposite palm. "Now that's an idea I can get behind."

CHAPTER THIRTY-THREE

Diana strode directly toward the enemy witch, determined to make her pay for attacking Rath. Where her rage had been a fiery thing before, it was now cold. The outcome was already determined. It was merely a matter of calling it into being. The woman threw fire at her, and she countered with her flame buckler, drawing power into her. She tried ice, and Diana's mind, entirely focused on her rival, was no longer a hindrance and instead, summoned a proper ice shield to drain more energy from her adversary's attack.

Sarah retreated, her expression suggesting that the look on the agent's face alarmed her. *As it should, witch.* The expected blast of darkness spilled from her wand, and she cast a force shield to intercept it. The tendrils came again and she smiled. She looped her force rope over them, drew it tight, and yanked it back to force the witch to choose between being hauled off balance or releasing the tentacles. She chose the latter, and Diana flicked the line at her face. Sarah brought her wand around to block, abandoned the shadow attack, and gave her the opening she had waited for.

With a yell to startle her, she attacked the witch, the distance now short enough that she could cross it before more than one counterattack could be thrown. She accepted the blast of shadow that struck her, ignored the emotions she associated with it, and pushed through the actual pain it caused. When she reached Sarah, she gathered all her momentum and channeled it into a leaping head butt and drove her forehead into the top of her enemy's nose.

The witch staggered, dazed, and Diana used the opportunity to raise her left leg, pivot, and drive it down into her knee. It shattered under the impact of the blow, and the witch screamed as she fell. Part of her registered that her target mumbled "stop" repeatedly but she had no interest in anything the woman might have to say. She powered the steel toe of her combat boot into the witch's hand to shatter the bones and knock her wand free. Diana knelt before her and summoned a force blade, shorter than her sword, and added a flaming outline to the edges. She grinned at her opponent, who seemed to have difficulty holding her head up. "So, the tentacles...they come out of your arm, right? Do you want to tell me which one, or should I simply dig until I find it?"

Her danger sense saved her again. She threw herself to the side as she felt a threat from above. The giant purple crystal that fell from the ceiling high above must have been nudged by magic somewhere along its path to trigger her power and provide the warning. She rolled once she saw it, but quickly stopped when she realized it was too big to evade. Instead, she created an outer shell of ice, a layer of force under it, one of fire beneath that, and a second layer of force that rested an inch above her skin. There was barely enough time to wonder if it would be sufficient before the mammoth stalactite struck.

The sound and pressure of the rock as it pounded into her shields was all-encompassing, and as it faded, it felt like she was alone on a barren planet. When the sounds ceased, she slowly pushed the single layer that remained intact outward. Voices became distantly audible, and she felt the weight vanish from above her. Finally, the rubble was cleared away, and the others—all the others, she was relieved to discover—stood above her. Hank offered her a hand, and she used it to climb to her feet. She searched for Sarah's body and groaned when she failed to see it.

Diana turned to Nylotte, who looked both very martial and very pissed off. "She did not get away again. Say these words to me. Please say these words to me." The Drow shook her head with a frown, and Diana threw her hands up in the air. "That witch has more lives than any nine cats."

Cara grinned. "Well, that's one for me and none for you, then."

She faced her second in command. "You got him?"

"Yep. He's toast." Hank snorted, and Cara raised a hand. "Do not say a single word about him being more like some other food or something equally stupid. Please don't." The big man laughed harder but refrained from speaking.

Rath said, "One-half for me, I think."

Nylotte nodded. "That sounds right. Maybe even two-thirds." Diana raised an eyebrow, and the Dark Elf explained. "Chief asshole Dreven arrived. I distracted him and the troll threw knives into his neck but he vanished before we could be sure he was done."

She sighed. "The important thing is that we're all alive and mostly well. And, of course, that the Remembrance had its ass kicked again."

CHAPTER THIRTY-FOUR

B ryant had come to visit, and the entire team was gathered in a closed restaurant. Sloan was present as well, looking haggard and stressed. Kayleigh and Duncan sat on either side of him. Diana couldn't hear and didn't want to pry, but imagined they were trying to convince him to leave his character behind and surface from his undercover gig. She'd given him the authority to choose his path. There was no denying their need for intelligence as the organization picked up the pieces or fell to pieces, but she was willing to find other options if he wanted out.

Bryant had been apologetic about his choice to stay on as head of ARES, but she had stilled his explanations with a kiss, fully cognizant that it would be the first time her people saw them do anything romantic. The team clapped and cheered, except for Cara and Hank who quickly drew judging numbers on their napkins and held them up, denying them even a shot at the bronze medal. She'd stuck her tongue out at them in revenge. They hadn't seemed moved.

The meal was all small plates, a tradition she and Rath and Kayleigh had started at home and wanted to bring to the others. There were traditional appetizers—the troll continued to be a big fan of mozzarella sticks—as well as fancier offerings drawing upon Spanish and Mediterranean cuisines. Several bottles of wine had been opened, and there had already been toasts to the techs for their investigative work and to Cara for ending the threat that Marcus posed. Rath also received one for hitting the biggest adversary with his blades and actually seemed embarrassed when everyone congratulated him. *Maybe Chan's style is rubbing off on him.*

Diana climbed onto the long table, stamped her feet, and raised her hands for silence. When she had everyone's attention, she put every ounce of pride, admiration, and caring into her soft words as she could. "We are more than co-workers. We are more than a team. We are family. In the recent past, we have gone through some really heinous stuff, one and all." She looked around the room as she spoke, holding each pair of eyes for a few seconds before moving on so each person knew she was talking to them. "And still, we are here. We are together. And we will take on any bastard who thinks they can break us apart and show them how very wrong they are."

She took the glass Bryant handed her and waited while everyone sorted their own out. Then she lifted it and managed to get out the words, "To family," before the emotions overcame her voice. The others murmured the same, and she slid from the table before she did something stupid to ruin the moment. There were a few moments of silence before Tony declared loudly, "Great job, boss. Way to kill a party. Someone, throw a pie."

The laughter resumed, Diana's among the loudest. *Best. Family. Ever.*

Far, far away, in a frigid basement on a different planet, Dreven struggled to breathe. He sensed the cold stone under his mostly naked form but couldn't move his arms or his legs. His eyes could only see the ceiling, and he had no way of knowing if he was tied down or paralyzed. When the portal appeared and he fell, he'd been entirely sure it was Lechnas saving him despite his promised reward for further failure.

Now he was much, much less certain. After what seemed like an eternity, measured in his second by second struggle to draw his next dismal portion of air, a loud crash sounded nearby. He heard footsteps, and his mind trembled with fear and anticipation. *A healing potion, that's all I need. Please. Save me.* If he could speak, he would beg, but there was no breath for it.

Iressa's face came as a world-shattering shock when she leaned over the table. The smirk she wore was as condescending as he'd ever seen on her face. She shook her head. "Dreven, Dreven, Dreven. Look what's become of you." He gaped and gasped and couldn't reply. Her smile widened. "You were a useful pawn for a while but now, that utility is at an end. I have dreamed of this day for so long and imagined the pleasure I would have driving a knife into your heart."

She raised a hand that had been hidden outside his line of sight and the light from above twinkled on the keen metal of the stiletto she held. The witch spun it lazily over his head, perilously close to his eyes, and laughed when he failed to respond. "Oh, this is beyond delightful, really. I'd always imagined you struggling when this moment came, but this is so much better." She paused and stared at him, then shifted her gaze to his opposite side. "Don't you agree?"

Sarah stepped into view, her bald head still healing from a wound that looked like it would scar. She looked at him and her voice was filled with satisfaction when she spoke. "Oh, I so very much agree." Iressa extended her hand across the table and offered her the weapon, and the witch took it with a smile.

She positioned it over his heart, and he imagined the cold point touching his chest but couldn't feel it. Iressa said, "Goodbye, Dreven." Sarah nodded and echoed, "Goodbye, Dreven," and began to push. The two witches' eyes remained locked on his as the hilt got lower and lower, and then he knew no more.

The story doesn't end here. Follow Diana, Rath and BAM's adventures in Arcane Ops.

CONNECT WITH TR CAMERON

Stay up to date on new releases and fan pricing by signing up for my newsletter. CLICK HERE TO JOIN.

Or visit: www.trcameron.com/Oriceran to sign up.

If you enjoyed this book, please consider leaving a review. Thanks!

AUTHOR NOTES - TR CAMERON

WRITTEN JULY 19, 2019

Geez, what a ride. Thank you for coming along with us!

Thank you for reading the *sixth* book in the Federal Agents of Magic series, and for continuing on to the author notes! I wake up every day unable to believe the good fortune that lets allows me to share stories with you. It is my deep pleasure to do so.

This book was *hard*. It's got a lot of moving parts, sure, but I think it's because of the characters. The cast is more or less complete, and trying to give them all an opportunity to grow and develop in their own ways within the confines of the overall story is like walking on a 2x4 over a pit of alligators. Alligators with metal teeth. *Sharp* metal teeth. I'm really happy with how it turned out, though, and hope you are too.

Looking ahead, the search for Fury will continue, as will the agents' efforts to untangle the knot of the forces arrayed against them. Plus, much to Diana's chagrin, the mobile armory continues to be a thing. Books 9 and beyond are coming together plot-wise, and so far all signs point to big fun ahead.

In personal stuff, I've got a busy fall planned! My best friend is having a wedding bash in August and I've got a couple of professional conferences on deck. It's definitely more scheduled than I usually am, travel-wise.

My daughter dyed her hair blue, so that's something. She's awesome, and wildly unpredictable. We're plotting and planning to do some more amusement park action before the summer's over. On our last trip to one, she insisted we ride the biggest, fastest coaster it had to offer seven times in a row. She wanted to go for ten, but was weaving when she walked, so I opted to be a good parent rather than a cool one.

Videogames: Finished the Spider-Man main plot, downloaded the DLC, can't get past the first mission. Like, "Hey you're awesome, oh, sorry, you actually suck, nevermind." *Thanks, Spider-man.* Red Dead 2 is on hiatus, as my gaming time is going toward Detroit Become Human, which is an amazing example of interactive cinematic storytelling.

Plot details for book seven are sketched out, but are going to take a couple of days to pull together fully. I've spun out a lot of strands that need to be gathered up in the next pair of books, and I don't want to let down y'all, or the characters, or myself, by letting anything slip by.

Quick media notes: *Endgame* broke my heart again the second time, even more since I'd seen *Spider-Man: Far From Home*, which had all the feels. I cheered out loud when JJJ appeared; great choice by Marvel and Sony on that one. *Killing Eve* season two is holding up well, but I'm sure it's not for everyone. *American Gods* is on deck, and I'm going to need to go back and see the amazing speech that Anansi gives on the boat again. *Still* trying without success to get the child to watch Star Wars: ANH, which I think makes me a complete failure as a parent. But I did get her to start on *Dr. Who* (Eccleson), so that's something, right?

If you want to chat media, the books, or whatever else, I check in pretty often on Facebook. Just search TR Cameron Author to find me. Or, less reliably, thom@trcameron.com.

Now, back to figuring out the next way to mess up Diana's life. Until next time, Joys upon joys to you and yours – so may it be.

My summer goal is to lose enough weight to fit into the smaller end of my closet. The larger end will be packed away in the garage like some kind of talisman to ward off fat cells. So far, I've lost a size and a half and only three to go. Progress.

That progress has not been a straight line, sort of. I started out strong doing the Runners World 8-Week Program and seeing a nutritionist, plus reading a few books on Mindful Eating. I'm telling you, I'm determined to make peace with all of this.

But then a trip to Scotland for almost two weeks and I was in a kind of holding pattern. I wasn't eating terribly and there were long walks involved but it wasn't the same. Main thing I learned though, was how well I felt when working out regularly and eating the right things for me. I see that kernel of knowledge as a victory. It gives me incentive to stick to my lane where there's plenty of great stuff to eat, none of it packaged food.

To motivate my keister into staying the course I've

signed up for at least one 5k in Chicago to run with friends there and celebrate my 60th birthday. It's the Hot Chocolate on November 3rd and I will do my best to turn down the Ghirardelli chocolate they give out at the end. No promises.

My goal is to run the whole thing and then go have brunch with friends. A perfect day. I'm looking for one or two in the Austin area as well. I've also been meeting a neighbor, Elaine at the gym that's a quarter of a mile from my house. Yeah, I could walk there if it wasn't 100 degrees outside right now. Frankly, I've run there plenty of times.

It also helps that Elaine likes to text me and find out when I'm going. Who can say, *never* to that? I'm telling you, we do our best work in community with others.

As the fall approaches and The Peabrain Society's big project to bring us all together and unfold our own dreams is gearing up. I'll be hanging out at a lunch for fans in the Austin area on August 17th for anyone who's around and I'll be toting swag. Bit by bit I will also get into shape and one day that entire left side of the closet will fit. Getting closer... More adventures to follow.

THANK YOU for not only reading this story but these *Author Notes* as well.

(I think I've been good with always opening with "thank you." If not, I need to edit the other *Author Notes*!)

RANDOM (*sometimes*) THOUGHTS?

So, I often read the author notes from my collaborators before I do mine. It's a version of hacking (I think) my life to help me get ideas since I've done so many of these in the last three years.

TR Cameron was just chilling in his notes, updating everyone about his game life, tv life, and his roller-coaster efforts with his daughter, which is cool. My challenge is my life isn't as cool.

Here is mine:

1) I bought a tricked-out XBOX One (best one available) early July. I probably, in some small way, need to blame TR for this episode. It's true that I've been wanting a game setup (re: man cave) for a couple of years. Since I'm

not getting a man-cave anytime soon, I opted to go with Xbox on my TV in the Condo in Vegas.

It was kinda ok.

I love Xbox, but I didn't like the games so far. I was told by fellow author JN (Jeff) Chaney to go Sony PlayStation and I think he was right.

The problem is I've been Xbox forever, and purchasing Sony seems like drinking Pepsi when I'm a Coke fan.

Xbox, you need better games.

Fortunately for me, I can say '@#%@# It!' and buy them both.

I have the money, I have the room under the TV - I just need my wife to go out of town for forty-eight hours...

2) I don't watch TV that much to speak of. Well, I guess that's mostly true, but not all the way true. I watch a S#%-TON of *Ancient Aliens* and *UFO* (something or another.). That stuff fascinates me.

Could be the same part of my brain that creates stories - it needs more input.

Regardless, I can't speak to cool series I'm watching or (most) movies I haven't seen, so, my pop-culture discussion is pretty pointless.

3) My kids. All of our sons are out of the house. One's in Dallas (Joseph) starting his third year at UT Arlington. One (Jacob) is in Katy (outside of Houston), living with family there, and one is also in the Katy Area (Joshua), and I'm working with him on the *Animus* project (and soon to be another project.)

I have a complete lack of ability to discuss roller-coaster rides.

My biggest project in the company is still under wraps.

I will slowly start dropping hints and stuff in the coming weeks.

I suppose I could talk about being in Paris at the moment, but that isn't as cool as the games.

I am waiting for Cyberpunk 2077... I think I'll take off two weeks to try to play that game.

AROUND THE WORLD IN 80 DAYS

One of the interesting (at least to me) aspects of my life is the ability to work from anywhere and at any time. In the future, I hope to re-read my own *Author Notes* and remember my life as a diary entry.

Le Salon Sarah Coiffure, Paris, France

Ok, I'm hanging in a hair salon (just got my hair cut) while my wife is getting her hair done. I am presently sitting in one of the chairs, my laptop on the little ledge connected to the mirror, type type typing this out.

Typey, Typey, Typey... I just like the way that sounds... Typie (hmmm, not sure which way to spell it.)

My reflection is only a couple of feet in front of me since I'm so close to the mirror. At the moment, all of my gray hair is faded into the lighter hair, and looks blond because of the yellow lights next to me.

I'm so young-looking.

I'm scared to get up, because natural lighting is going to show the grays are taking over.

Do I get my hair colored? If I do get it colored, should I go with my natural color, or screw around with it?

(No, I'm not going blue. I'm old fashioned.)

Damn, I just admitted to being old-fashioned. I'm one banana-peel-slip away from a curmudgeon.

I need a Coke.

FAN PRICING

$0.99 Saturdays (new LMBPN stuff) and $0.99 Wednesday (both LMBPN books and friends of LMBPN books.) Get great stuff from us and others at tantalizing prices.

Go ahead. I bet you can't read just one.

Sign up here: http://lmbpn.com/email/.

HOW TO MARKET FOR BOOKS YOU LOVE

Review them so others have your thoughts, and tell friends and the dogs of your enemies (because who wants to talk to enemies?)... *Enough said ;-)*

Ad Aeternitatem,

Michael Anderle

JOIN THE ORICERAN UNIVERSE FAN GROUP ON FACEBOOK!